Keri Arthur is author of thrilling
paranormal romances. She's a dessert and function
cook by trade, and married to a wonderful man who

KNOWSLEY LIBRARY SERVICE
Knowsley Council

Please return this book on or before the date shown below

You may return this book to any Knowsley library
For renewal, please telephone:
Halewood: 443 2086, Housebound/Mobile: 443 4202
Huyton: 443 3734, Kirkby: 443 4289
Prescot: 443 5101, Stockbridge Village: 443 2501
Or online at: http://www.knowsley.gov.uk

www.facebook.com/knowsleylibraries

Also by Keri Arthur

Chasing the Shadows

Keri Arthur

PIATKUS

PIATKUS

First published in Great Britain as a paperback original in 2008
by Piatkus Books
First published in the US in 2002 by ImaJinn Books,
A division of ImaJinn, USA

A CIP catalogue record for this book
is available from the British Library

ISBN 978-0-7499-0893-5

Typeset in Sabon by Phoenix Photosetting, Chatham, Kent
www.phoenixphotosetting.co.uk
Printed and bound in the UK by CPI Mackays, Chatham, ME5 8TD

Papers used by Piatkus Books are natural, renewable and recyclable
products made from wood grown in sustainable forests and certified
in accordance with the rules of the Forest Stewardship Council.

Mixed Sources
Product group from well-managed
forests and other controlled sources
www.fsc.org Cert no. SGS-COC-004081
© 1996 Forest Stewardship Council
FSC

Piatkus Books
An imprint of
Little, Brown Book Group
100 Victoria Embankment
London EC4Y 0DY

An Hachette Livre UK Company
www.hachettelivre.co.uk

www.piatkus.co.uk

With thanks to Terry Matthies, who went above and beyond the call of duty in answering endless questions about San Francisco

One

Michael? Where are you?

The sharp voice swam through his consciousness, scattering any remnants of sleep. He opened his eyes and watched the moonlit landscape sweep by the cab's windows. Only a few more miles and he'd be with Nikki.

Michael? This time, Seline's piercing mind voice held a hint of concern. *Can you hear me?*

He sighed. How could he not hear her when she was all but screeching? *Yes, I can hear you.* He just wasn't concentrating. All he wanted to do right now was get home to Nikki. They'd been apart for nearly three weeks, and it felt like forever.

After living alone for over three hundred and sixty years, it was amazing how quickly he'd become accustomed to having her in his thoughts and in his life. He needed her, not just physically, but emotionally.

You sound tired, Michael.

He was. Tired of chasing vamps gone bad. Tired of killing. Or maybe he was just tired of doing it alone, though he had no intention of giving in to Nikki's demands to let her share this part of his life. One killer in the family was more than enough. *It's been a long three weeks, Seline.*

It was a tougher case than I'd originally thought. I'm sorry.

He smiled wryly. That was a first—her apologizing. She *had* to be after something. *What's the problem?*

1

You know me too well. Her amusement swam down the mental line between them, yet it was mixed with an anger that burned so sharply he could almost smell it.

Curiosity stirred, but he thrust it away. He'd never refused Seline anything she'd asked him to do, but after one hundred years, he was getting a little weary of helping everyone else at the cost of his own existence. Especially now, when he had someone to exist for. *Seline, I'm tired, I'm almost home, and I'm in no mood for games. Get to the point.*

She sighed. *I think we need your help on another case.*

I've just finished this one. I need a break. Needed time to regain some sense of normality—something that had been sorely missing in his life until Nikki had come along.

I know, and I'm sorry. But vamps are your area of expertise, and this case has a bad feel to it.

Was there ever one that didn't? For a moment, he studied the softly glowing aspens lining the road, then glanced at the cab driver. "It's the next left." Ten more minutes, and he'd be with her. The longing that had sat like a weight in his gut these past three weeks lifted, and something close to excitement bubbled through his veins.

What are we dealing with? he asked eventually.

That's it—we're not exactly sure.

Then how do you know it's me you need? Impatience edged his words, and her smile shimmered through his mind.

I'm a witch. Some things I just know.

He rubbed his eyes. *Seline . . .*

Okay, okay, I'll come to the point. She hesitated again, then all sense of amusement disappeared, replaced by a bluntness that spoke of fury. *Two weeks ago, the wife of a wealthy restaurateur was kidnapped from a high-profile hotel in San Francisco, and a ransom subsequently demanded. The husband paid the ransom, but his wife wasn't returned, and the money hasn't resurfaced.*

He frowned. As yet, it didn't seem the sort of case that the Circle would get involved in, let alone one that would need his expertise. *And . . .?*

Four days later, another woman was kidnapped. From a private home this time, but otherwise, everything was the same.

So the police are dealing with a serial kidnapper?

Yes. And there was a third victim—she was taken two days ago. They found the body of the first victim yesterday.

He raised his eyebrows, surprised by the fierce undertone of anger washing down the mental lines. *How did she die?*

They'd drained her. The autopsy revealed half a dozen different puncture wounds.

Meaning six vamps had fed off her? That *was* unusual, because most vampires didn't like sharing their meals. Yet it didn't really explain the anger he could feel in Seline.

Apparently. But that's far from the worst of it. She hesitated, and again the anger surged—a wave of red heat that roared through his mind. *These vamps weren't just after blood and money. They were after far more than that.*

What did they do? In over one hundred years of knowing her, he'd never heard her so riled—and they'd tackled some pretty damn tough cases in their time together.

The bastards mutilated her—they shaved off her

3

hair, pulled all her nails, scarred her face and slit her nose. And cut off her breasts for good measure . . .

Her voice faded, but her anger remained, sizzling his mind with its heat.

So basically, they destroyed her self-image before they killed her. Or at least, took away practically everything that defined her as a woman. Obviously, they weren't just dealing with vampires, but vampires with some serious psychological problems.

A shudder ran down the mental line. *I want these things caught, Michael. I want them killed quickly, before they can do this again. No one who is capable of something like this has a right to life—whether they're human or not.*

He scrubbed a hand across his eyes again. He didn't want this case, but he knew he had no real choice. Seline was right. Vampires *were* his field, and this sounded particularly nasty, though he'd heard—and seen—much worse over the years. This sort of defilement certainly wasn't new.

I can't leave right away. I need to see Nikki first. Lord, wasn't she going to be ecstatic over him leaving again so soon?

Fine. I'll send the helicopter over to pick you up. It should be there by four.

He glanced at his watch. That gave him six hours with Nikki. After three weeks of abstinence, it was nowhere near enough. *How do you want to play this?*

I want you to go undercover. I've set you up with a new profile—and seeing you don't want Nikki involved in any of these cases, I'm sending Katherine to play the part of your wife.

He'd worked with Kat a few times in the past, but her forthright manner tended to get on his nerves—

as did her raucous laugh. *Kat comes as a pair with her grandmother. I really don't think she's the best choice . . .*

And I really don't care what you think of the woman. She's the best choice for the case, and she lives in San Francisco.

He bit down on his irritation. He knew it came from tiredness more than any real annoyance. *Is she there at the moment?*

Seline hesitated. No. *But I can pull her off the other case easy enough. This is more urgent.*

She's being used as bait, and you know I don't like doing that. I really do prefer to work alone.

We haven't the time on this one, Michael. We have to flush them out fast. Katherine can defend herself well enough, believe me.

He knew she could defend herself. He just didn't like setting anyone up as bait. No matter how carefully you planned, things always went wrong. And more often than not, the bait became the victim. As annoying as Kat could be, he didn't want her dead. *Where are we staying in San Francisco?*

The three kidnappings happened within a radius of two blocks from each other. The third victim was taken from the Diamond Grand—and that's where you'll be staying.

He frowned. He'd heard the hotel mentioned recently, but he couldn't remember where—or why. *Surely they won't hit the same place twice?*

Instinct tells me the Diamond Grand has a major part to play in this. But it also tells me it's not the location that matters as much as the people themselves. The victims have three things in common— they all originally came from Boston, they all married extremely wealthy men, and they all attended a fund raising benefit at the Hyatt two and a half weeks ago. Kat attended that benefit, which is why I wanted her along.

Michael raised an eyebrow. *Does that mean you think all the women who attended the benefit might be potential victims?*

I doubt it, though it's not beyond the realm of possibility. That benefit went badly wrong—six men broke in just before dessert and took everyone's cash and jewelry. It's linked to the kidnappings, I'm sure of that. I'm just not positive how yet.

How did the thieves get past security?

No one knows. They disappeared just as easily, as well.

What about the security tapes? They been checked? Even vampires wrapping themselves in shadows would not escape the camera's eye—simply because no hotel could afford to have foyers or corridors half-lit these days.

Yes. Nothing was found. The people behind the theft or the kidnappings aren't getting into the hotels through any normal means.

If vampires *were* behind all this, then all it took was one employee under their control to leave open a window, and they were in undetected. *Did Kat give you much of a description of the men involved?*

She said there were six of them, and that they were all vamps. They wore leathers and motor bike helmets, so it was impossible to see any features. But she did say there was one maker and five Loop members.

Which suggested two things—not only that the head vampire was gay, but that he liked more than one partner. Though five was taking it a bit far. Even Elizabeth at her worst only had four lovers at any one time—and they were never created *at* the same time. Controlling a fledgling was often difficult. Dealing with a Loop of them—whether that Loop contained three, five or more vampires, would be overwhelming.

Did she sense anything else?

Only that she thinks robbery was not the true motive. The Loop's creator was skimming the minds of the older women there.

That could mean he had a definite target, and the robbery was little more than a means of collecting recent information about them. What's the police thinking on this one?

They're not saying much, officially or otherwise. The Feds have been brought in, of course.

Have there been any other unusual killings or disappearances outside of these three women? If vampires *had* moved into San Francisco, then surely there'd be more bodies about. Three women weren't likely to contain the hunger of six vampires for very long. *A jump in the rate of homeless deaths, perhaps?*

Nothing more than what you'd expect. We'll keep checking, though, just in case.

He glanced out the window again and saw the familiar formation of cottonwoods and pines that led into his driveway. He shifted again, half-tempted to just tell the driver to stop here so he could get out and run. The need to hold Nikki, to breathe in the rich scent of her, had become so strong his whole body was beginning to ache. It was only for appearance's sake that he remained in the cab. The driver was a local, and Michael didn't want any gossip started up that could eventually force him to move.

His house came into view—a large, rambling cabin half-hidden by surrounding pines, aspens and cottonwoods. There were no lights visible through any of the windows. He glanced at his watch again and frowned. Nikki was a night owl and rarely went to sleep before midnight. At the very least, he should have seen the soft glow of the television in the front room.

He reached out with his thoughts, but he was met by silence. Either she was asleep, or she wasn't there.

I've done a reading on the case, Seline continued. *But I can't seem to get any clear image. All I can feel is hate.*

That's a given, considering what they're doing to these women. He paid the cab driver, then grabbed his bag and climbed out. The wind whispered through the trees, and the smell of balsam tainted the night air. He switched to the infrared of his vampire vision and scanned the house. There was no life anywhere inside.

Concern knifed through him. She'd made no mention of going anywhere the last time they'd talked— though the phone connection had been bad and had made it hard to hear what she'd been saying.

Something must have happened. He shouldered his bag and raced up the steps.

Michael, I get the feeling you're not exactly paying attention to what I'm saying.

Sorry. I've just arrived home to find that Nikki's not here. He opened the front door and walked through.

Cinnamon and vanilla lingered in the air, mixed with the stronger scent of pine. The house was still warm, so she hadn't been gone long.

Seline's amusement whisked down the link. *Maybe she's teaching you a lesson.*

Lesson? He walked into the living room and smiled. A huge Christmas tree dominated one corner of the room, its top branches bending across the ceiling. Ribbons, tinsel and various other bright baubles hung off every branch, glittering faintly in the moonlight streaming in through the windows.

Yes, you know, Seline continued, *don't expect her to be the good little wife waiting meekly for you to come home.*

She's not my wife. He hesitated, wrapping his fingers around the small package in his pocket—one he'd carried all the way from his farm in Ireland. One he intended to give her on Christmas Eve. *And I certainly don't expect her to wait meekly for me to come home.*

Seline's mental snort stung his mind. *Then what the hell do you expect her to do out there in the sticks? She's a city girl, born and raised, and used to working. With the agency temporarily closed down, you off on cases and refusing her help, it's a wonder she hasn't gone stir crazy.*

It was her choice to stay here, he said, more than a little annoyed at the old witch's sarcasm. Damn it, he didn't need his friends taking Nikki's side against him. *I even offered to pay for a vacation, if that's what she wanted.*

Seline sighed. *After three hundred and sixty years of existence, I thought you'd have learned something about the female species.*

I have—even the old ones can be damn irritating sometimes. He walked into the kitchen. Santas danced around the edges of his refrigerator door, but none of them held notes. All that was on the table were several unopened envelopes and a half-finished Christmas wreath.

Michael, if you really want this relationship to last long-term, you'd better start thinking a little clearer.

He frowned and headed for the stairs. *What do you mean?*

She sighed again. *Have you even discussed the future with her?*

He'd known the old witch long enough to realize she was actually asking if *he'd* thought about the future. Which he had, especially in the last three weeks. But it wasn't something he was about to discuss with Seline, no matter how close a friend she was—not until he'd talked to Nikki first. *We've been living together less than four months. I hardly think she's worrying about the future just yet.* He took the stairs two at a time, then walked down the hall to the bedroom.

She's a very independent individual. Remember that, or you may just get yourself into trouble.

The note was on his pillow. He switched back to the infrared of his vampire vision and picked it up, quickly scanning it. The uneasy tension sitting in his gut intensified, and he sat down on the bed, staring almost blindly at the paper.

Seline's concern whisked through his mind. *What's wrong?*

What wasn't wrong? *Don't bother sending Kat on the helicopter.*

Why?

He crushed the note in his fist and threw it across the room. *I already have help. Nikki's in San Francisco investigating the disappearance from the Diamond Grand.*

Two

"Nik!"

Nikki spun at the sound of her name and grinned as she saw Jake's blond head bobbing up intermittently from the sea of humanity streaming towards the airport exits.

She shouldered her bag and made her way towards him. He grabbed her arm and pulled her into a bear hug that darn near squeezed every ounce of breath from her lungs.

She laughed when she finally could and planted a quick kiss on his cheek. "I missed you, too," she said, then stepped back and studied him critically. "You look good."

No longer was he the pale-looking wraith she'd seen off at the airport only a month before. There was color—and weight—back in his cheeks and a sparkle in the blue of his eyes. And his suit fit him comfortably, rather than looking as if it were hanging on a rack.

"I feel good, too." He wriggled his left arm and fingers. "See, full movement."

She smiled. He'd had a stroke on the operating table, and for a while there, the doctors had feared he might lose mobility down the left side of his body. "I'm glad."

"So am I." He grabbed the bag from her shoulder and swung it across his own. "You wouldn't believe how boring it's been at the hotel—until recently, that is."

"Oh, I'd believe," she said dryly. "And it couldn't

be any more boring than sitting alone in front of the TV all day, with no one to speak to except the mail carrier."

Jake raised his eyebrow, blue eyes amused. "I take it from that comment that Michael managed to escape on another case without you?"

"Yeah. This time he went to Ireland, and I couldn't even keep in mind contact with him. I've spoken to him three times in as many weeks."

"So why didn't you just stay in Lyndhurst?"

She looked away from the intensity of his gaze and studied the blush of dawn visible through the windows. "I guess I was getting a little sick of people gossiping behind my back." Sick of people giving her those sideways glances. She felt guilty enough over Matthew Kincaid's death. She didn't need everyone else dumping on her as well.

"Ah." Jake took her arm and guided her toward the exit. "So why not take a vacation? Michael offered to pay for it, didn't he?

She snorted. "Yeah. But I'm not some chattel he can toss money or a trip at when he wants to get rid of me. If I want to go on a vacation, I'll damn well pay for it myself."

Jake glanced down at her, eyebrow raised again. "That sounds like trouble brewing in paradise."

"Maybe." She frowned, not sure she could make him understand how she felt—especially when she still didn't really understand it herself. "He just takes it for granted that he'll pay for everything. He never lets me contribute money-wise to anything we do. Anything I want he gets for me, and it's gotten to the point where I'm afraid to express an interest in *anything*."

Jake's smile was wry. "Some women would kill for a man like that."

"I know—and I know I haven't got a lot of money to contribute, anyway." She hesitated and shrugged again. "I just hate being dependent on him, I guess." Hated the feeling that she wasn't his equal in *any* way.

"Have you talked to him about this?" Jake steered her towards a waiting limo. The chauffeur opened the door and gestured her inside.

"Nice," she murmured, running her fingers across the plush leather seats as she sat down. "The hotel's, I gather."

Jake nodded and sat down opposite her. "And from your avoidance of the question, I gather you haven't tried talking to him."

"Well, no." She sometimes thought it would be easier to talk to a brick wall than to try to get serious with Michael—at least when it came to what *she* was supposed to do with her life. As far as he was concerned, he loved her and he would support her. End of story. No discussion required.

And as yet, she hadn't really pushed it. A tiny part of her feared to do *anything* that might shatter the magic that had been the last four months.

Jake was regarding her quizzically. "Why not?"

Heat crept into her cheeks, and she looked away again. "We . . . umm . . . get distracted."

He grinned. "At least one part of your life together is still working well."

Very well, she thought with a smile. She'd never thought sex could be so varied—or so damn good. She glanced out the window and wondered if he was home yet. Wondered if he ached to be touched as much as she did.

Wondered how he'd react when he discovered she wasn't there.

"You need to talk to him, Nik," Jake said into the silence. "Remember, he's the old-fashioned type."

"Considering his age, you'd have to say *very* old-fashioned." She leaned back into the seat's luxuriousness. Time to change the subject. Talking about Michael stirred up longing in all the wrong places. "So, tell me about the case."

The amusement died from Jake's face. "Do you remember Mark Wainwright? You met him at one of Mary's dinner parties just before we took on the Kincaid case."

She frowned. "He was that bald-headed man, with the white-haired wife, wasn't he?"

"Yeah. They came to San Francisco three weeks ago for business reasons and have been staying at the Grand." He hesitated. His voice, when he continued, was low and very controlled—yet his anger seemed to burn the air. "Two days ago, his wife, Dale, disappeared. A ransom note turned up yesterday, demanding a million dollars in cash."

As ransoms went, it wasn't particularly large—not when you were as rich as Mark Wainwright supposedly was. "I gather the police have been called in?"

Jake nodded. "And the Feds. But Mark has asked if we'd mind investigating as well."

She raised an eyebrow. "Does he know about our spate of unsuccessful cases?"

"He does." Jake's voice was grim. "Trouble is, he knows Dale's time is limited anyway, and he's willing to try anything."

"Why does he think her time is limited? Isn't he going to pay the ransom?"

"He is, but neither he nor the police are holding out much hope. This isn't a singular kidnapping, you see, but the third within two weeks. The body of the

14

first victim apparently turned up yesterday. The whispers I've heard say she was pretty mutilated."

She raised her eyebrows. "Didn't her husband pay the ransom?"

"He did. And that's what has Mark worried."

"So you want me to have a go at finding her?"

Jake nodded. "It may be Dale's only chance."

If *they* were this woman's only chance, she could be in big trouble. "My gifts have taken some strange turns lately, Jake. I can't guarantee anything."

He shrugged. "If the unconventional doesn't work, we'll go back to the conventional. We're a pretty good team, you know, and we solved an awful lot of cases without the benefit of your abilities."

And even more *with* them. They relied on her gifts far more often than he seemed to think. "So what does Mary think about you getting involved in this case?"

After all, Mary had dragged him to San Francisco not so much to recover from his injuries, but to get him interested in the security job here at her family's hotel—hoping, of course, that he'd give up his investigating days and settle down in a position she considered far less dangerous. And far more respectable.

He sighed. "She's angry with me. Says I have no right to get involved with a police investigation."

"Never stopped us before," Nikki commented, smiling. "And I thought Dale was one of her friends?"

He shook his head. "They barely know each other. I went to college with Mark. We studied law together."

Nikki stared at him in surprise. "You never told me you were a lawyer."

"That's because I'm not. I failed the bar." He

shrugged. "I didn't really care, because by that time I'd realized I just wasn't cut out for the courtroom scene."

In all the years she'd known him, he'd never mentioned how close he'd come to being a lawyer—though maybe it did explain his somewhat cynical opinion of them. And if Mary had known him from college, or at least had known how close he'd come to being a lawyer, maybe that was the reason for the often disappointed note in her voice whenever she spoke about him.

"So you became a private investigator instead? Why?"

"It's something I fell into, thanks to Mark. I was bumming around, looking for something to do, and he asked me if I'd track down a witness for this case he was defending. The rest, as they say, is history."

Then she owed Mark a note of thanks, because if Jake had become a lawyer instead of a private investigator, she probably would never have met him. And beyond Michael, Jake was the one truly good thing that had happened in her life. "Is Mark waiting for us at the hotel?"

Jake glanced at his watch. "Yes. I told him to hunt up some of Dale's things."

Her stomach stirred. She hadn't used her psychometry skills for a good four months—not since she'd tried to find Matthew Kincaid and had become one with him instead, sharing his pain, his fear. Goose bumps trailed across her skin, and she rubbed her arms. What if it happened again? What if she became a part of whatever was happening to this Dale and couldn't escape?

She took a deep breath and pushed the fear away.

16

She had to try, for Jake's sake. He never asked much of her, and this was important to him. "Has he told the police he's asked us to investigate?"

Jake shook his head. "It's not just the police, now, but the Feds as well."

"And won't they be pleased to have a couple of amateurs bumbling about," she said, voice dry.

He shrugged. "Won't be the first time we've crossed swords with the police, and I doubt it will be the last."

She raised her eyebrows. "Then you have no intention of becoming the Diamond Grand's next chief of security?"

"Hell, no." He shuddered and scrubbed a hand through his thinning blond hair. "I'd rather die in the field than die of boredom."

She couldn't hide the surge of relief, and yet in many ways, she knew she was being selfish. Jake had been badly hurt in their last two cases. The next time he just might get his wish. "Mary is making some sense, you know. It would certainly be a lot safer, health-wise at least, if you took the security job."

"Nik, if I wanted safe, I would have become a lawyer." He leaned forward and opened the door as the limousine came to a halt. "And here we are."

She climbed out. The wind whistled around her, damp and cold. She zipped up her jacket and studied the Diamond Grand Hotel. It was smaller than she'd expected, being only nine or ten floors high. It was also a lot older. Ivy climbed randomly over the red-brown brickwork, gently framing the white wooden windows and Juliet balconies. The entrance was a huge, white stone arch, intricately carved with wreaths of flowers and ivy. Two old-fashioned gas lamps sat on the wall either side of the arch, and a canopy curved over the sidewalk, protecting guests from the worst of the weather. Christmas lights climbed around it, twinkling like stars in the fading night.

"It's pretty," she said.

Jake joined her on the sidewalk, her bag slung over his shoulder. "It's that, if nothing else," he said and motioned her forward. "I would still rather be stuck in our paint peeling office than here for the rest of my life."

She glanced back at him as she climbed the steps. "Have you told Mary this?"

The doorman nodded a greeting at them both and opened the door. The warmth of the lobby swirled around her, rich with the scents of freshly-baked bread and strawberries. Her stomach rumbled a reminder that she hadn't eaten since lunch yesterday.

Jake touched her back, guiding her through the doors. "Yes. She's just not listening—as usual."

The lobby was pale yellow and cream and dominated by a huge chandelier that hung in the center of the room. The delicate chains of crystal glittered like gold in the warm yellow light and spun fingers of light through the entire lobby. Under this, on a carved mahogany table, sat the biggest bunch of flowers she'd ever seen. But their pale pinks and greens offset the golden glow of the room and counterbalanced the fiery red cushions that were scattered about on the various chairs.

"This is nice," she murmured, running her fingers across the top of one of the plush velvet chairs.

"This is expensive," Jake replied. "And I've put you in our top room."

18

"You can't—"

"I can," he interrupted. "And I have. No arguments. Consider this little slice of luxury a Christmas gift. I've booked you in for a couple of weeks, so if you want to stay and do some touristy stuff after we solve this case, you're quite welcome to."

He sounded awfully confident that they *would* solve it, even though past experience had taught them both nothing was ever as simple as it seemed. She leaned forward and planted a kiss on his leathery cheek. "You don't have to bribe me to get me to stay, you know. All you have to do is ask."

He smiled. "I thought you might have wanted to spend your first Christmas alone with Michael."

"He wasn't sure whether he was going to make it home in time or not." She shrugged and tried to hide the familiar sense of disappointment. "Besides, Christmas is a time for families—and you and Mary are all the family I have. I was planning to come out here, anyway."

"Good." He stopped at the desk and signed her in.

"There's a message for you, Mr. Morgan." The receptionist handed him a slip of paper along with the room keys.

Jake scanned the note quickly and grinned as he handed it across. "Looks like you might be celebrating Christmas with Michael after all."

Her hands were actually trembling as she took the paper and read it.

I'll be there by ten, it said. *Tell Nikki not to do anything until I arrive.*

Disappointment, and just a little anger, shot through her. She crushed the paper into a ball and tossed it into the nearby waste basket. Why hadn't he left something for her? He knew she was here—even a "can't wait to see you again" would have been nice.

She forced a smile and glanced up at Jake. "Let's go up and meet your friend."

He frowned, blue eyes concerned. "You sure you don't want to wait for Michael?"

"Do you think we can afford to?"

"Well, no, but—"

"No buts," she said with a smile. "Besides, all I'm going to do is see if I can trace her through her possessions. It won't make a difference if he's here or not."

Which was not exactly the truth, especially if her abilities took her into this woman's mind and made her share her experiences. Michael had once warned her she could lose herself if she wasn't very careful. So doing this alone, when he wasn't there to pull her out, was more than just a little dangerous. But she wasn't about to tell Jake that.

He still looked doubtful, but guided her toward the elevator. "If the Feds are still with Mark, it might be wise to try to find Dale in your room."

"It might be better to do that anyway," she commented as the doors closed. "The Feds certainly won't want us involved in the case." And she certainly didn't want them walking into the middle of everything—especially if things went wrong.

Jake nodded. "In that case, I'll escort you to your suite, then go and collect the items you'll need from Mark."

"Good," she said, despite the sliver of unease that curled through her stomach.

They stopped on the top floor and got out. The golden theme from the lobby was extended here, lending the long corridor warmth. Flowers cascaded over tables in corner nooks, and palms sat either side of the elevator doors, their fronds waving gently in the breeze of air conditioning.

"There are only two suites on this floor," Jake said, as he swiped the key card through the lock. "And the other one's not occupied. You and Michael can come and go as you please without disturbing anyone."

He thrust open the door and waved her through. Nikki stopped in the middle of the living room and shook her head in amazement. Talk about opulent! The walls were again pale gold, offset by burnt umber chairs and curtains of rich red and gold. The windows looked out over a leafy park, though the trees were little more than shadows in the fog.

"You have a look around," Jake said, dumping her bag on the ornate mahogany coffee table, "and I'll go see Mark."

She nodded and headed into the bedroom. The bed was big enough to hold a party and was framed by a canopy of red and gold curtains. She touched the comforter, her fingers sinking into its rich redness. The mattress underneath was firm, but not overly so. Just the way she liked it. Directly opposite the bed was a fireplace. She smiled and flopped back onto the bed, closing her eyes as she imagined lying here in Michael's arms, the warmth of the fire caressing their bodies. . . .

Heat stirred through her, and she sighed. Three weeks without his touch was *way* too long.

She lay there for a while, listening to the growing hum of traffic and the musical peal of a bell as a cable car rolled past the hotel.

Then she heard the ding of the elevator returning

and soft footsteps. She sighed again and pushed up from the bed. Time to get to work.

"We'd better shift some of the furniture," she said, walking back into the living room. "The last time I tried this I ended up—"

She stopped abruptly, a cold feeling of dread enveloping her. It wasn't Jake who'd entered her room.

It was a vampire.

Three

He was young and scruffy-looking, dressed in jeans and a black leather jacket decorated in biker's colors. His face was pale, gaunt, and his brown eyes haunted.

Hasn't been turned all that long, Nikki thought. Which only made him all the more dangerous.

She clenched her fist against the energy burning across her fingers and shifted her stance slightly, ready to dive out of the way should he attack.

"What do you want?" She kept her voice flat and low, not wanting to provoke him in any way.

"Are you Nikki James?" His voice was guttural, thick.

A sliver of fear ran through her. How did he know her name? She'd just arrived in San Francisco, and no one but Jake and Mark really knew she was here. "And what do you want with her?"

He smiled, revealing long, sharp canines. It was rather obvious what he intended to do—suck her dry.

"You're her, ain't you?" His gaze travelled the length of her body and back again, and an excited light crept past the haunted look in his brown eyes. "Gonna enjoy tasting you, I am."

His gaze seemed to intensify, and power slivered through the air between them. She frowned. He was obviously trying to get a mind-lock on her, but thanks to what she'd become, she was basically immune to the mind-control attempts of most vampires. Despite her earlier fears, she suspected even Michael couldn't really force her to act against her wishes—not that he'd ever tried.

Evidently, this vampire had no idea his mind assault wouldn't work, which was odd. Elizabeth, the now-dead vampire who'd turned Michael so long ago, had taken one look and known she was a thrall. Had known mind control wouldn't work simply because Michael had, in a sense, created her. So why couldn't this one tell?

She shifted her weight from one foot to the other and continued to watch him, her hands still clenched against the energy burning across her fingertips. Sweat tickled down his hollowed cheeks, and after a few seconds, he frowned.

"Well, hell," he muttered. "That ain't working, is it?"

"No, it's not," she replied. "Who sent you here to kill me?"

"Yeah, like I'm going to tell you that." He snorted and produced a knife from the side pocket of his dirty jeans. "Ready to die?"

Fear slid through her. The knife was long and sharp and gleamed silver in the room's warm light— and it was not the sort of weapon you could easily conceal. He should never have been able to get past hotel security with a weapon like that stuck down his pants. There had been at least two discreetly positioned guards near the hotel's main entrance, and it would have taken a lot of psychic strength to control their minds enough to slip past unnoticed. More strength than what this vampire had, anyway. And she had no doubt that after the recent kidnapping, security would have been doubled on every exit.

So, if he hadn't come through any secured entrance, where in hell *had* he come from?

And why was he using a knife when he was a damn vampire?

He snarled silently and sprang, slashing wildly with the knife. She dove out of the way, but he was faster than she'd expected. The blade nicked the sleeve of her jacket and sliced into her arm as easily as butter. Biting back her yelp, she hit the carpet and rolled back to her feet. The vampire was little more than a blur, the knife a streak of silver as it arced toward her. She thrust out her hand, hitting him with the pent-up energy.

He flew across the room and smashed into an expensive looking painting. The frame and glass shattered, showering the vampire with shards as he hit the floor then scrambled back to his feet.

She thrust out kinetically again, this time retrieving rather than pushing away. The vampire's eyes went wide as two jagged pieces of frame flew across the room.

She caught them deftly and forced a grin, feigning a confidence she certainly didn't feel. Warmth flowed down her arm, and the cuff of her sweater was growing damp. She had to end this quickly before she started bleeding all over the carpet.

A wild light entered the young vampire's eyes. He could obviously smell the blood, even if he couldn't yet see it. "How'd you do that?"

"Magic," she said and waved the stake in her right hand, catching his gaze. "Want to see more?"

He sneered again. "I'm going to kill you, you know. You can't beat me. I'm a vampire. I'm invincible."

She snorted softly. "You've been listening to a few too many fairy tales, kid. No vampire is invincible. Not even the old ones."

He launched across the room, his body blurring. She twisted out of the way and slashed through the shadows, stabbing one of the stakes deep into his leg.

He hissed, a sound full of anger and pain, then twisted and threw the knife. She ducked and heard the blade thud into something solid. Heard the whistle of air and twisted desperately away—but not fast enough. His fist smashed into her chin and lifted her off the ground. She flew across the room and crashed into the wall. Air whooshed from her lungs, leaving her gasping and seeing stars as she slumped to the floor.

A warning tingled across her skin. The vampire was coming at her again. She thrust out her hand and reached again for kinetic energy. He slammed into her wall of power, abruptly stopping. Pain slithered through her head, a warning she was beginning to push her limits. She ignored it and climbed slowly to her feet.

Warmth trickled down her fingers. She thrust her hand into her pocket and met the vampire's gaze. It was filled with desperation and hunger.

"Tell me who sent you here to kill me," she said.

He didn't answer, just twisted desperately, fighting her hold on him. Every movement stabbed red-hot pokers through her head. She had to end this quickly, while she still had some semblance of control.

"Tell me." She thrust him backwards, towards the windows and the pale beams of sunlight beginning to filter into the room.

His struggles grew more violent, the pain in her head sharper.

"Tell me," she repeated and pushed him closer.

Light caressed his left arm and, almost instantly, his fingers went a deep, dark red. He screamed. It was a sound filled with fear and anger, and shuddered right though every fiber of her being. Not very old at all, she thought, and pulled him back a little.

"I can't." His eyes were haunted, frantic. "He'll kill me."

She wondered how young he really was—or how young he'd been when he'd been turned. Despite the bravado and the tough words, she suspected he was only in his mid-to-late teens. A babe in human or vampire terms. But then, Jasper had been a lot younger, and he'd been one of the most depraved bastards she'd ever met. She raised an eyebrow. "And you think I won't?"

He stared at her for a heartbeat. His desperation singed the air as he began to struggle again. Red-hot pokers gnawed at her brain, and pain shuddered through her entire being. She couldn't hold him for much longer—and when the net of power failed, she'd be in trouble.

"Are you really so desperate to die?" she said, thrusting him back into the light.

He screamed again. "I can't," he said, twisting severely. "If I go back without killing you, I'm finished."

"Then don't go back. Run for it."

"You don't know these people . . ."

He gave a final twist and shattered her hold on him. Agony locked her mind tight, and she fell to her knees, fighting tears and the red tide of pain threatening to engulf her. She wrapped her fingers around the remaining stake and thrust it out in front of her, knowing it would be as useless as a toothpick against a snake.

But the young vampire didn't attack.

He ran for the window and the sunlight instead.

"Don't—"

The rest of her words were lost in the shattering of glass. She scrambled to her feet and staggered over to the window. The vampire's body became flame the minute he fully hit the sunlight, and the fire consumed him with a fierceness that turned her stomach. There was nothing left of him but black dust by the time he hit the pavement.

"What the hell has been going on here?" Jake said from behind her.

The cavalry has arrived. But too late, as usual. An insane desire to laugh bubbled through her, but what came out was more a sob. She slid down the wall and closed her eyes.

"Nik? What happened? Are you all right?" Jake knelt beside her and touched her arm. She flinched, and he cursed.

"You're bleeding. Henry, get the hotel doctor up here immediately."

She opened her eyes a slither and saw a big man in an official-looking black and gold uniform walk over to the phone. Henry, obviously. "Are all the exits in this hotel guarded?" she murmured.

Jake frowned. "Yes. Why?"

"Because a vampire just waltzed into my room and attacked me with a very large knife he'd stuck down the leg of his jeans."

Jake glanced quickly at the man on the phone and lowered his voice to ask, "Are you sure?"

"Sure that it was a vampire?" She forced a smile and rubbed her forehead with her good hand. "Oh yeah, I'm sure. If you look down at the pavement below this window, you'll see his dust."

"Did he say anything?"

"Other than they wanted me dead, no."

"The doc's on his way," Henry said as he put the receiver back down. "And I called the cops."

Jake cursed under his breath. "Thanks, Henry. Do you mind standing guard outside the door until the police arrive?"

The big man nodded and headed for the door.

"He knew my name, Jake," she said when Henry had disappeared. "It was no mistake."

"But you're not registered here under your name—only as my guest. How the hell did they even know you were here? You'd barely arrived."

"I haven't got any answers. He killed himself rather than give me anything."

Jake thrust a hand through his hair. "I don't like this."

"Join the club," she murmured and looked past him as a gray-suited man carrying a heavy bag bustled into the room.

"About time," Jake said, rising to make room for the stranger. "She's bleeding pretty heavily from her left arm."

"It's just my arm that's injured, not my tongue," she muttered.

The gray-suited stranger knelt beside her, then reached into his bag and grabbed some gloves. "You able to remove your sweater, or shall we just cut it?"

"Cut it," she said. The less she moved right now, the better it was for the pain in her head. She closed her eyes again, leaning her head back against the wall while the doctor sliced open the sleeve of her sweater.

"Pretty nasty," he murmured after a while. "And you're losing a fair bit of blood. You should really go to the emergency room."

"No. Just stitch it up, Doctor. I'll be fine."

"I really think you'd be better in emergency. The

29

wound is very deep, and might have caused serious muscle damage."

She bit back her annoyance. The last thing she felt like doing right now was arguing—especially when her head felt ready to explode. All she wanted to do was take some painkillers and lie down in the dark until the pain drifted away.

"I don't care what you really think," she snapped. "Just stitch the wound up. If you're worried about being sued, write up a release form, and I'll sign the damn thing."

The doctor glanced around. "Mr. Morgan? This could come back on the hotel, you know."

"It won't. Just do as she asks," Jake said.

The doctor muttered something under his breath. She closed her eyes again, trying to ignore the sharp sting of the needle as he began stitching her arm.

Time slithered by. "Here," he said eventually, "is a prescription for painkillers. If you see any sign of infection near the wound, get yourself to a hospital immediately. Try not to use your arm much for the next few days."

She opened her eyes and accepted the white slip from him. He shoved the bloody cloths in a bag, peeled off his gloves and placed them in a medical-waste bag, then picked everything up and headed out the door.

"You want me to get that prescription filled?" Jake said into the silence.

She nodded and handed it to him. "Don't bother with a guard near the door, either."

"Nik, I can't leave you here unprotected."

"Why not? A guard wouldn't have stopped that vampire, believe me." She rubbed a hand across her eyes, trying to ease the ache. "Besides, it may have been just a random attack."

Jake snorted. "When he knew your name? You can't honestly believe that."

She didn't. But right now, she just wasn't up to looking for answers or worrying. "Look, I'll be fine—the vampire won't be missed for a few hours yet. I'll just catch some sleep, and then I'll do the search for Dale."

Footsteps sounded outside. She tensed and didn't relax any when two burly police officers appeared in the doorway. Sleep, it seemed, was a ways off yet.

She answered their questions as civilly as her headache allowed, wishing all the while everyone would just leave her alone. They "tutted" over the window, gouged the knife from the mahogany sideboard and eventually said they'd get back to her.

Not that she expected to hear from them anytime soon. Knife attacks, it seemed, weren't big news. Especially when nobody was missing or dead.

By that time, Jake was back with her painkillers. She climbed wearily to her feet and gave him a tired smile. "Thanks."

"I've arranged for you to be put into the next suite. We have to get the window here fixed anyway."

She nodded, though she had a suspicion changing location wasn't going to make a great deal of difference to whoever was after her. She collected her bag and followed him into the next suite. It was almost identical to the original one.

"I've already told Mark it'll be this afternoon before we can try to find Dale. Go get some sleep, Nik. You look like shit."

"Gee, thanks, Boss. It's nice to know you're always there with an encouraging word."

31

He grinned and handed her the keycard. "I'll head downstairs and keep an eye out for Michael."

She glanced at her watch. "It's barely even seven."

"Yeah, but your boyfriend has a habit of turning up when he's least expected. I'd hate for him to walk in and find you like this. He can get pretty temperamental when it comes to your safety."

She grinned. "Anyone would think you were scared of him."

The sudden seriousness in Jake's expression surprised her. "Look, I know he would never hurt you, and probably not me— but I've seen what he can do, Nik. And part of me still does fear him." He hesitated, then shrugged. "It's not just the vampire factor, either."

She touched his arm, squeezing gently. "I know what you mean." Because she did. She loved Michael, and she trusted him. But there had been a few times in the past when his reactions, his anger, had frightened her. He may have controlled his dark half, but it was still a part of him, and none of them could really afford to forget that.

Certainly Michael never did.

"Henry's stationed near your door, and there's another guard near the elevator." Jake wagged a warning finger in front of her nose. "No arguments, missy. They'll stay until Michael gets here."

"Fine," she muttered, too tired to argue any more. "Wake me at twelve, and I'll try finding Dale."

"You wake when you wake. Just get reception to page me when you do. Sleep tight."

She watched him disappear out the door before heading into the bedroom. She grabbed a glass of water from the bathroom and took a couple of painkillers, then stripped and climbed into the party-sized bed.

Shame I'm alone, she thought and snuggled deep into the silk sheets. But as sleep drifted in, dreams stirred.

Dreams that warned of death striking down someone close to her.

Someone she loved.

Four

Michael climbed out of the cab and glanced up at the sky. It was close to ten, but the fog had hung around, muting the full force of the sun. Even so, he could feel it itching across his skin.

He collected his bag and strode towards the hotel. He'd barely entered the lobby when the feeling that something was wrong hit him.

A feeling not helped when he saw Jake striding towards him.

"Michael," Jake said, holding out his hand. "Nice to see you again."

He restrained the urge to read Jake's thoughts and shook his hand impatiently. "What's wrong?"

Jake sighed. "You're almost as bad as Nikki. There's no hiding a problem from either—"

"Is she okay?" he said sharply.

"She's fine. I'll take you there now." Jake motioned Michael towards the elevator. Once the doors were closed, he continued, "She was attacked this morning by a vampire. She took care of him, but he managed to nick her arm with a knife, and I think she overextended her abilities."

Relief ran through him. At least that explained the haze of pain he'd been getting from her all morning. "I gather it wasn't a random attack?"

Jake shook his head. "He knew her name."

"Did she get anything else from him?"

"No. He jumped through the window and fried rather than tell her anything."

He frowned. That sounded more a compulsion

than fear. If Nikki had overstretched her abilities, she certainly wouldn't have been much of a threat to the vampire—psychically, anyway. He could have escaped if he'd wanted to.

If it *was* a compulsion, it could mean real trouble. There weren't many vampires strong enough to force their will upon another brother of the night. Elizabeth had been capable of it. So was he. He knew of maybe three or four others, but none of them were currently in America. All of them were what he termed 'master' vampires—vampires who had lived long enough to fully understand and control all the gifts vampirism endowed.

And he had no doubt that this attack was somehow connected to the vampires who'd snatched the three women. It was too much of a coincidence, otherwise.

"How many people know she's staying here?"

"Besides me and Mary, only Mark. Nik's helping me find his wife."

"Yes, I know all about that." The elevator came to a halt, and the door opened, revealing a burly security guard. Michael glanced at Jake. "Thanks for taking extra precautions."

Jake smiled. "I love her, too, you know."

Michael nodded and tried to curb the growing need to see her. To take her in his arms and breathe in the sweet, warm scent of her. "Has she tried to track Dale Wainwright yet?"

"No. But only because of the attack."

At least he had something to thank the attacker for. He had no doubt she would have tried it otherwise—despite the dangers involved. Sometimes, she could be incredibly blind to her own safety.

Jake swiped the card through the lock. "How did

you know it was Dale Wainwright we're looking for?"

Michael waited until they were in the suite and the door closed to answer. "The Circle sent me here to sort it out. We think a gang of vampires are behind the kidnappings."

He dropped his bag on the sofa and walked over to the bedroom, pausing in the doorway to breathe deep. She smelled of cinnamon and vanilla. Of life and love, and everything he'd ever longed for.

She was asleep, facing away from him, shoulders bare and one arm exposed. His body stirred at the thought of holding her close, caressing the warm silk of her skin—something he could not do just yet. She was here, she was safe and, for now, that was all he needed to know.

"Oh great," Jake said behind him. "So Dale could be dead right now, for all we know?"

"Not necessarily. The first victim lasted almost two weeks before they killed her." Two weeks that had surely been hell, but there was no need to tell Jake that. "You want to show me where the attack against Nikki happened?"

Jake led him into the other suite, and he walked across to the window. The glass had yet to be replaced, and soot still dusted the balcony below them. "What time did the attack happen?"

Jake frowned. "A little before seven. Why?"

He shrugged. "Just curious." At that hour, the rising sun had little strength. The only way it could have killed Nikki's attacker was if the vampire was fairly new to his condition. If that were the case, even the sunrise would have been deadly. So how did he get into the hotel, if not via the streets?

"Has the Circle given you any idea what we're up against?" Jake continued.

Michael glanced toward him. "We're?"

Jake's expression was resolute. "You're not getting rid of either of us on this one."

He'd known he couldn't stop Nikki's involvement—he might as well try to stop the San Francisco earth from ever shaking. But he had hoped to avoid dragging Jake in as well, especially since he'd just recovered from major surgery.

"What does Mary think of you getting involved?"

Jake shrugged. "Mark's a good friend. I've known him all my life. Mary understands that."

Michael studied him for a moment. Mary might have understood his friendship with Mark, but if Jake's thoughts were anything to go by, she certainly didn't understand his need to get involved with the case and perhaps endanger his life again. One long-time relationship headed for the rocks, Michael thought, and remembered Seline's warning.

He frowned and crossed his arms, watching the stirring breeze brush the remnants of the vampire from the balcony.

"Did your boss provide you with any other clues?" Jake continued.

Michael smiled. Seline would laugh at the thought of anyone calling her his boss. She gave him assignments and ran the Circle, yes, but she was far from his employer. "Other than there being six vampires involved, no."

Jake grimaced. "We barely survived Jasper and Monica—how are we going to survive six of the bastards?"

"Not all vampires are as sick as Jasper." He couldn't help the edge of self-derision in his voice. Mainly because many of them were—even him, in times past.

And given what Seline had told him, these six certainly rated high in that category.

"Great." Jake took a deep breath. "Look, I'll let you go back and get some rest. I told Nik to page me when she wakes."

Michael returned to the other suite and walked into the bedroom, stopping near the bed. He watched her breathe and listened to the steady beat of her heart—a siren's song that stirred the darkness in him despite his tight leash of control. He let his gaze drink in her face, from the fullness of her mouth to the small lines of laughter beginning to appear near her eyes. Lines that had not been there when they'd first met.

He stripped and climbed into bed. She stirred, her thoughts touching his, warm and fuzzy with sleep, yet still flushed with pain. Closing his eyes, he reached into her mind, easing the surface turmoil, drawing in her pain. After a while, she sighed, and her frown disappeared. He wrapped an arm around her waist and pulled her close. And, for the first time in weeks, felt a sense of peace. Coming home had never felt so good.

Heat wrapped around her, pressed against her. Hands caressed her, hands that were strong and yet so gentle as they explored her body and teased it to life.

Nikki sighed, enjoying his touch until it became an ache that thrummed through her entire being. Only then did she turn. She met his gaze, her stomach flip-flopping as she momentarily lost herself in the ebony warmth of his eyes.

"The wanderer returns," she murmured, trailing her finger down his cheek, gently outlining his full

38

lips. "All I need now is coffee, and my life is once again complete."

He raised a dark eyebrow, amusement in his eyes. "Really?" His hand slipped between her legs. "You sure I can't interest you in anything else?"

Pleasure rippled through her. "Well, maybe there is *one* other thing I might be interested in." Her voice came out a little breathless, and she growled in frustration when his touch left her.

He smiled and caught her hand, kissing her fingertips. "I have discovered something over these last three weeks."

"What's that?" She hooked a leg over his hip and pulled him close, so that the hard length of him rested against her. Gently, she began rocking her hips.

Heat slithered through the link between them, wildfire ready to explode.

"I've discovered that celibacy is not something I care for."

"Well, don't come to me looking for pity. You're the one who won't let me accompany you."

"I know, but someone has to keep you safe." He leaned forward and kissed her with a tender urgency that shivered through her entire being.

"I don't want safe," she said against his lips. "I just want you."

His gaze met hers, rich with desire and love. "You have my heart, you have my soul, and right now, you can have as much of my body as you can handle."

She raised an eyebrow, a grin teasing her lips. "I can handle quite a lot, you know."

"I certainly hope so," he murmured and rolled on top of her.

She shifted her legs to accommodate him, and he slid deep inside. "Oh my," she whispered, wrapping her legs around him. "That's an awful lot of missing you have there."

He grinned at her. "You haven't felt the half of it yet, my love."

And he proceeded to show her just what he meant.

The scent of fresh coffee stirred her sometime later. She yawned and stretched and decided she felt like a cat who'd just feasted on cream—deliciously wicked and terribly contented. It was, she thought with a smile, amazing just how much several hours of good loving could improve your outlook on life.

Michael appeared in the doorway. He'd obviously taken a shower because his dark hair was still damp. He was barefoot, and looked damn sexy in thigh hugging jeans and a black cotton sweater—one, she noted with pleasure, that she'd bought him just before he'd left for Ireland.

"Coffee, ma'am," he said, placing a tray on her bedside table. "And breakfast."

She scooted up in the bed and accepted the coffee he handed her. She took a sip—it was strong and sweet and just the way she liked it—and sighed in contentment. "Now I *am* a happy woman."

"So easily pleased," he teased and sat down beside her. "How is your arm?"

She glanced down in surprise, having totally forgotten about it. The doctor had placed a clear plastic film over the wound, and it was easy to see that there was no sign of infection. "Fine. Doesn't even hurt when I move it."

He touched her arm, gently probing around the wound. "It should nearly be healed, but we'll leave the film on until tomorrow."

She nodded and tried to ignore the sliver of unease. When he'd shared his life force with her, he'd also shared his amazing healing capabilities. It was something she was still trying to adjust to.

"Tell me about the vampire who attacked you."

She shrugged and sipped her coffee. "There's not much to tell. He had to be a fairly new vampire, and he was pretty much convinced of his invincibility."

"Most newly turned are," Michael said, voice dry. "Comes with the condition, I'm afraid."

She raised an eyebrow. "Were you?"

His dark gaze searched hers. She wondered why. "Yes," he said after a moment, "though it took me less time than others to realize my mortality."

"Why?"

He hesitated. "Elizabeth generally liked her men young and in harems. I was but one of three she turned that year, and the shock of learning that—combined with having to fight for her affections—brought me to my senses sooner."

Pain slithered through her, even though she knew it was ridiculous. They both had pasts—and ex's—that were best forgotten. Yet she hadn't given up life and everything she'd ever known for her ex. "So why did you stay with her?"

He smiled—a gentle, loving smile that warmed her entire being. "I have never said I was very bright back then."

Which didn't entirely answer her question, but she didn't push.

"Can you remember anything else about this vampire?" he asked.

She frowned. "He was wearing a leather jacket. And biker colors."

Though he raised an eyebrow, he didn't seem surprised. "Did you recognize them?"

She shook her head. "I wasn't exactly concentrating on them. But he knew my name, which has to mean he somehow knew I was coming."

"Yes. And until we know exactly why that vamp was after you, we had better be doubly careful." He glanced at the clock. "Jake will be up here in a few minutes. Apparently his friend is getting pretty worried."

It was close to four, so no wonder. Nearly nine hours had passed, and no attempt had been made to find his wife. "I'll just finish this, then I'll dress."

He touched her cheek, his fingers warm against her skin. "Are you sure you're up to this? It could be pretty bad."

She frowned, her gaze searching his. "You're here because of the kidnappings, aren't you?" *Not* because of her. Disappointment mixed with anger, and she looked away, trying to conceal her hurt.

Which was stupid, really, when he could read her thoughts as easily as he breathed.

He touched her chin, bringing her gaze back to his. "Do you doubt that I love you?"

"No, but—"

His voice was gentle yet unyielding. "Do you have any doubt about how much I needed to see you?"

She grinned faintly. "After this morning's efforts? Not one."

"Then do not doubt me when I say that no matter where you were, that is where I would have gone first. Nothing else was more important to me."

His words sang through her heart, yet part of her remained stubbornly angry. "But you could have told—"

He stopped her with a kiss that stole her breath and left her dizzy.

"That," she said when she could, "is not playing fair."

"Eat." He smiled and handed her a sticky, fruit-filled bun.

She did, but only because she knew he wouldn't let her out of bed until she did. Under normal circumstances that might not have been a bad thing, but she wasn't here to enjoy herself—not right away, anyway. She had work to do first. She drained the remains of her coffee, and he took it from her, placing it back on the tray.

"Why will it be bad?" she asked.

"We think there's a gang of vampires behind the kidnappings. They killed their first victim by draining her blood—but not before they'd brutalized her."

She swallowed. Was the vampire who attacked her connected to the vampires who might be behind these kidnappings? She suspected he was, and that only made the attack more frightening. It suggested they thought her some sort of threat, but how had they known she was even coming here? Only Jake, Mary and Mark had known. A chill ran through her, and she rubbed her arms. "Brutalized how?"

"They shaved her head, scarred her face, and—" He hesitated. "Cut off her breasts."

She shuddered and crossed her arms over her chest—not that she had an awful lot to protect. "Why on earth would anyone do something as . . . depraved . . . as that? They're sick. Totally sick."

"Yes. And we have to stop them before they can do it again or take any more women."

"We? You're not going to play the heavy and order me to stay put and out of danger?"

"Would you listen if I did?"

"No."

"Exactly. You'd gallivant off with Jake, and no doubt fall headfirst into trouble. At least if you're with me, I can keep an eye on you."

Anger stirred again. "I don't need you to play nursemaid. I *am* able to look after myself, you know."

"You barely survived Jasper," he reminded her softly. "And there are six of them this time."

Memories rose, and once again she felt Jasper's heated touch against her skin, his teeth in her arm, sinking into her flesh. Saw the desire in his eyes as he sucked her life away. She shivered and thrust the images away.

"You can't be looking over your shoulder trying to protect me all the time. That'll only lead us into trouble." She hesitated, her gaze searching his again. The resistance she could feel in his thoughts was evident in his eyes. "If we are going to have any hope of pulling this off, we have to work as a team."

He touched her face, trailing his fingers down to her lips. "Are you asking me to ignore what I feel?"

His caress flushed heat against her skin and sent shivers of desire pulsing through her. She pushed his hand away. They needed to have this conversation, and for once, she would not be distracted.

"No, what I'm asking is for you to trust me."

He frowned. "I do trust—"

"No, you don't," she interrupted. "Not when it comes to taking care of myself. You cosset me, Michael, and it's not what I want. It's not what I need."

His frown deepened, his thoughts suddenly wary. Confused. "After three hundred and sixty years of searching for my heart's desire, you certainly cannot blame me for wanting to pamper you."

"Pamper away—just don't go overboard. Don't wrap me in cotton and expect me to remain happy. I'm not built that way, Michael." She hesitated. What she was about to say would hurt him, yet it needed to be said, and said now, before time and resentment put real force into the words. "I need to be a full partner in your life, not something you pull out to play with every now and then."

Anger surged briefly through the link, a wave of red heat that damn near blew her senses. He stood up abruptly, his face expressionless, dark eyes stony.

"Do you really think that is all you are to me? A toy I will eventually grow tired of?"

That's not what she'd said at all, and they both knew it. Yet, deep down some small part of her *did* think that. Had always thought that. Eternity was a long time. She had no doubt that he loved her, but how could he say now that he would never tire of her? He'd loved Elizabeth enough to give up life for her, and yet he had remained with her less than a century.

She rubbed her eyes. "You're missing my point."

"No, you're missing mine." He glanced around sharply. "Jake's coming. You had better get dressed."

She cursed silently. "We need to finish this conversation."

"Maybe," he said, voice flat, free of the tension she could feel in the link. "For now, just get dressed."

He walked away. She picked up a pillow and tossed it at his retreating back. It hit him between the shoulder blades, and he glanced back, irritation flaring in his eyes. "If you want to be a full partner, start acting like one."

She clenched her fists and somehow resisted the temptation to kinetically smack him against the nearest wall. God, he could be *so* annoying. "I'll start acting like one when you start treating me like one."

He didn't answer, just walked out the door. But she knew his thoughts. He wasn't about to let her walk completely by his side—not when it came to sharing the dangers of his life.

And if he didn't, it would eventually tear them apart. He couldn't honestly expect her to sit at home for the rest of eternity while he went out and risked his life. The last four months had given her the taste of what *that* would be like.

She heard the door open, then Jake's voice greeting Michael. She sighed, gathered some clothes, then headed into the bathroom for a quick shower.

When she entered the living room ten minutes later, Michael was on the sofa reading a newspaper, his bare feet propped up on the ornate coffee table. He looked casual, at ease—an image at odds with the tension she could still feel in him. She didn't bother trying to read his thoughts, simply because she knew he'd block her. Next to his feet were two plastic bags. Dale Wainwright's belongings, no doubt.

Jake was standing near the windows. He glanced around, but his welcoming smile failed to mask the concern in his eyes. "I hate to hurry you, Nik, but we really need to get moving on this."

She sat down opposite Michael, who made no comment at her choice of seating. "What's happened," she said, picking up the plastic bag with the bra in it. Images skittered through her mind, muted flashes of color and sound. She only had to reach a little and she'd be with Dale Wainwright, sharing her thoughts and her feelings. Nikki licked her lips, not sure she was ready to face all that again.

"They found the second victim," Jake said grimly. "From what the cops said to Mark, she was pretty beaten up. Worse than the first victim."

"Then we'd better hurry." She took a deep breath and met Michael's dark gaze. "I don't like the feel of the images coming from this. You'll pull me out if things get too heavy, won't you?"

Irritation seared the link, though his face remained expressionless. "Of course."

She opened the plastic bag and let the bra fall into her hand. Images surged, too fast and too sharp to capture fully. She frowned, trying to gain some focus, trying to see where Dale was.

Control it, Nikki. Don't let yourself be pulled too deeply into her mind.

Going deep might be the only way I can find out where she is.

The images flowed past her, quicksilver thrusts that refused to be pinned. She bit her lip and pushed a little deeper. Fear swam around her, a cloying scent that clogged her throat, making it difficult to breathe.

It's too dangerous. Just sort through the images, and we'll see where they lead us.

They didn't have the time—Dale didn't have the time. She could feel it in the other woman's fear—feel it in her hurt and humiliation.

Nikki's breath caught in her throat, and her heart began to pound so fast she feared it was going to gallop out of her chest. *Oh God, I don't want to do this.* Her fingers twitched as she battled the urge to drop the bra and break the contact.

Then don't. Pull out.

I can't. Not if she wanted to be his partner rather than merely a spectator.

Concern and annoyance washed down the link. *Now is not time the time or the place to be trying to prove anything to me. If you think it's too dangerous, pull out. We'll find her another way.*

But they'd never find Dale in time to save her. That much was evident from the images. It left her with no real choice. Taking a deep breath, she clenched her fingers around the bra and dived deeply into the pool of memories.

And became one with Dale Wainwright.

Five

Dale drew her legs close to her chest and wrapped her arms around them. She felt cold, so cold—like it had seeped deep into her bones and she was never going to get warm again. The air itself was damp, its touch icy against her bare skin. But it wasn't so much the cold chilling her bones, but fear.

Her lip trembled, and she closed her eyes, trying to ignore the sounds outside her cell. The slap of flesh against flesh, the groan of ecstasy. Laughter, high and insane, followed by a quick, desperate whimper.

Don't think, she thought. *Don't imagine*. But how could she not, when all she could see was darkness and all she could hear was those sounds?

She knew it was only a matter of time before they came for her. Before they started doing to her what they were doing to that other woman.

Terror rose, and for a second, she couldn't even breathe. Her chest felt so tight it ached, and her left hand tingled. She frowned and wriggled her fingers, wondering if it was just the cold or something more.

She shifted slightly, trying to get more comfortable. The mattress scraped harshly under her buttocks—it was little more than straw and scratched like sandpaper. But it was softer, and warmer, than the bricks—her only other choice of seating.

A gurgling broke the momentary silence, followed by the sound of someone slurping. Messy drinker, Dale thought distastefully. She licked her lips and wished they'd give her some water. Then thought better of it. The less she saw of her captors, the better off she'd be.

The whimpering died, but the silence was, in some ways, more frightening. She stared into the darkness, unable to see her toes let alone the door six steps away. For several moments, all she could hear was the rattle of her own heart, the harsh sound of her breaths. Then the lock scraped, and air stirred as the door opened.

She couldn't see him, but she could smell him. He reeked of death and blood and water long gone stagnant. She edged back into the corner, a small whimper escaping her lips.

He laughed. The sound crawled over her skin and sent her heart into overdrive. The aching in her chest leaped into focus.

"Just a taste. Just a little taste," he murmured. His voice was childlike, innocent, and yet somehow evil. "I need it. He has to see that, he can't deprive me of that."

He ambled towards her, something she heard rather than saw. "Just one little taste," he continued.

He skimmed a hand up her leg, his touch fiery against her skin. She screamed . . .

. . . the silent scream reverberated through Michael's soul. He drew Nikki into his lap and sat back down. She didn't say anything, just wrapped her arms around his neck and hung on tight. He rubbed his hands up her arms and lightly touched her thoughts, carefully detaching the remaining threads holding her mind to Dale's.

She sighed. *Thank you.*

Her mind voice was clear, unfettered by pain or shadows that belonged to Dale. Relief surged through him, and he brushed a kiss against the top of her head. She never seemed to realize just how dangerous this developing ability of hers could be—or if she did, she didn't seem to care. What worried him more, though, was the fact it seemed far stronger now than it had been the last time she'd used it.

I'm going to have to teach you how to control that gift of yours.

Uneasiness washed through the link. *I'm not sure it's something I really want to control.*

Are you intending to stop using it?

She hesitated. *No.*

Then you must learn to control it. I don't want to lose you in the mind of another. He caressed the silk of her hair. She'd cut it sometime in the last three weeks. It now brushed her shoulder blades rather than the middle of her back, but had more of a wave in it than before.

She shifted slightly, and her gaze met his. Fear lurked deep in the rich amber depths. "Can that really happen?"

"Yes," he said softly. He brushed a strand of hair from her eyes. "And I don't really have to tell you that, do I?"

She bit her lip and didn't answer. She didn't have to. The fear washing through the link was answer enough.

"Promise me you won't try that again without me nearby," he continued.

She hesitated and met his gaze, her expression suddenly defiant. "Are you going to reconsider your position about me working with you?"

He bit down on a rush of anger and said as calmly as he could, "No."

"Then I will make no promises." She pushed off

his lap and moved back to the other sofa. "I found her," she added, looking across to Jake.

"I gathered as much," Jake said. "What's happening to her?"

He was still standing near the window, but his arms were crossed, and his expression annoyed. And with good cause, Michael thought, glancing at Nikki. Every second they sat here arguing was another second in which Dale might die. Heat flushed Nikki's cheeks, but she gave little other indication she'd heard his silent rebuke.

"She's alive and relatively unhurt." She hesitated again, and fear flashed through the link between them.

Dale might be alive, but something had certainly happened to her. He wondered why she wasn't telling Jake. Wondered why *he* could no longer see the images in her mind. Had her ability become so strong she was somehow able to block him? "Did you see or hear anything that would give us a starting point?"

She shook her head. "No. It was pitch black—no external sounds, other than—" She paused, and cleared her throat. "Someone having sex nearby. A vamp came into the cell she was in, and he smelled like blood and putrid water."

"Nothing else?" he asked softly, knowing from her fear that there was.

She rubbed her arms and glanced at him. *The vamp was about to feed on her.*

I gathered that. Why aren't you telling Jake?

Tell him that his best friend's wife is currently some desperate vampire's meal? I'm not that insensitive.

Her mental tone implied that *he* was. He pushed away his annoyance and met her glare. *Jake is aware we are hunting vampires.*

52

Maybe. But he doesn't need to know what is happening to her right now. How could he keep the horror of that from Mark? They've been friends all their lives. Mark would see it in Jake's eyes.

Jake has been a private investigator a long time. I think he'd be able to conceal a truth or two from a client.

Not this truth. Not everyone is as an accomplished a liar as you, you know.

His annoyance rose another notch. *I have never lied to you.*

She gave a mental snort. *How true. You work on a need-to-know basis—and I never seem to need to know it all, do I?*

Nikki, it's—

For my own safety, she finished tartly. *Yeah, I know.*

He pushed away his growing irritation and the need to keep arguing. Now was not the time for this sort of quarrel. *We have a woman to rescue. Let's save our petty squabbles until after that job is done.*

This is far from petty, believe me.

Not when compared to what has already happened to two women, and what might currently be happening to Dale.

She stared at him for a minute then looked away, but not before he'd glimpsed the brief sheen of tears in her eyes. He frowned, not sure whether the cause was his continuing refusal to discuss her working with him or the thought of Dale's life being sucked away. Either way, it didn't really matter—he still felt like a bastard.

Damn it, why couldn't she just see sense and give this insanity up?

"So you saw nothing that gives us a clue as to where she might be?" Jake said into the silence.

"No." She hesitated and glanced at the bra on the table. "But I can try to track her. If the bra is in the plastic, maybe I can hold the images at bay long enough to get a fix on her direction."

She didn't sound convinced, and *he* certainly didn't wish her to risk going into Dale's mind again so soon—especially if the vamp was still feeding on her. He studied the daylight behind Jake for a moment, then said, "Maybe you won't have to."

Nikki raised an eyebrow. "Why not?"

He pointed towards the window. "How did that vampire get into the hotel? Wasn't dawn rising when you arrived?"

She nodded thoughtfully. "And he was carrying the mother of all knives, yet he wasn't a strong enough telepath to take over the mind of more than one guard at a time. Jake has two stationed at the exits."

He nodded. "So, if not secured exits, where from?"

"Basement?" She glanced at Jake. "Or parking garage?"

"They're one and the same," Jake said. "It won't hurt to check, though I know the cops have gone over them thoroughly."

"The cops do not know they're looking for vampires," Michael commented. "It gives us a certain advantage."

"I'm not sure it's an advantage I really want." Jake pushed away from the wall. "I'll go collect some flashlights, just in case we need them, and meet you down in the lobby."

Michael nodded and headed into the bedroom. Nikki followed him but stopped in the doorway, her expression an endearing mix of fear and determination. "Why does knowing we're after vampires give us an advantage? Surely if there was anything to find in the basement or parking garage, the cops or FBI would have found it."

"Not necessarily." He sat on the bed and pulled on his socks. "Vampires have become very adept at hiding. Many of us have literally had centuries in which to learn. Getting in and out of buildings is just another method of concealment."

"So you think they have a hidden entrance somewhere?"

"It would be the most logical explanation." Though it didn't exactly explain how they'd gotten into the second victim's home. They certainly wouldn't have been able to cross the threshold without her inviting them.

She frowned. "But how would that help them avoid the sunlight?"

"They're probably using the sewer system to get around. It wouldn't be the first time it has happened." He slipped on his shoes and walked across to her.

Her gaze searched his. "The vampire who attacked Dale smelled like dead water."

He wrapped his arms around her waist and held her close. Her pulse was a rapid beat that pounded through her body and his. "Then that would certainly suggest my guess is right." He brushed a kiss across her lips and wished they had the time to do more. This morning had been wonderful, but he still wanted her. Would always want her, physically *and* emotionally—something she still didn't seem to understand. "You *will* do as I ask down there, won't you?"

Her expression was the picture of stubbornness. "Just don't try ordering me out, because I won't go unless you leave with me."

He smiled and tucked a stray strand of hair behind her ear. "Right now, I have no plans to go anywhere without you."

Amusement and love washed through the link, and a smile touched her lips. "Good. Because I have no intention of letting you go."

"So I discovered," he said dryly. He caught her hand, weaving his fingers through hers. "Shall we go?"

She sighed and cast an almost wistful glance towards the bed. "Yes."

On the way out, he grabbed the plastic bag containing Dale's bra, tucking it into his pocket. If the vamps were in the sewers, they could literally be anywhere. And with Dale Wainwright slated as the next victim, speed was of the essence. As much as he hated using Nikki's unpredictable psychometric abilities, it might be their only real chance of finding this woman alive.

Jake was waiting in the lobby. He tossed Nikki a flashlight and led them towards an exit. "This will take us down to the basement." He swiped a keycard through the lock and opened the door. "From there we can get into the parking garage."

"Do the elevators go down to the garage?" Michael touched Nikki's elbow, stopping her from entering before he could. Her annoyance clouded the link, but he ignored her, his gaze searching the darkness for any sign of life—or *unlife*—below in the basement. Nothing moved, and the only heartbeats he could hear were Nikki's and Jake's. Both were erratic.

"One does," Jake said, locking the door behind them. "But there are several security cameras in the structure, and they're monitored twenty-four hours a day."

"Did the cops check the tapes?" Nikki asked, her voice soft yet edged with tension. He wondered what it was she sensed.

"Yeah, but they didn't find anything," Jake said. "Whoever took Dale didn't take her out through the parking garage."

Nikki's flashlight beam swept across the darkness. He wondered why she was bothering. Her night sight was almost as good as his these days. If he could see in this darkness, she certainly should be able to.

Not that there was anything to actually see. He swept his gaze past the huge clumps of machinery and frowned. Nothing stirred, and yet something waited in the far corner. A hint of depravity and death. Frown deepening, he led the way down the stairs. Both Nikki and Jake made a racket on the metal steps and the noise seemed to echo across the room.

"Are the garage cameras still being monitored?"

"Yep," Jake said. "And I checked them earlier. Nikki's attacker didn't appear on any of them."

No surprise there. Michael reached the basement floor then stopped. Nikki paused beside him, and apprehension stirred the link.

"There's something here," she said.

"Yes," he replied, wrapping his fingers around hers. "But I'm not sure what."

"It doesn't feel human, whatever it is." Though her voice was steady, her trepidation shimmered through him.

"Vampire?" Jake queried, stopping on the last step behind them.

"No." Michael glanced at him, noticing for the first time the slight bulge in his jacket pocket. "And you know from experience guns are not an effective weapon against them."

Jake merely grinned. "Maybe, but it sure as hell makes me *feel* a little safer. You have to let an old man have his illusions."

Nikki snorted softly. "Old man my ass. You could probably outrun me, bad heart and all."

"Damn right, especially if it's a pack of vampires on our tails." Though he grinned, his tension was evident in the set of his shoulders. "So if it's not a vampire, what the hell is it?"

"Something that isn't scared by a lot of noise," she muttered. "Something that has been dead for some time."

Jake groaned. "Not a zombie. That's all we need to complete the party right now."

"No, it's not a zombie," Michael said. "You'd be able to smell it by now if it was."

"What then?"

"I don't know." He met Nikki's narrowed gaze and almost smiled. She wasn't going to let him get two steps away from her side—not that he wanted to, especially until he knew why that vampire had been sent after her. "Keep close behind me. If you sense anything, tell me, no matter how insignificant you think it is."

She raised an eyebrow and nodded. He tugged her forward and switched to the infrared of his vampire vision. The cloak of darkness lifted completely, and a hazy, humanoid figure appeared in the far corner of the room. One that didn't have a heartbeat or take a breath.

He wove his way through the network of noisy machines and air conditioning units and approached the far wall. The body he could see was behind it.

Nikki stopped in front of the wall and pressed her right hand against the plaster. "It's not solid," she murmured. "And it holds back death."

He glanced at her quickly. Her expression was as distant as her thoughts, and unease slithered through him. Was this yet another mutation of her psychometry talent? When he'd shared his life force and made her as immortal as he, had he somehow altered her psychic essence? Even now he wasn't sure, and neither he nor Seline had been able to find much in the old texts about thralls—other than one warning that stated it was better not to turn those with psychic talents. It didn't say why, which was damned frustrating. Seline was still looking, but he had a horrible feeling they'd better hasten the search. It wasn't just her talents mutating. There were signs of other changes too—like her night sight.

"Sure looks solid," Jake said into the silence. He slapped the wall, then frowned and stepped back, running the light across the ceiling and down to the machines behind them. "You know, I thought there was more of a gap between the wall and this unit."

"Maybe there once was—there's another wall behind this one," Michael commented, his attention still on Nikki. She was moving away, her fingers trailing across the wall, as if feeling for something. "There is a gap of about four feet separating them."

Jake frowned. "Why would anyone want to build a false wall like this?"

"Maybe someone who wants to conceal a hidden entrance."

Nikki stopped near the end of the wall, and energy stirred, tingling briefly across his skin.

"Here," she murmured. "There's an entrance here."

Jake flashed his light across the plaster. "Nik, that wall is as solid as the rest of it."

Michael probed the wall with his fingers and found a hairline crack in the plaster, one that extended ceiling to floor. He moved around Nikki, found another four feet along and looked up. There was a minute gap between the ceiling and the wall, barely noticeable and yet telling. As was the metal rod he could see in the middle of the plaster, thrusting from the ceiling into the floor.

"She's right. It's a doorway of some kind." He pressed the wall near the crack. He could see the catch—it was just a matter of finding the right way to spring it.

Nikki blinked and for a second looked like a dreamer just awakening from a dream. "The entrance is on this side, the exit your side." She reached up on tippy-toes and pressed her palm against the wall. The whole wall rotated aside, revealing a two-foot gap.

The air that rushed out was thick with age and death. Nikki shuddered, her face white. "There's a body in there somewhere."

He caught her fingers, squeezing them in gentle reassurance. "Yes. Do you wish to remain here while I check it out?"

Her gaze flashed to his. "I think you already know the answer to that."

He smiled grimly and tugged her forward. "Then prepare for the worst. It will not be a pretty sight. This one has been dead for a while."

"How can you tell?" Jake asked as he followed them in. The beam of his flashlight danced across the darkness, crisscrossing Nikki's and creating crazy patterns on the cobwebbed brick walls.

"I am a vampire, remember. I saw the body long before you were able to smell it."

"Even through the walls?"

"Yes."

"Damn—"

Jake's voice died as the beam of the flashlights centered on a huddled, shapeless form at the far end of the small gap. Beside it, there was a hole that led into a deeper darkness. Nikki stopped abruptly, as did Jake.

"Someone's been feasting on the poor fellow," she said, voice holding a slight tremor.

Her revulsion seemed to curl through the link, a wave of horror that stirred his senses, even though death and he were old companions.

"Probably rats coming up from the sewer," he said, squeezing her hand before releasing it. He squatted beside the body. It was a male, and what remained of his clothes indicated he was a guard of some kind—probably hotel security. If the state of decay was anything to go by, he'd been dead a good two months, if not more—though it was hard to be certain because damp conditions like this often hastened decomposition.

"Has the hotel had any personnel go missing of late?" he asked, examining the corpse's neck and arms.

"Not since I've been here," Jake said. "But I've only been here a month. It could have happened earlier."

"Can you check the files? Ask around?"

"Yep." Jake hesitated. "Was he killed by vampires?"

"Yes." Given the extent and manner of his injuries, it was undoubtedly fledglings who'd attacked him.

No vampire who'd been on this earth any length of time was this messy. Or this careless. Leaving a body here like this was nothing short of stupidity—unless, of course, they didn't intend to hang around all that long.

The vampire who attacked me was a fledgling.

Michael met Nikki's gaze. He saw in her expressive eyes the fear so evident in her thoughts, yet he knew it wasn't fear of the darkness or the body or even the fledglings. It was fear of what awaited them. An evil they couldn't yet see, but whose presence tainted the very air around them.

Not that *he* could feel anything beyond the chill of the stinking air. Whoever was behind the kidnappings was nowhere close; otherwise, he would have been able to sense their presence. The evil he *could* smell was little more than a psychic overflow from Nikki. Somehow, she was sharing what she sensed with him. He wondered if it was deliberate, or yet another worrying mutation of her abilities.

It's a presence that doesn't feel very old, he said.

Jasper wasn't very old, either. Nor was Cordell. She hesitated, rubbing her arms. *This feels far worse than either of those.*

If the mutilations were anything to go by, then yes, it was. *It's not near, Nikki. We're safe for the moment.*

For the moment. Her trepidation swam around him, yet it was a fear he knew she would not retreat from. Aloud, she said, "Where does that hole lead?"

"A sewer tunnel, by the look of it."

"Wonderful," she muttered. "And here I am wearing only sneakers."

He smiled. "The nasty stuff is all piped."

She snorted. "A lot of shit flows down the storm

drains, you know, and I'm not just talking about human waste."

"You could stay here if you want."

She raised an eyebrow. "One of these days you're going to get sick of hearing the answer to that question."

"Never." Nor would he stop asking it. Her safety would always be a priority, whether she liked it or not. He threaded his fingers through the warmth of hers again. "Let's go."

They climbed carefully through the gap. The brick tunnel beyond was little more than three feet wide and five feet high. Not much room for maneuvering if they were discovered.

"They've gone to some trouble to conceal that sewer entrance," Jake said, sweeping the light left and right as he came through the hole. "Wonder why?"

Michael shrugged, his reply almost absent as he listened to the silence for movement. "It would suggest the hotel has some major part to play in their schemes."

"But they haven't yet hit the same place twice, so why go to the bother of building a false wall?"

"Maybe they haven't hit the same place twice simply because they haven't yet needed to."

Through the hushed darkness came the tremulous sound of a heartbeat. It was distant, full of fear, full of pain. If it was Mark Wainwright's wife, then she needed medical help fast. Even from this distance it was evident her heart was struggling.

"This way," he said, leading them to the right.

"Are there any vampires nearby?" Nikki's soft question seemed to melt into the darkness, a hushed sound edged with apprehension.

He glanced back at her. Her eyes gleamed with a cold, gold fire in the shadowed darkness that surrounded them, looking almost otherworldly. His uneasiness rose several notches. He wished he'd taken a chance and talked to Elizabeth about thralls. She probably had forgotten more than they could ever discover in the old texts. But Elizabeth was dead, and it was too late now for regrets. He just had to hope Seline could find some clue as to what might be happening to Nikki. And him.

"Not yet. Why?"

She hesitated. "There's something here. An essence, watching us. And I hear voices. Lots of voices."

He couldn't hear anything, which in itself didn't mean anything. If she was sensing the other vampire, maybe she was also hearing what he could hear.

And if the vampire behind all this *was* clairvoyant, he could certainly be watching them through psychic means. It would explain how he'd known about Nikki, and why he'd sent someone to kill her. But it still didn't explain how *she* could sense him. "We'd better hurry."

Because if they *were* being watched, they'd undoubtedly face opposition as soon as they got anywhere near Dale Wainwright. That he couldn't hear or smell another vampire just yet didn't mean anything—not when even the youngest of vampires could move faster than the wind.

They continued on, quickly making their way through the damp, dirty darkness. The twin beams of the flashlights danced across the path ahead, highlighting the rubbish swept down from the streets above.

"Is it true alligators can be found in sewers," Jake

asked, swinging his light not at the water near his feet but towards the slimy roof they had to bend to avoid.

They came to a junction, and Michael stopped, studying each tunnel arm. "I've traveled through a few sewers in my time and have yet to come across one." The heartbeat was coming from his left. He tugged Nikki in that direction.

"That's almost disappointing," Jake said. "I rather liked the myth of giant alligators roaming the sewers, munching on the unwary."

"There's something much worse than alligators roaming these sewers ready to munch on the unwary," Nikki said. Her gaze met Michael's, filled with the fear beginning to explode through the link. "They're coming."

He still couldn't sense anything other than Mark Wainwright's wife, but he didn't doubt her. In many ways, her senses were far more powerful than his. "We haven't got that much further to go. Let's move it."

They splashed through the shallows, the twin beams of light creating crazy patterns across the darkness ahead. The tremulous sound of the heartbeat got stronger, but across it, he could now hear others.

Six of them.

They came to another junction and skidded to a halt. In the middle of the intersection lay a scantily-clad body. She hadn't been dead long—a little less than an hour, if the heat still dying in her body was any indication.

Jake's light swept across the sad form. "Hooker. Probably hasn't even been missed yet."

"No." Michael released Nikki's hand then stepped over the woman's body. The tunnel directly ahead had been walled off except for a doorway. The unsteady heartbeat was coming from inside.

"No woman deserves to die the way this woman did," Nikki said softly. "Not even a prostitute."

Michael glanced back at her. She was still standing near the body, her arms crossed, her expression a mix of horror and sorrow. But as much as he wanted to walk over and take her in his arms to offer the comfort she so clearly needed, he didn't. Maybe it would convince her of the futility of her quest to share his life, because this death was far from the worst she would ever see if she did.

"Death is an ever-present danger of the trade, and every client a potential nut case," Jake said with very little sympathy in his voice. He moved around the body and centered his light on the door. "Odd place to build a wall, isn't it?"

"It's a cell. Dale Wainwright is in there."

Michael twisted the handle, but the door was locked. So he leaned a shoulder against it and pushed as hard as he could. The door had been built to withstand the strength of a human, not a vampire, and it gave way with very little resistance.

"It's a wonder the Department of Public Works hasn't done anything about this," Jake said. "It would surely be stuffing up the storm water flow."

"Remember that most vampires can easily read and control a human mind. People might have been sent down here to investigate, but maybe they report back only what they're told to report back." Michael glanced over his shoulder. Nikki was studying the shadows behind them, her thoughts a haze of rising dread.

I know they're close, Nikki. We have to move as quickly as we can.

We won't make it.

Had he been alone, he would have. But she knew that as much as he did. *We can try*.

She studied him for a moment, thoughts closed to him, then nodded and moved back to his side. He wrapped his fingers through hers again and entered the cell.

Dale Wainwright lay on filthy straw in one corner of the small room. She was naked, curled up like a babe, her breathing rapid, pulse weak and irregular. Even though he wasn't using the infrared of his vampire vision, he could see the bruises marring her torso and legs. She'd been sexually assaulted more than once already.

Anger rose like a wave. He'd never understood the mentality that enjoyed inflicting pain on others—even though he'd been turned by a woman who'd certainly thrived on it. But at least Elizabeth had restricted her games to those she'd turned. Most of the time, anyway.

Jake's soft curse filled the night, a sound Michael felt like echoing. Nikki disentangled her fingers from his and hurried over.

"Dale's alive." She stripped off her sweater and draped it over the other woman. "But she needs help fast. Jake, you got your cell phone handy?"

"Certainly have."

Behind them, the darkness came alive with the sensation of evil. The time to escape or to call for help had slipped away. Michael wrapped a hand around the phone, preventing Jake from dialing.

"Wait," he said softly. "Because we are no longer alone."

Six

A blanket of evil wrapped around Nikki's senses, almost smothering her. She rose slowly and studied the darkness beyond the cell door. Though she could hear or see no movement, she knew they were there. She could smell them. It was almost as if the air recoiled from their presence.

Jake pulled the gun from his pocket. The sound of the safety being clicked off was almost bullet loud. "What now?" he asked, voice soft but harsh.

Whether that came from anger or fear she wasn't sure. Michael's gaze skated past Jake and met hers.

"Fledglings," he said, voice as expressionless as his face. "I'll face them alone. You two stay here."

"You can't," Jake said.

"Definitely not," she echoed. She crossed her arms and stared at him defiantly. The link between them was void of emotion, which only meant he was controlling himself very tightly. "You can't face six of them alone."

"I've done it before."

"And still bear the scars," she retorted. "Stop letting your concern for me overwhelm common sense."

His annoyance briefly seared her mind, even though his expression remained impassive. He stared at her a moment longer, then said, "Very well."

Unease stirred. He had to be up to something because he'd never give in so easily otherwise. Power spiked her senses, then the darkness swirled around him, whisking him from sight. A heartbeat later the door slammed closed.

Anger surged, as did kinetic energy, crackling like lightning across her fingertips. If he thought a closed door would stop her, he was sorely mistaken . . .

This is my job, Nikki. This is what I do. Let me do it without having to worry about you.

We're full partners or we're nothing. The sooner you accept that fact, the better off we'll be.

He didn't answer. The sound of fighting filled the air, punctured with grunts of pain and the snarl of things not long dead.

"Damn fool," Jake muttered. "Nikki, get that door open."

"Willingly." She flung out her hand. The pent-up energy surged, wrapping the door in sparks. She pulled back and wrenched the door off its hinges.

Air stirred, rushing at them.

"Vamp!" She hit him with a lance of kinetic energy, thrusting him back against the wall. "Nine o'clock high."

Jake fired the gun. There was a howl of pain then shadows unraveled, revealing a leather-clad vampire. Jake's shot had taken him in the shoulder. His eyes were bloody, hostile, showing little sign of the human he'd been as he struggled against her hold. Jake fired again. The vampire's head jerked back, and blood and other matter splattered the wall behind him. She let him drop and briefly closed her eyes, trying to control her rising nausea. Would seeing someone die, human or not, ever get easier?

She hoped not. At least it meant part of *her* was still human, no matter what else she had become.

Air stirred again, stronger this time. "Two more," she warned, and kinetically picked up the door, throwing it sideways at the vamps.

There was a grunt of pain, then the sound of a

body hitting the wall. Several more gunshots bit into the night. Then she was hit and thrust backwards onto the ground, the weight of someone—or something—holding her down.

The shadows rolled back, revealing the gaunt, needy face of a man who looked no more than twenty. He was snarling, canines extended and dripping, his body quivering with the force of his bloodlust. Memories of another time and another vampire, rose, but she thrust them away and raised her fist. He caught the blow long before it landed and twisted her wrist brutally. Agony tore up her arm, almost blinding in its intensity. Then his teeth sank into her flesh, and horror filled her as he began to greedily suck her life away.

Energy surged, a wave so strong she shook with the intensity of it—a wave she had no hope of fully controlling. It rolled from her body and battered the vampire away, smashing him though the brick wall and out into the darkness of the junction beyond. And there it consumed him. Literally.

The smell of burning flesh stung the air, and his screams echoed. Bile rose in her throat, momentarily overwhelming the pain beginning to pound through her entire body. The light of the flames danced across the brick walls—walls across which shadows danced. Michael, still fighting.

She pushed upright. Her legs were almost boneless, and it felt like her brain was on fire. But she ignored both and staggered over to the shattered remains of the wall.

Jake came up beside her and fired another shot. The sound seemed to echo through her brain, making her wince. The bullet took the fledgling in the shoulder, spinning him half-around. Michael quickly finished the young vampire off.

Nikki sank down on her haunches, closing her eyes as she rested back against the wall. It was over. She could relax. And ache.

"How in hell did that vampire catch fire?" Jake asked.

"It was Nikki's doing." Michael's voice was little more than a harsh growl. He knelt beside her, a warm, angry presence she felt rather than saw. "Are you all right?"

She nodded fractionally. The smell of burnt flesh still stung the air, and her stomach continued to roll. Nor was it helped by the hot lances of fire digging into her brain. If she moved too much right now, she'd throw up for sure.

He touched her wrist, fingers firm against the wound caused by the vampire's bite. Stopping the flow of blood, she suspected, and wondered how savage the fledgling had been. But she didn't open her eyes to find out. Didn't dare. Not with the way her stomach was rebelling.

"Jake, you'd better call the cops." Michael's voice was again emotionless, but even though the link between them was lost to the haze of pain consuming her mind, she could feel his anger.

"You can't wrap me in cotton forever," she said softly.

"But surely I *can* expect you to listen to common sense."

Wisps of fury reached past the barrier of pain separating their minds, and for first time in her life, she was thankful for the agony that came with overextending her abilities. She wasn't ready to face the full extent of his anger just yet, even though she knew she'd have to eventually.

"They were only fledglings, Nikki. Six of them would never have taken me."

"Yet you once told me a fledgling was more dangerous than a vampire who'd passed the bloodlust stage."

"To humans, not to a vampire."

"But I'm neither, am I?" *Because I'm a thrall and stand somewhere between the two.* Just where, she wasn't entirely sure—and she had feeling Michael wasn't, either.

"Being a thrall doesn't make you invincible."

"Just like being a vampire doesn't make you invincible."

"That's different."

"How?"

She felt his gaze on her, could almost taste his frustration. "Now is not the time to discuss this."

"It never is," she said, unable to hide the hint of bitterness in her voice. God, why wouldn't he just listen?

"The cops are on the way," Jake said. "I told them to come through that hole we found in the hotel's basement. Easier than trying to find the nearest street entry, especially seeing I can't tell them where exactly we are."

"And the paramedics?"

"On their way as well." Jake hesitated. "What about those bodies out there in the tunnel?"

"I'll move them if you'll come over here and keep pressure on this wound."

His touch left her, to be quickly replaced by Jake's cooler grip. "How are we going to explain this wound, your bruises and the blood on the wall?"

"We don't. I'll ensure they won't see or question it."

Touch their minds, take it all away, she thought with a shudder. "Michael, you can't—"

"I can and I will." He rose, and though she heard no footsteps, she knew he'd moved away.

Jake took a deep breath and released it slowly. "I don't think I've ever seen him so angry."

She snorted softly and opened her eyes. Pinpricks of red light pranced crazily everywhere she looked— even across his face. They weren't real, just a side effect of the hammering in her brain. She blinked, and the spots faded a little. She wished the pain would ease as quickly.

"He doesn't like being disobeyed."

Jake smiled. "You'd think after living with you for four months, he'd be used to it."

"You'd think," she muttered and glanced at her wrist. The vampire had certainly done a number on it. No neat pinprick holes for him, that was for sure. She dug her other hand into her pocket and dragged out a handkerchief. "Here, use this. Better than you being attached to my wrist until the police and paramedics get here."

Jake grabbed the handkerchief, but the minute he released her arm the blood began to pulse freely. Even though she knew she couldn't die from blood loss, it was still an alarming sight. And one that explained Michael's sudden departure. Maybe it wasn't so much anger as the need to distance himself from the smell of her blood. It was little more than ten months ago that she'd sliced her wrist in an effort to save his life, and in doing so had almost destroyed his control over his demon half. Had almost brought the vampire fully to the surface. His struggle for control continued, though he would never admit it to her. But she'd seen it in his eyes, seen the flicker of darkness the one or two times she'd cut herself. She loved him and she trusted him—but even so, she sometimes wondered if one day she'd wake up and find herself tied to a stranger. A stranger desperate to kill her.

"How's Dale doing?"

Jake finished tying the handkerchief then rose and walked over to the other woman. "Not good," he said, touching her neck. "Pulse is still thready, and her skin is clammy. It suggests heart problems to me."

She remembered the tingling, achy sensation in her chest and arm when she'd been in Dale's mind, and knew that Jake was more than likely right. "Let's hope the paramedics get here soon, then."

"They're on the way," Michael said, appearing by her side once more. "I can hear them. Hear their heartbeats."

"And no doubt the person behind all this will, too."

He reached out, brushing something from her cheek, his fingers so warm against her skin. "You tell me. You've been sensing him, haven't you?"

"Sort of." She frowned, not sure she could really explain. It wasn't so much that she could feel the other vampire's presence—not in the way she'd been able to sense Jasper or Cordell. This vamp was evil, but in a totally different way from those other two. His evil was born more of anger. An anger so deep it had all but consumed him.

Michael raised an eyebrow. "Are you saying these murders are the result of a need for revenge?"

She shrugged. "That's what I'm sensing." She hesitated, listening. Footsteps echoed in the hush. The police and paramedics were finally here.

Michael glanced at Jake. "Why don't you go meet them while I disappear. For the moment, it's better if I remain an unseen partner in these investigations."

Jake nodded and moved out of the small room. Michael leaned forward and kissed her. "I'll be close," he said, breath brushing warmth against her lips. "And I agree with what you said earlier. You and I really do need to talk."

She stroked his cheek and wondered if she'd ever tire of his touch. Ever stop wanting him. "Only if you intend to listen."

"I'll listen, if you promise to do the same. It's a two-way street, my love."

The endearment stirred her heart. Yet as she stared into the depths of his beautiful eyes, she could see only determination. In reality, that two-way street was still headed one way—his, not hers. He wasn't ready yet to hear what she had to say, no matter what he said. But she had to try anyway.

Voices drew closer. He kissed her again, harder this time, stealing her breath and leaving her dizzy with wanting. Then the shadows wrapped around him and he disappeared.

"Damn you," she muttered. It was bad enough that she had to face the police and their endless questions. Doing so when she was feeling hornier than hell was only going to make the experience all that much more uncomfortable.

His soft chuckle stirred air past her ear. *I promise to relieve your tension once we're alone.*

Knowing the cops, that's going to be an unpleasant amount of time from now.

The wait will be worth it.

She raised an eyebrow and half grinned. *Now*

there's a statement from a man totally confident in his own abilities.

After three hundred and sixty years of life, I should be. Shadows caressed her cheek, warm and gentle. *Yet in all that time, I have never felt anything like this. What we share is special, Nikki. And so very rare.*

She sighed. *Even the very rarest of jewels can be smashed if care isn't taken.*

That's all I'm asking you to allow me to do. Care.

And that was the whole trouble. He cared too much, and it was smothering her. She glanced up as the first of the police officers arrived. The look in his eyes told her it was going to be a longer night than even *she'd* anticipated.

She sighed again and slowly climbed to her feet. She was *not* looking forward to the next few hours.

In the end, it wasn't as bad as she'd anticipated, though it was every bit as long. The San Francisco police seemed a whole lot more accepting of her abilities than the cops back home, which really shouldn't have surprised her, given the reputation for tolerance the city had as a whole. Even the Fed's seemed willing to accept the *concept* of her abilities, even if one or two of them had looked skeptical.

A paramedic treated her wrist and reluctantly gave her some painkillers for her headache. A heartbeat later, power stirred the air. Michael, enforcing his will on the medic. The same thing happened any time one of the officers took notice of the blood staining the wall. His mind took theirs, bending their attention towards something else.

Her anger rose several notches every time. She

understood his reasons, but understanding didn't make what he was doing any easier to accept. Didn't make it right. And it was just another thing in an ever-growing list they would have to talk about.

It was close to midnight by the time they were finally allowed to leave. By then, the pounding ache in her head had eased to a softer thud. A police officer escorted them back up the tunnel, and another helped them past the guard's crumpled body and out through the brick wall. It wasn't until they neared the lobby exit that Michael finally stepped free of the shadows.

He wrapped a hand around hers, but his attention was on Jake. "Are you going to see Mark Wainwright?"

Jake shook his head. "He'll be at the hospital with Dale, and I very much doubt if they'll let me in to see them tonight. I'll wait until morning."

"When you see him, ask him if she knew the other two women. If Nikki is right and these kidnappings are based on revenge, then there has to be some connection among the three victims. We need to find out what it is."

"Then you don't think the vamp behind all this will give up and make a run for it?"

"No. There's too much planning gone into it."

Jake sighed. "Thought I might have been a little too optimistic. I'm heading off to bed before Mary decides to kill me. I'll see you two in the morning."

"Night Jake," Nikki said as Michael pulled her into the elevator.

Jake waved a sketchy good night and disappeared up the stairs. Michael wrapped an arm around her shoulders and drew her close. She yawned and leaned her head against his shoulder and closed her eyes.

Being held had never felt so good. So safe. "I'm so tired it feels like my legs are shaking."

"I know." He brushed a kiss across the top of her head. "I'm afraid it's sleep not loving for you tonight, my love."

She glanced up at him, a grin touching her lips. "I don't have to stand to be loved, you know."

His warm, sexy smile sent shivers of desire skating across her skin. "True. But you do have to be awake."

She raised an eyebrow. "Have I fallen asleep on you yet?"

"No, but there's always a first time."

"It won't be this time, believe me." Not when the ache for his touch was so bad it was almost painful.

He caressed her cheek, running his finger down to her lips. "Are you sure? Given what happened tonight, it might be better—"

She stopped the rest of his words with a kiss. She didn't want to think about what had happened tonight. Not now. Not yet. Because thinking would mean acknowledging that her gifts were changing in ways she couldn't even begin to imagine. That *she* might be changing just as much as her gifts.

Heat slithered through the link and burned through her senses. Michael groaned and pulled her so close their bodies were almost one. Their kiss deepened, became a long and sensual exploration that left them both panting with need.

The elevator came to a halt and the doors opened. Michael swung her into his arms and carried her out.

"Saving my energy, huh?" She wrapped her arms around his neck and lightly nibbled his ear.

His smile shimmered through the link, a glow she felt clear down to her toes.

"Definitely. You fall asleep on me now, and I'll be one very frustrated vampire."

"No chance of that." She undid the buttons on his shirt and ran her fingers across the hard plane of his chest.

"Good grief, woman, wait until we're inside."

She laughed softly. "I do believe the vampire is shy."

"No. Just not an exhibitionist." He kicked the door shut, his gaze hot and filled with passion. "But I'd make love anywhere you want, anytime you want. I will never be able to get enough of you."

She touched a hand to his cheek as her heart did an odd flip flop. "Never is a long time."

"With you by my side, it won't be."

She kissed his cheek. "I do love you, you know." Even if his old-fashioned ways sometimes frustrated the hell out of her.

"There's only one frustration I'm interested in curing right now." He placed her on her feet and began to undress her. "The rest can wait."

"For now," she agreed softly. "For now."

Michael brushed a kiss across Nikki's shoulder, then slowly disentangled himself from her. She stirred slightly, murmuring something he couldn't quite catch. The link between them came briefly to life, and a contented rush of love swam around him. He smiled, gently brushing the hair from her closed eyes.

It was hard to believe that only four months ago he'd been considering walking away from all this. Odd how swiftly things had changed. He couldn't even begin to imagine life without her now.

He kissed her cheek, then rose and went into the

living room. After pouring himself a wine from the bar, he walked over to the window and studied the fog-blanketed street below.

Seline? he said, reaching out with his mind.

Here. Her instant reply suggested she'd been waiting for his call. *Did you find Nikki?*

Yes. Nose deep in trouble, as usual.

Seline's smile shimmered through his mind. *I'm liking this girl more and more. You're really going to have to introduce us.*

That would probably create more havoc than I can handle. The last thing Nikki needs is you telling her all the ins and outs of getting around my moods. She has enough tricks of her own.

Seline laughed, a warm, throaty sound. *Sounds like you're starting to hit trouble.*

That he was—though he still didn't entirely understand why Nikki refused to listen to common sense. But he had no intention of admitting *that* to Seline. All he'd get was an I-told-you-so. *We've rescued the third victim. She s been sexually assaulted and looks to have suffered a heart attack, but the doctors seem reasonably confident of a recovery.*

At least she's alive. I gather you found nothing on the fiend behind all this?

No, but Nikki seems to think it centers around revenge. If that's true, then it means the three women are all connected somehow.

They are. Apparently all three went to the same high school in Boston.

Did they know each other?

From all reports, they were classmates rather than friends.

There had to be some deeper connection than that. The man behind these kidnappings didn't just want revenge, he wanted to destroy them—emotionally as much as physically.

Can you get a list of everyone who was in their classes and do a crosscheck? I've got a feeling we'll come up with a lot more missing women.

Doing it as we speak. She hesitated. *Why does Nikki think it's revenge behind all this?*

She is sensing him. He sipped his wine, watching the lights of an approaching car flare against the wall of white fog. *Have you found anything else about thralls yet?*

We found an old journal from one of the ancients that looks promising. It's just taking a little time to translate it. Worry whisked down the line between them. *How is Nikki sensing him? I thought her only gifts were telekinesis and psychometry?*

They were. And yet she has been able to sense my thoughts from the beginning, which suggests a latent ability in telepathy.

Telepathy is not clairvoyance. She shouldn't be able to sense this fiend with telepathy.

Nikki was starting to do a lot of things she shouldn't be able to do, and it was worrying the hell out of him. *Her gifts are mutating faster, Seline. And that's not all—remember the flame imps?*

Remember them? Had a chat with them a month ago. Wonderful creatures, they are.

Wonderful or not, they appear to have given Nikki the ability to produce flame with just a thought. And if it were a developing gift, it was one they had to get under control fast.

Pyrokinesis is a rare talent these days. And a dangerous one. She hesitated again, and her confusion swirled around him. *What about you?*

He frowned. *What do you mean?*

There's been a connection between you and Nikki from the very start. It's that connection that allowed you to share your life force and make her a thrall. But unlike most thralls, Nikki was given eternal life out of love, not necessity.

So? The car crested the hill and the light separated, becoming twin beams of brightness before abruptly dying. The fog swirled around the vehicle, almost washing it from sight. He smiled. Whoever was in that car would undoubtedly regret their parking choice in the morning. They were stopped in a tow-away zone.

So what if you shared more than you were meant to share? And what if that sharing went both ways?

Both ways? He certainly hadn't developed any of Nikki's talents ... the thought stopped cold as he remembered this afternoon. Remembered sharing the sensation of evil with her. *I don't get what you mean,* he said. Even though he was beginning to.

She sighed. *Remember, I'm only theorizing, but what if that warning we found—the one that suggested it was better not to turn those with psychic talents into thralls—was more a warning of the dangers involved to the maker, not to the thrall?*

How can it be dangerous to the maker? Other than the initial shock of transferring his life force, he'd felt no different, nor had he noticed any change in his psychic abilities—until this afternoon.

Thralls are generally created as little more than servants, are they not?

He gave a mental nod. Servants, or, as in Elizabeth's case, obedient lovers.

So what if turning someone with psychic talents created a thrall who was not a servant but an equal? One who could not be ordered around?

82

He raised his eyebrow. Nikki would certainly be pleased to hear that snippet of information. *I can see where it would create problems for those vampires who did not care for their thralls.*

Indeed. And what if turning someone you loved into a thrall took it one step further?

He took another sip of wine and watched the silent car as the implications of her statement swirled through his mind. *You think there's been some sort of psychic sharing between us?*

No. What I think is happening is more a merging. And if that's the case, you're both going to have to be very careful until you discover the full extent of the merger.

People can't share psychic talents, Seline.

You're right. People can't. But you and Nikki are no longer just people. Amusement threaded her mind voice. *The possibilities of this union are damn exciting, let me tell you.*

The only union I'm interested in with Nikki is one of the heart. I don't want her joining the Circle. I don't want her accompanying me on missions.

And what of her wants?

Nikki had voiced her wants loudly enough, but he had no intention of giving in. It was just too dangerous—for them both. Her pain this evening had been a knife stabbing deep inside, momentarily freezing him. Had he been fighting older vamps rather than fledglings, he could have been in real trouble.

You can't keep her wrapped in cotton for the rest of eternity, Michael.

Nikki had said much the same thing. He wondered if the old witch had been talking to her behind his back. *It's only been four months. Cotton is allowed, I think.*

He chuckle surrounded him. *Three hundred and sixty years old and still so much to learn.*

Better than being one hundred and eighty and thinking I know it all, he said, amused.

I don't claim to know it all, but I do claim to be a very wily old witch. The wise listen to me.

He smiled. *And how often has that gotten me into trouble in the past?*

Only three or four times. Her mind voice was prim.

You forgot to add the dozen in that amount. No one had gotten out of the car yet. Curious, he switched to the infrared of his vampire vision. *Listen, when you're doing the cross-check for classmates, could you also check how many of them might currently be in San Francisco? It could give us a lead to the next victim.*

In other words, mind my own damn business and stay out of your love life. Her cackle spun around him. *You know that's impossible. And the check is being done as we speak. I should have the results in the morning.*

Then I'll talk to you in the morning. He broke the connection between them and studied the car with a frown. The couple inside were not getting passionate, as he'd half expected, but simply sitting there. He mentally reached to touch their minds. Only it wasn't their minds he found, but that of another vampire.

Seven

Brightness flashed in the foggy darkness. Michael ducked to his left, and a heartbeat later a hole was torn through the window. The bullet blasted past, so close it stirred his hair and sent heat rippling across his skin before it thudded into the opposite wall.

If that heat was any indication, they were using silver bullets, not ordinary ones—which meant even a wound would have been dangerous to him. Anger rose in a wave, almost engulfing him. If it had been Nikki standing there, they would have killed her. That bullet had been aimed at his head, not his heart.

Bullets can't hurt you, can they? Fear and confusion mingled in Nikki's still sleepy mind voice.

He looked around. She was standing just inside the bedroom door pulling on a sweater. His sweater, not hers. *Bullets aimed at my head can destroy me as easily as they can you. And these were silver. Stay there.*

She nodded, arms crossed, hands lost in the sleeves. *Be careful.*

Always. He wrapped the shadows around him and opened the window. Fingers of fog brushed dampness across his skin as he leaped from the balcony. He hit the ground with enough force to jar every bone in his body—any higher, and he might have broken bones.

He rolled swiftly to his feet and ran towards the car. The gun was still pointed out the car window. The other vamp could obviously control the couple, but not to the extent that he saw what they saw.

Which was odd, because he'd obviously had enough mind-power to put the compulsion on the young vampire who'd attacked Nikki, forcing him to leap out the window rather than revealing anything.

He grabbed the rifle, wrenching it from the man's grasp, and tossed it aside. Then he smashed his fist through the half-open window and grabbed the driver's face, plunging deep into his mind, chasing the essence of the vampire and surrounding him with energy. It was a psychic cage, but one he wouldn't be able to hold very long.

Who are you?

No enemy of yours. The voice that came out of the depths of the stranger's mind was older than he'd expected and, oddly, full of respect.

Then why are you trying to kill me?

I wasn't even aware of your presence. We were waiting for the witch. I thought it was she seeking to touch my mind again.

A chill ran through him. That bullet *had* been meant for Nikki. *Why waste silver on a witch?*

Because this witch is not human. She shifts, becomes something else.

He thought her a shapeshifter? Why? *So what harm will a shifter cause a vampire?*

She has the power to destroy my dreams. I have seen it.

Sweat was beginning to trickle down his face. He wished he could invade the other vampire's thoughts and discover where he was, but his mind-strength was just a little too strong to attempt both capture and invasion. If he let the net slip to attempt it, the fiend would slither away—or try an invasion of his own. And while he very much doubted the other vamp had the strength to succeed, it was a risk he wasn't willing to take. Not when Nikki's safety was at stake.

I have the power to destroy your dreams if I ever feel your presence like that again.

I apologize. I didn't realize there was another brother in the city, let alone this hotel. He hesitated. *Perhaps we should get together tomorrow evening. I have not spoken to someone close to my age in years.*

He raised his eyebrows at the soft yearning so evident in the other vampire's voice. Obviously, despite his clairvoyant abilities, this vampire had no idea who *he* was. *Why should I trust you?*

Ah. A man who has been around longer than me, obviously. We shall meet somewhere public, if you wish.

He knew it was a risk, but one worth taking simply because it might lead to the chance of killing this fiend and ending all their problems. *Where?*

The Hard Rock Café on Van Ness Avenue. You know it?

I can find it.

Then I look forward to meeting you.

I give no guarantees to be there. Better to let the fiend think he was far from eager for this meeting.

Of course. But if you do show up, ask for Farmer.

At least they now had a name. He released the net and let the other vampire slither from his grasp. The two people in the car blinked, dreamers just waking from a dream. He touched their minds, swiftly searching their memories. They'd just left a restaurant in Hyde Street when the other vampire had taken control. Hyde Street wasn't far from the hotel. The other vampire couldn't have been, either, simply because he wasn't strong enough to hold these two captive over any great distance.

Keeping them mind-blind, Michael punched a hole into the windshield to give them a plausible excuse for stopping, and rebuilt their memories around that excuse. Then he wrapped the shadows around himself, grabbed the gun and walked away. Within a minute, their curses filled the night, then the car started up and they drove away.

Nikki appeared in the window. What little light there was seemed to caress the pale skin of her bare legs, and he found himself wishing he could do the same.

Are you really intending to meet him?

So she *had* been listening in. Obviously the link between them worked on a far different, far deeper, level than telepathy because he certainly hadn't felt her presence when he'd been questioning the other vampire.

Or had it simply gotten so strong over the last few months that either of them could read the other's thoughts without really trying? That perhaps from now on, it would take a conscious effort to keep the other out?

Yes. You want to throw me some clothes, then get dressed yourself and come down here?

She pulled off his sweater, giving him a tantalizing but all too brief glimpse of her firm, high breasts. She tossed the sweater down to him before disappearing inside. *Why?*

Because I want to go for a walk and see if I can sense the presence of the other vamp, and I have no intention of leaving you in the hotel alone.

He's nowhere near. I'd feel him if he was.

I'd still like to check, just in case.

He caught the sweater and pulled it on. It smelled faintly of cinnamon and vanilla. He smiled and hoped she was right. Hoped they didn't find the scent, just so he could walk hand in hand with her. They'd spent too little time simply being lovers of late.

More clothes tumbled down to the pavement. *Be there in five.*

Wait. Catch this rifle and tuck it safely under our mattress.

She appeared in the window again. He checked to ensure the safety was on then tossed the rifle up to her. She caught it deftly, if a little gingerly, and disappeared. He quickly dressed then walked down to the hotel entrance to wait for her.

She bounced out four minutes later, wearing a short black skirt that showcased her wonderful legs, and a dark red sweater that clung to her breasts and highlighted the fact she wasn't wearing a bra.

"You look entirely too energetic for someone who has had so little sleep," he commented, wrapping his hand around her waist and pulling her close. "Are you going to be warm enough in those clothes?"

"The look in your eyes will keep me hot enough, believe me." Her grin was pure cheek. "And we can always find a secluded foggy spot in which to warm each other up."

That definitely sounded more enticing that hunting a vampire. He kissed her, long and tender. Her pulse was doing a double-time dance, and with the heat of her body pressed against him so wantonly, he really didn't want to go anywhere but back to the hotel room. Which was obviously the effect she'd been after when she'd donned these clothes. "You're incorrigible," he said eventually.

Her eyes twinkled with amusement and desire. "I

try hard. Are we walking, or do you have something else in mind?"

"Walking."

Her sigh was dramatic. "Such a spoil sport."

He smiled and led her down the street. The fog was a blanket of white dampness that swirled sluggishly around them, muffling the noise of passing traffic and the late night laughter of partygoers. Street lights twinkled like forlorn stars in the distance, and from the direction of the bay came the haunting cry of fog horns. The night was peaceful, untainted by the touch of evil. It was doubtful he'd find any hint of the other vampire, but he kept walking anyway. He was enjoying the night. Enjoying doing something semi-normal with Nikki.

"Why do you think this vamp wants to meet you?" she said.

He shrugged. "Loneliness. The night can be a desolate place after a few years."

Her expression was curious. "Was it for you?"

He nodded. "You asked why I stayed so long with Elizabeth. Perhaps there lies your answer."

"Yet you survived it. And her."

He smiled at the slight emphasis she placed on *her*. "Thanks in part to the friendships I formed. But the lifestyle of many vampires does not allow them to form true friendships."

"Because they drink human blood?"

"Yes."

"Can two vampires ever become truly good friends?"

He hesitated. "There are a number of vampires in the Circle, and I would call them friends. But not close. It is never truly comfortable for us."

She raised her eyebrows. "Why?"

"It's the nature of the beast." He shrugged. "Vampires are hunters. Hunters tend to be territorial."

"And no true hunter likes another in his territory?"

"Yes."

"Then why is this vampire inviting you to dinner?" She hesitated, and amusement spun through the link, warm and sexy. "Maybe he's taken a fancy to you."

"Wouldn't be the first time it's happened."

She pulled him to a stop, her expression slightly shocked. "What?"

He grinned and kissed her nose. "Both sexes seem attracted by my natural good looks and charm."

She snorted softly and whacked him lightly on the arm. "Yeah, right."

He raised his eyebrows. "It's true. I've been propositioned by many a male, both before and after death."

She stared at him for a moment. "Before death?"

"Not all our English landlords were as straight as they claimed." He tugged her across the intersection and continued on up Hyde Street hill. "I was barely twelve at the time."

"What did you do?"

"Kept well out of his way, and hid whenever he came to our farm." He shrugged. "He found other sport to chase after a week or so."

"Good grief."

He chuckled softly. "You spent quite a few years on the streets as a teenager. Surely you saw more shocking sights than old men chasing young boys."

"Well, yeah. It's just I never figured you were one of those young boys."

"I ran very fast," he said solemnly. "Believe me, he never caught me."

"And after death?"

"They quickly found their attention directed elsewhere."

She raised an eyebrow, amusement touching her full lips. "Including the females?"

"Of course. How could you think otherwise?"

"Something to do with the expertise you show in certain fields," she said dryly. "What if this vampire intends to lure you into a trap?"

"I doubt he'd do anything in a crowded café."

"What if he's seizing the opportunity to size up the opposition?"

"Then that'll make two of us, won't it?" He studied her for a moment. "What is it about this meeting that worries you?"

"I don't know. He doesn't sound anything like Jasper or Cordell. He sounds normal, and he's very obviously not." She bit her lip for a moment, her gaze sweeping the fog-enshrouded darkness around them. "I think it's going to be a lot harder to stop him than it was either of them."

"Which is why—"

Anger flared through the link, singeing his senses. "Don't say it," she warned, pulling her fingers from his. "Not unless you want an all-out argument right here on the street."

He didn't want to argue at all, here or anywhere else. *You keep complaining I don't listen to you, and yet you refuse to consider my reasons.*

Her gaze searched his, expression annoyed. "Maybe you're right. Maybe you should fully explain your reasons."

He reached out, brushing the moisture from the tip of her nose. "Not out here. It's too wet."

"The fog may be damp, but the night isn't really

cold." She shrugged. "I want you to talk to me, Michael."

He didn't want to talk. He just wanted to enjoy the night and her company in this brief window of peace they'd been given. But her determined expression suggested *this* time she would not let it go. He twined his fingers through hers again and kept walking. On a clear night, the bay would have stretched out before them. Tonight, there was little more to be seen than fog-muffled lights.

"I have been with the Circle since its beginning," he said. "In that time, both the Circle and I have gained a fair number of enemies. There are some alive today who would stop at nothing to destroy either of us."

"I'd think that would be a natural fallout from the type of work you do," she said, voice flat. "You can't run around killing bad guys without the bad guys' friends and relatives getting a little pissed about it."

He smiled, despite his annoyance. "True. The point is, these people will do all in their power to destroy me and everything I hold dear. That has never worried me because, until you, I had no one in my life whose destruction would destroy me."

She stopped, her gaze searching his, eyes glittering liquid gold in the damp night. "Then you know precisely how I feel when you go off on one of your missions and leave me behind."

He brushed his fingers against her cheek. "You're stronger than I am. You would survive my death. But I have spent over three and a half centuries alone, and I could not survive another three if I lost you."

"And you think I'd want to go on if I lost you?"

"No. But I think you'd survive the loss. I think you

would go on. I think in many ways you are far stronger than I ever will be."

She turned away and continued down the hill. "You're wrong. So wrong."

He followed her, watching the sway of her fog-dampened hair across her shoulders. "I don't want you to become a target. If you join the Circle, become a part of what I do, you will be."

"Isn't that a risk everyone in the Circle takes?"

"Yes. But because of me, the risk will be doubled for you."

"What if I said I understood that risk and was willing to take it?"

"I'm not."

She swung around to face him again. Her anger seared the night, burned through the link. "So what the hell am I supposed to do with my life for the next three or four centuries? It's not as if I can stay home and watch the kids, is it?"

Shock coursed through him. God, he'd never even thought . . . He reached out to pull her close, but she slapped his hand away.

"Loving you was my choice. Everything else that has happened between us has been yours. You can't keep making decisions for me, Michael. It'll destroy us."

He took a deep breath and released it slowly. Pictured her slender body heavy with his child. It stirred an ache fiercer than anything he'd thought possible. And while it could never be, he couldn't help the brief wish for humanity. For the chance.

"Did you want children?" he asked softly.

She swung away, but not before he caught the glimmer of moisture on her eyelashes. "No. Yes." She made a helpless gesture with her hand. "I don't know. It's something I never really thought about until you came along."

"I'm sorry."

She crossed her arms and walked on. "Don't be. You made me a thrall to save me from Jasper."

"No," he corrected gently. "I made you a thrall because I love you and couldn't bear the thought of losing you."

She glanced at him. Tears still gleamed faintly in her wonderful eyes, but a smile touched her lips. "First time you've actually admitted that, you know."

"You knew how I felt. You have always known."

"Knowing and hearing it said are two entirely different things."

"Words can lie. Thoughts can't. That's where we share an advantage over most couples."

"We don't share all thoughts."

No, they didn't. He'd certainly never sensed her regret over losing her humanity—anger yes. But not regret. Had never suspected she'd ached to have children. Guilt rose, but only briefly. He couldn't really regret his actions when they were responsible for bringing her into his life.

They continued on in silence, walking side by side but not touching. Below them, the masts of a tall ship loomed, and the salty tang of ocean became stronger.

"I have buried far more friends than I care to remember," he said eventually. "I have no wish for you to join them."

"I think we can safely say death is something neither of us wants." Though her voice still held an edge of annoyance, it was softer than before. "And neither of us is exactly an easy kill, anyway."

"But we are not immortal, either."

"No. But finding death by your side is better than dying slowly inside every time you leave me." She hesitated. "Will you at least consider the possibility?"

He didn't want to, but he didn't want to lose her, either. He was beginning to see that their relationship truly was at stake over this. She'd walk away rather than settle for what she considered second-best. It was odd how quickly things had turned around. Only four months ago he'd been the one wanting to walk away—to keep her safe from the very dangers she was now fighting to share.

"I'll consider, if you'll agree to think about Jasper—and Cordell—and remember that there are things out there ten times worse than either of them. Those things could be hunting me even as we speak. You join me on missions, and they'll quickly be hunting you as well."

Her fear swirled briefly around him. "You can't keep your home life and your working life separate forever. Sooner or later that's going to happen."

He touched a hand to her back, guiding her across the road towards the park. "I'd prefer it happened later rather than sooner."

"So would I." Her gaze met his again, full of determination. "I know the risks and I don't care. I need to be a full partner in your life."

"I'll think about it." Which was certainly more than he'd been prepared to do only a day ago.

"For now, that's all I'm asking." She twined her hand through his and led him through the park. A building that oddly resembled a cruise ship loomed out of the fog. "Have you caught any scent of the other vampire?"

"No."

An impish smile touched her lips, and her eyes twinkled. Trouble headed his way. And he very much suspected it was the sort of trouble he was going to enjoy.

"And people? Any one in the nearby vicinity?"

He let his gaze roam the foggy darkness. The red haze of life burned near the wharf, and in some of the shops that lined the street. "No one close."

"Good." She stopped at a park bench and pushed him down on it. "Guess what?"

She straddled his lap, and he slipped his hands under her sweater, caressing the aroused points of her breasts. "What?"

"I'm not wearing any panties."

He slid his hands past her waist and hips, then up the inside of her thighs until he discovered she was indeed telling the truth. The muted ache that had sprung to life in front of the hotel leaped into renewed focus. "Wicked wench," he murmured. He gently cupped the triangle of her curls, delved carefully into their moist heat. She was as ready for him as he was for her.

"You did say anywhere, anytime." Her voice was teasing, her gaze hot. She slipped back on his lap and undid the zipper of his jeans. "I think it's time to prove you meant what you said."

"This is a little *too* public for my liking. You'll end up getting us arrested." But as much as he wanted to pick her up and run back to the privacy of their hotel room so he could love her more fully, he didn't move. Couldn't move. Not when every part of him quivered to be inside her. To feel her warm, moist heat wrap around him.

She shifted again, capturing him, thrusting him deep. He groaned out loud at the sheer pleasure of it.

"You'll sense it if anyone comes close, won't you?" She dropped tiny kisses from his cheek to his chin, her breath a sweet caress across his skin, but one that seared deep.

"With you sitting so snugly on my lap, I very much doubt if I'd sense a herd of wild elephants running past." He caught the end of her sweater and pulled it gently over her head. Her skin gleamed in the misty night, nipples dark and erect.

Amusement and passion shimmered through the link. "I doubt you'd have to worry about that happening."

"This is San Francisco. Anything can happen." Including him making love in the middle of a park for every passerby to see to the woman who held his heart.

"Just think." She slipped her hands under his sweater, her touch cool compared to the fever of his skin. "If we were a team in the full sense of the word, there'd be no more lonely nights, no more long weeks of frustration."

"But there'd be more distraction, which could only lead to more danger for us both." He cupped her breasts, gently kneading the puckered nubs. "Don't think to use sex as a means to change my mind. It won't work."

"I'm not." She began to rock, ever so gently. Heat slithered through the link, wildfire ready to rupture and blow them both into bliss. "I'm just intent on showing you what you're missing out on."

"I'm very aware of what I'm missing out on, believe me."

The last three weeks in Ireland had certainly been hell. Loneliness was something he'd thought himself well accustomed to—until she'd stepped into his heart and made him dream of things he'd long thought impossible. Losing her would be like snatching the sunshine from the sky. He couldn't survive the plunge back into darkness. Wouldn't want to survive.

"I need you emotionally far more than I need you physically." He cupped a hand around the back of her neck and drew her lips close to his. "And I rest far easier at night knowing you are safe."

"I'm not safe. Not really." Her breath tingled across his mouth, her gaze holding his. "It's just an illusion you draw for yourself. Your work is your life. Either I'm a part of that life, with all its inherent dangers, or I'm out. Standing halfway between the two, like I currently am, is the most dangerous place of all."

"You're wrong." He brushed a tender kiss across her full lips. "And what we're doing now is the true danger. Distractions can kill."

"We are lovers, Michael. Occasionally it's nice to act like it." A teasing smile touched her lips. "But if you're really worried, just tell me to stop."

He slid his hand down to her waist and held her in place. "The Man of Steel wouldn't have the strength to tell you to stop right at this moment."

"Then stop worrying and just start loving."

"You are an extremely bossy woman, you know that?"

"And you are the most talkative male I have ever met." She wrapped her arms around his neck. "How about we concentrate on the business at hand before daylight comes and we really do get arrested."

As you wish.

He kissed her hard and began concentrating.

The harsh rap of knuckles against wood jerked Nikki awake. She kept her eyes closed, listening as her heart galloped in her chest. There was no sensation of danger, no hint of evil. The knock at the door echoed again.

The bed bounced as Michael rose, and she opened her eyes. The sunshine filtering past the hotel's curtains was warm and bright, so dawn had come and gone. She glanced at the clock. It was just after eight. They'd been asleep for a little more than three hours.

She sat up and looked around. The warm light played almost lovingly across Michael's well-toned back and shoulders as he pulled on his pants.

"What's wrong?"

"Jake's at the door." He leaned across the bed and quickly kissed her. "And from the feel of it, he's not happy. You'd better get dressed."

She tossed off the blankets and rose. "Something's happened."

"Obviously." He pulled on his sweater and walked quickly from the room. A heartbeat later she heard Jake's angry tones.

She hurriedly pulled on some clothes and walked out. "What's wrong?"

Jake threw the newspaper he was carrying onto the coffee table between them. "That's what's wrong."

The headlines screamed at her. Another woman had gone missing overnight.

Eight

She looked quickly at Michael. "It must have happened after that couple tried to kill us."

"Not us. You." He picked up the newspaper and studied the front page.

"Hang on," Jake said. "What am I missing here?"

She waved towards the window. "Someone took a potshot at us through the window last night. Turns out the fiend behind these kidnappings was psychically controlling a couple with a gun."

Jake's glance shifted to Michael and back again. "So why is he trying to kill you and not Michael?"

"Because he sees Nikki as the threat, not me."

"Why?"

"He's clairvoyant."

"Meaning?"

"Meaning," she answered with a smile, "he can see things other people can't. Sometimes this can include the future."

"That obviously means you're going to catch the fiend."

"Not necessarily. The future is not set in stone, you know. And knowing it means you can do something to change it."

"Well, that's just great." Jake dropped down onto the sofa and glanced at Michael. "You'd better turn to page three while you're reading that thing."

He did, and though his expression didn't change, a wave of annoyance singed her senses.

"What?" she said.

He folded the paper and showed her the headline.

Psychic recovers kidnap victim, it all but screamed. Complete with a picture of her that had been taken during the inquest into Matthew Kincaid's death.

"Oh, that's just great." Just the sort of headline she needed while trying to stop a killer.

"It mentions the agency in the article," Jake said. "And about an hour after that edition hit the streets, I got a call from Jeff Harris, the husband of the woman who's just been kidnapped. He wants you to try to find his wife."

And why wouldn't he, given what had happened to the other victims? She bit her lip and met Michael's gaze.

You don't have to, he said gently.

Yes I do. I couldn't live with myself if I stood back and did nothing, only . . .

Only this time it might very well be a trap, he finished for her.

She sighed. *Yes.*

He studied her for a moment, then threw the paper back onto the coffee table. "You remember what we did when Jasper kidnapped Jake, and we had to find him?"

She nodded. "Merged minds."

"It might be worth trying something like that again. I'll direct your abilities and hold them in check."

"But what if this Farmer fellow senses you?"

"I doubt he has the psychic strength."

"Can I ask who Farmer is?" A hint of exasperation tinged Jake's voice.

"The fellow behind the shooting last night," Michael said. "I have a meeting with him tonight."

"Is he the killer?"

She shrugged. "We're not sure. Probably."

Jake glanced at Michael, his expression hard. "He's a dead man?"

"If I can discover for a certainty he's behind the killings, yes."

"Good." Jake's gaze returned to her. "Are you up to helping Jeff Harris?"

"I have very little choice, really. You've arranged a meeting?"

He nodded. "Much to the annoyance of the police and Feds, I think." He glanced at his watch. "Mary wants us to have breakfast together, then we'll head on over. I said we'd be there by nine-thirty."

"That's not leaving much time for breakfast. Mary won't be amused."

"She never is." He pushed up from the sofa. "I'll see you in the dining room in ten minutes."

He strode from the room and slammed the door closed. "A marriage in trouble," Michael said softly.

"Yeah, and you'd better take note, buddy boy, because that's us a few years down the road if you don't start listening to me."

His dark gaze met hers, as unreadable as ever. "You and I are far different."

"Bull. Mary's taking no more notice of Jake's desires than you are of mine."

He raised an eyebrow. "And is Jake taking any notice of Mary's desires?"

"He's here, isn't he?"

"Only to recover. You and I know he has no intention of taking the security position permanently."

She crossed her arms and all but glared at him. "Mary knew what Jake did for a living when she married him. She has no right trying to change him this late in the game."

"Yet you have the right to try to change me?" A

slight smile touched his lips. "I have never made any secret of my opposition to you joining me in my work."

"I'm not asking you to stop like Mary's asking Jake. All I'm asking is to be included in that section of your life."

"And in the meantime, deliberately ignoring every opposing argument I give. A marriage works two ways, Nikki. It's give and take."

She raised an eyebrow. "We're not married."

He hesitated. "No. But the principle is the same."

"So you're saying I take and don't give?"

His frustration flitted through the link between them. "No, that's not what I'm saying at all."

"Then what *are* you saying?"

"That for any relationship to last long-term, there has to be some sort of give and take between the wants and desires of both people."

She crossed her arms and glared at him. "And just what have you given up in this relationship? Your solitude and loneliness? Gee, that's mighty big of you."

"Sarcasm will not get you anywhere."

"But neither is simply trying to talk to you."

He made a cutting gesture with his hand, and the frustration in the link became clouded with anger. "I said I'd think about it. Leave it at that, Nikki."

"God, you're so damn frustrating at times."

"So are you," he retorted. "Go have a shower."

She thrust her hands onto her hips. Energy tingled at her fingertips, but she resisted the temptation to knock him against the nearest wall. "Stop treating me like a child and giving me orders all the time."

"Fine," he said, voice tight. "Don't have a shower.

Do what you please. I'm heading downstairs to the dining room."

She swept the newspaper off the coffee table and threw it at his retreating back. He didn't even look back at her, just walked out the door and slammed it closed. She watched the sheets of newsprint flutter to the ground and sighed. She seemed to be doing that a lot lately—throwing things at his retreating back. And while she knew it was only a venting of her anger, it was one she'd definitely have to control. It wouldn't take much to slip into using her kinetic powers instead, and that was far more dangerous.

Besides, he was right in what he'd said yesterday. If she wanted to be treated like an adult, she should start acting like one. Throwing things at him might provide short-term satisfaction, but in the long run, it wouldn't help either of them.

With another sigh, she walked over to the door and picked up the newspaper. After dumping it onto the coffee table, she walked into the bedroom.

And discovered a stranger standing in the middle of the room.

Michael rubbed his eyes as the elevator doors slid shut. He hadn't meant to get angry, but it was just so damn frustrating that she *wouldn't* listen. He'd agreed to consider her request—was it asking so much that she do the same?

The elevator slid open, and he strode into the dining room. Jake was nowhere to be seen, but Mary sat at a table near one of the windows. He hesitated, but in that moment she turned around and saw him. He smiled at her raised hand and wove his way through the tables towards her.

"Michael, so nice to see you again," she said, voice warm, cultured.

He clasped her offered hand gently, her fingers like cool parchment against his own. "As it is nice to see you again." He kissed her fingertips then pulled out a chair near the wall. While it was nowhere near ten and the sun itself offered no danger, he wasn't about to take a risk after last night's attack. "Jake been called away?"

She nodded, a small, tight smile touching her lips. "It's always one thing or another."

Her voice was edged with the bitterness he could read in her thoughts. Mary, the loving, patient wife, had just about had enough. He hesitated, not sure he really should interfere, but unwilling to sit back and watch two people he liked drift apart. He smiled slightly. Nikki was certainly a bad influence. A year ago he wouldn't even have sat here, let alone been thinking about discussing Mary's personal problems when he had enough of his own.

"Jake will never change."

She leaned her chin on her clasped hands, her gaze touched with amused weariness. "Don't you think I know that?"

"Then why—"

"Why am I complaining so?" she cut in. "Because I have spent thirty years of my life loving him and supporting his endeavors. I think it's beyond time he started supporting mine."

"But your desires lie here in San Francisco. His do not."

She raised a finely penciled eyebrow. "And you think I desired to spend thirty years of my life in a town like Lyndhurst?"

"No one could want to spend thirty years in a town like Lyndhurst," he said with a smile.

"Except Jake. And possibly Nikki." She sighed softly. "I love San Francisco. And I love Boston, where I grew up. They are so much more . . . refined . . . than Lyndhurst. Is it asking too much that he move his business to either city?"

The sharp premonition of danger stabbed his mind, and he raised an eyebrow. Why had no one mentioned the fact Mary had grown up in Boston?

"No," he said slowly, "I guess not."

"There. Someone finally agrees with me. Perhaps you should talk to Jake for me.

"Perhaps." He touched her thoughts, lightly controlling. The spark of awareness left her eyes. "Tell me, did you attend high school in Boston?"

"Yes," she repeated dutifully.

"Were any of the following women your class-mates at that high school?" He reeled off the names of four kidnap victims.

She frowned. "All but Dale Wainwright were in my class."

He wasn't entirely surprised. "Did you know Dale at all during school?"

"We met afterwards, when she married Mark. I believe she was three years my junior."

"Did anything unusual happen during your years at high school?"

"No."

"Think back a little more." He pressed his mind control a little deeper.

"Nothing." She hesitated. "There was *one* prom that was somewhat tragic."

"In what way?"

"Two girls got drunk and leaped from the roof of the hall."

"Any idea why?"

"No."

"How did the alcohol get into the hall then?"

"No idea."

This was getting him nowhere fast. If Seline was checking the records, she'd undoubtedly find mention of this incident. He'd talk to her later this morning.

He crossed his arms and stared at the window for a moment. "Did these three girls do anything unusual during the evening?"

"Nothing different from the rest of us."

"And nothing else happened?"

"No."

He released his hold on her mind, and she blinked. "Now, what was I saying?"

"It's not me who needs to talk to Jake," he said, giving her the prompt. "But you." And knew the irony of the words even as he said them.

"We have talked. I talk, he talks, and still we get nowhere. I think we've both grown more selfish over the years, and it's me who's cracked first."

"You've spent too long together to simply walk away now."

She sighed. "It's the only reason either of us is still here."

He reached across the table and squeezed her hand. In that instant, he was slammed by the rush of fear running through the link.

Nikki. In trouble. He thrust upwards. "I'll be back in a moment."

Mary smiled gently. "Don't worry. I've grown used to men running out on me of late."

He hurriedly kissed her cheek, then ran out of the dining room. He didn't wait for the elevator, but blurred his form and raced up the stairs.

A heartbeat later he reached their room and shoved open the door. Nikki spun as he entered, hand raised, energy dancing in sparks across her fingertips. She relaxed the instant she saw him.

What's wrong? He quickly looked around the room but could see or feel no immediate threat.

We have a visitor.

Who?

She nodded towards the bedroom behind her. He strode to her side, sliding his hand down her arm until his fingers were twined through the warmth of hers. In the center of the bedroom stood a man. He was ordinary looking—short, plumpish, with thinning red hair and pale blue eyes. His face was pockmarked, leftover evidence of the acne he must have suffered as a teenager. He was dressed in black boots, faded jeans, a black T-shirt and a leather jacket.

But he wasn't real.

Wasn't actually there.

His image rippled, sparked, and energy caressed the air, raising the hairs along Michael's arm. *Have you talked to him?*

She shook her head. *I was about to, when you came in.*

Then do so. He released her fingers. *I'll remain silent, so he doesn't sense I'm here.*

She walked into the room and stopped in front of the flickering image. "Who are you?"

The man jerked, like a mannequin brought to life. Michael very much suspected that this wasn't the true form of the man behind the murders. And if the marks on the image's neck were anything to go by, he was also very dead.

"I'm sending you a warning. Leave this city now, or I will destroy you."

The image's lips didn't move. The voice was disembodied but familiar. It was the man he'd talked to last night.

"And why would you want to do that?" She circled the image, studying him from all angles. She paused when she saw the man's neck and glanced across at Michael. *This man is dead.*

By several hours, I'd say. He crossed his arms and leaned a shoulder against the door frame. But he didn't entirely relax. This image might well be the forerunner of another attack.

"What I do is nothing more than justice," the voice said. "You have no right to stop me."

"What you're doing has nothing to do with justice, and everything to do with revenge. Don't lie to me or yourself."

The image's mouth slid into the gruesome replica of a smile. "You are more intuitive than I'd originally thought."

"And you're sicker than I'd originally thought." Nikki stopped near the front of the image again. "And I have no intention of going anywhere until I stop you."

No reply came. The image hung in the room, waiting for its master to give it life once more.

It might not be wise to antagonize him, Michael advised. *We're working with a sick mind, and it's doubtful his reactions will be predictable.*

Antagonizing him might be our only way of stopping him. At least if he's coming after me, he's not kidnapping other women.

110

I wouldn't be too sure of that. This plan, whatever it was, smelled of precision. Their killer *might* be mad, but madness certainly hadn't incapacitated his brainpower. *He's here for a reason. He's not here just to deliver a warning.*

An image can't harm me.

It can if it's meant as nothing more than a distraction. He glanced over his shoulder. While he could hear no sound or movement, the awareness of ... something ... surged across his senses.

She glanced at him, eyebrows raised. *You think he plans another attack?*

Yes.

But it's daylight, so his vamps can't move around. And the cops have the hotel monitored.

Fledglings could take them easily enough. Yet it wasn't fledglings he could sense. It was something else, something undefinable.

Something that felt vaguely human, though he could neither smell blood nor hear a heartbeat.

Zombie?

Remember what they smell like.

She shuddered. *No disguising that.*

No. He pushed away from the bedroom door frame and moved to the center of the main room, trying to get some sort of directional feel for whatever it was he sensed.

"Are you sure you just won't give up this madness and go?" the voice said.

She glanced at Michael. He moved back until he was near the suite door, then nodded.

"Oh, I'm sure."

"Then I apologize, but you really leave me no choice."

The image disappeared. For several seconds, neither Michael nor Nikki moved. Barely even breathed. The happy tune of a cable car bell mingled with the rumble of traffic rising up from the street below. On the floor immediately underneath them, people moved, talked or made love, the pulse of their hearts a distant but flavorsome beat.

Nothing and no one seemed to be approaching their room. Yet that sense of disconnected humanity continued to come close.

Get ready, Nikki. It comes.

She flexed her hands. Energy danced across her fingertips, brighter than he'd ever seen it before. Someone knocked loudly on the door. He glanced at her. She cleared her throat, then said, "Who is it?"

No answer.

After several heartbeats, the knock came again. There was no heartbeat, no thoughts, nothing to indicate there was anything human, vampire, or anything else vaguely alive, standing on the other side of the door. It could almost have been a zombie, except for the fact there was no smell, and no shambling step.

He nodded at Nikki again.

"Hang on a sec," she called. *What now?*

Say you're coming, then step back.

Humor momentarily chased its way through the tension in her expression. *I'd rather be coming right now than facing an imminent attack from a madman, let me tell you.*

So would I. He reached out through the link, momentarily caressing her mind with warmth and love.

She smiled. *And I love you, even if you are the most irritatingly stubborn man at times.*

112

He reached for the door handle, and her smile faded.

The door was rapped a third time.

Do it, he said.

"Coming, coming," she called and stepped backwards, out of immediate sight.

Michael turned the handle and pulled the door open.

Nine

It wasn't a zombie.

It wasn't anything, human or non human.

Just a bunch of flowers.

Michael stared at them for a heartbeat, then leaned out the door and studied the hall. Nothing. No smell, no sign of anything human. Whoever—or whatever—had delivered these flowers had disappeared as fast as they'd arrived.

He glanced down at the flowers again. Why would anyone deliver flowers . . . A chill ran up his spine. Maybe they were meant as a gift—but not a gift of life.

He whirled, his form blurring as he raced towards Nikki. He swept her up in his arms, not stopping as he raced toward the bathroom.

What the hell . . .?

I think it's a small bomb.

Her fear swirled around him, sharp and acrid. He jumped into the large tub and pushed her head down, then covered her body with his own. A half second later there was a rush of almost deafening noise. Heat and dust swirled through the air, covering them in a fine blanket of grey.

Alarms sounded, and the sprinklers dropped down from the ceiling, the fine spray quickly soaking them. He glanced down at Nikki. "You okay?"

She nodded and wiped the muddy droplets from around her eyes. "He's crazier than we thought. He could have killed everyone in the hotel with a stunt like that."

"Unlikely." He pushed upright, then offered her a hand. "The explosion wasn't large enough. I think he only meant to blow up the person holding the flowers."

She shivered. He pulled her into his arms and brushed a kiss across her forehead. Then he simply held her close. Held her tight. Her heart raced so hard it felt like his own, and the fear that tainted the link was as much his as hers. If he hadn't been here, she might have picked up those flowers. Might well now be dead.

"If we can find that woman today, I will kill him tonight." Though he tried to keep his voice flat, anger reverberated nonetheless.

She shifted slightly, looking up at him, amber eyes sparkling gold in the morning light. "You can't kill him in the middle of a crowded restaurant."

He could. And had done so—twice in the last hundred years. Why people thought there was safety in numbers he never knew. In most cases, a crowd only made it far easier to both kill and escape.

He caressed her cheek with his fingers and journeyed down to her full lips. "I'll do what I have to do."

"He's not a fool, Michael. He may not have suspected last night that you were with me, but he'll put two and two together soon enough."

"Perhaps." But it was still a risk he had to take. The heavy tread of footsteps approached their room, hearts beating fast. Jake and others. He kissed her. Her mouth was so soft and sweet against his own that he just wanted to keep on tasting her forever. But he couldn't—not right now, anyway. She sighed when he pulled away, a sound he felt like echoing.

"We have guests," he said, stepping out of the tub.

115

"Nikki! Michael!" Jake's voice, edged with panic.

"Here," he said, helping Nikki out of the spa.

Jake came in, grinning when he saw them. "You both okay?"

Nikki nodded and ran her fingers through her sodden hair. The sprinklers had stopped their rain, but ever inch of her was soaked, and the chill was creeping past her skin and settling deep inside. But she suspected it wasn't so much an effect of the cold, but rather the fear of what this madman would try next. "Better than the living room, I suspect."

"Actually, the damage is constrained to the door and a bit of the wall. What was it? A bomb of some sort?"

"Of some sort." Michael's reply was grim. "Meant to destroy nothing more than the person holding the flowers in which it was delivered."

A security officer dressed in the hotel's uniform stuck his head around the comer. "Police and Fire Services are here, Mr. Morgan."

"Tell them we'll be out in a minute." Jake glanced at Michael. "It might be better if you remain hidden."

"I agree."

Power surged, and Nikki knew without asking that Michael was adjusting the guard's memory so that he remembered seeing only her. She bit back her instinctive annoyance, knowing he wouldn't listen, and wouldn't care.

"I'll keep to shadows in the bedroom," he said once the surge of power had faded. He hesitated, then added, "Hadn't you better contact Mary?"

Jake swore and thrust a hand through his thinning blond hair. "Damn it, yes."

His expression was filled with annoyance—at himself, more than anything else, she suspected. He usually kept Mary up-to-date with what was happening. But when a case got as nasty, as this one was, she was never his highest priority, unless the case threatened to backwash and involve her as well.

"I guess this'll be another black mark in the book," he continued, a touch bitterly.

"Mary will understand," she said, even though she knew the lie. Mary was past understanding. Or perhaps tired of understanding. She hungered for something Jake couldn't—or wouldn't—give her, and though Nikki didn't really understand what that *something* was, she could certainly understand Mary's frustration. And *she'd* only put up with her own frustration for four months. Mary had been battling it for thirty years.

Official-sounding voices drew close. Michael squeezed her fingers lightly, then stepped past Jake and disappeared into the shadows still filling the bedroom.

She glanced up at Jake. "We're not going to make it to Harris' place by nine-thirty."

"No. I'll give him a call and let him know what's happened. We'll just have to get there when we can."

He touched a hand to her back and ushered her out into the living room. As he'd said, there wasn't much damage to the room as a whole, except for the fact that everything was soaked. A gap stood where the door had once been, but other than a chunk of missing plaster on either side of the door and scorch marks, there was nothing else to really indicate someone had tried to blow the hell out of her.

The police turned as they entered, notebooks in hands and questions she could almost read evident in their eyes.

She rubbed a hand across her eyes. Talking to the police had never been a favorite pastime, but it was something she seemed to be doing a lot of lately.

Sighing softly, she plopped down on one of the sodden sofas and got herself comfortable for a long few hours.

Michael crossed his arms and leaned a shoulder against the wall. From his position in the bedroom, he could see Nikki and not much else. She was sitting on the sofa, legs tucked underneath her, dark chestnut hair drying in waves that fluffed around her expressionless face. She looked absurdly young and almost delicate—neither of which she truly was.

A cop sat in front of her, writing notes and occasionally asking a question. He didn't appear inclined to hurry. Michael bit down on his frustration. Needing to do something, he reached out to Seline instead.

'Bout time, she grumbled. *Been waiting for hours.*

What, the cat's suddenly grabbed your tongue, has it? Actually, knowing her cat, it was more than a possibility. It was a big black-and-white monstrosity that only possessed one eye and half a tail, and was the meanest thing on four legs he'd ever met.

I was being discreet. Didn't want to interrupt you and Nikki at a delicate time.

He smiled. *You and discreet are not two words I've ever associated before.*

Her amusement swam down the mental line. *That's because most times I don't want to be. It's more fun being a pushy old witch.*

And you do it so well.

Thank you. Her voice was prim. Schoolmarmish.

Which she had been, at one point in her life. *We've discovered there are eight women who attended Boston High currently either living or visiting San Francisco.*

I gather the first three victims were from this eight?

Yes.

And would one of the remaining five be Mary Morgan?

I'm afraid so.

Which meant they had to get Mary out of San Francisco, and the sooner the better. No easy task when the only other place she wanted to go appeared no safer. *Did you run a check to locate the other classmates?*

Certainly did. One disappeared in Boston last year and has never been found. Two disappeared from New York, though the body of one was found floating in the river. Apparently she bore mutilations similar to the first two victims in San Francisco. Another woman was found drained of blood in a hotel room in Albuquerque two years ago.

But not mutilated?

She hesitated. *Not to the extent of the rest. The police put it down to rough sex.*

Any before that?

No. She was the first.

So what was the trigger? What did this woman do that started a madman down his bloody path? *Did the police reports say anything else?*

Yep. Apparently, she'd lost her husband a few months before and decided to do the tour they'd always planned. She'd stopped at the hotel for the night, and the manager said that while she booked in alone, she came back later with a man.

She picked up her killer?

So it would appear.

But was that man the same man who was now kidnapping and killing women here in San Francisco?

Was there a description?

Medium height, medium build, brown hair.

Mr. Joe Average, in other words.

Well, that's what he made the manager see, at least.

Is there any connection at all among these women, other than the fact they all attended the same school?

None that we can see, beyond the fact the current three victims all attended that fundraiser. But he's not going after all the women who attended that year of school, though. There are still at least one hundred girls living in or around Boston, and none of them have been attacked.

So what is it about these women?

Discover that, and we'll discover our motive, I think.

Nikki glanced his way, an intent look on her face. Listening in again. He raised his mental shields a little more, and annoyance rumbled through the link, a distant but threatening thunder.

When you were going through the Boston High records, did you find any reports about a couple of girls suiciding on a prom night?

Yeah, I did. Curiosity swam through Seline's mental tone. *Why?*

Just a feeling I've got. When I was talking to Mary, she said there was no alcohol in the building, yet both girls were apparently drunk. Might be worth investigating.

Seline paused. *Michael, when did you start developing precognition?*

He raised his eyebrows. *I haven't.*

You said you had a feeling.

It was just an insight, a guess, nothing more.

It was more. I can see it in your thoughts. Has Nikki any precognition skills?

He hesitated. *She can sometimes sense danger or evil, but beyond that, no.*

Which could mean this merging is bringing out latent talents in you, as well.

All I've ever had are telepathy and telekinesis. And his telekinesis wasn't anywhere near the strength of Nikki's.

That doesn't mean there aren't more talents. It only means they're the only ones you've acknowledged.

You've tested me more than once over the years, Seline.

But you are a far stronger telepath than I'll ever be. It's possible that you could have been subconsciously blocking me.

Why would I want to do that? You know more about me than any man or woman ever has—alive or dead.

But still I don't know all your secrets. You were a man used to keeping his own council when we met. I doubt whether that man has entirely disappeared, even after I've spent over a hundred years civilizing you.

He smiled. According to Nikki, that man had *not* disappeared at all. *I met a vampire last night. He was psychically using a young couple in an attempt to kill Nikki.*

Seline's amusement shimmered around him. She was well aware he was steering the conversation back to more comfortable topics. *And he still lives? Michael, you're slipping.*

I never had much hope of finding him in a city this

size—*he could have been anywhere in a one- or two-block radius, and his scent was nowhere to be found. But I am meeting him tonight, and if he is our kidnapper, I'll kill him if I can.*

If? You sense problems?

A fourth woman has been kidnapped.

Damn. She hesitated, her anger heating the link. *Which one?*

Her married name is Harris.

Anne Harris, that would be. She's one of the eight I mentioned. Her husband is involved in shipping.

It's not her present that's the problem. It's her past. Perhaps you'd better talk to Mary some more.

I've probed her memories. As far as she's concerned, nothing unusual happened.

Then probe deeper. Obviously, something else happened either that night or during the year—something that involved these twelve women.

I'll try. When Nikki wasn't around to protest. He wasn't up to any more arguments right now. *If you give me the names and addresses of the remaining women, I'll visit each of them and impress upon their minds the urgent need to leave.*

Good idea. Seline's thoughts touched his more fully, burning the information into his memory. *Though it may drive our killer underground again.*

Better us chasing him than him chasing these woman. And at least now we have some idea of who his targets are.

True. And instinct tells me it'll end here in San Francisco, anyway.

He didn't bother asking which way it would end. If she knew, she would have told him. *Listen, have you got a charm or spell or something that will stop this vampire using his clairvoyant abilities to track*

Nikki? We have to use her skills to find these women quickly, but he basically knows our every move, thanks to the lock he has on her.

Seline's frown was something he felt—a wash of darker light through the link. *A tricky one. I think I remember a spell that'll create a sort of dead zone around her. He won't be able to track her psychically, but you may not be able to, either.*

I don't think it'll matter. The link we share works on a far deeper level than telepathy.

Which only provides more evidence of the merging. Everything I've read on thralls suggests it's a one-way street. The thrall usually only has basic telepathy skills with its master.

We had this link before she became a thrall.

Yes, but now it's deepened. She hesitated. *You know, you both really should come into headquarters so we can test what's happening. I've got a feeling it could be very interesting.*

And he had a feeling that if he let Nikki anywhere near the Circle's headquarters, it would be the end of any hope he had of stopping her from joining them. *Let's concentrate on getting this case solved first.*

Do you have a name for this vampire you're meeting?

Farmer.

I'll check through the records and see what we find. I'll also check out that suicide incident.

And the charm for Nikki?

I'll work on it this afternoon and have it couriered across. It'll be tomorrow morning before it gets there, so be careful until then.

I will. Thanks Seline.

The link between them died. He glanced up and

met Nikki's gaze. She raised an eyebrow, expression annoyed.

Why do you keep locking me out?

Why do you keep listening in on private conversations?

Heat touched her cheeks, and the thunder in the link rumbled closer. *I thought we were going to work together on this case?*

We are—though if I had any choice in the matter, I would make you, Jake and Mary leave San Francisco so you'd all be away from this madman's grasp.

Don't I know that. Her retort stung his mind. She considered him for a moment, gaze narrowed. *Tell me—were you and Seline ever lovers?*

The question caught him by surprise. He barely managed to keep his laugh in check, but his amusement echoed down the link, momentarily drowning the sound of thunder. *No, we were never lovers. Why do you ask?*

She gave a mental shrug. *You don't want me to meet her. You don't want me to listen in on your conversations with her. It's the sort of secretive behavior of two lovers, isn't it?*

Perhaps it is. But we are not, have never been, and never will be. They were friends. Good friends. He trusted her more than any person on Earth, except Nikki. Yet he had never once felt the slightest bit of sexual interest in her. And it was a disinterest that was shared.

Why?

He shrugged. He'd never psychoanalyzed his relationship with Seline. He'd simply enjoyed. After two hundred years of darkness, distrust, and entrenched loneliness, she was the true beginning of his path towards the light. For too many years beforehand he'd walked the knife's edge, not quite falling on either side, yet slowly slipping back into the darkness from which he'd emerged after his years with Elizabeth. He might never have found Nikki had it not been for Seline.

I do not know, and I do not care. But I think the friendship Seline and I share would not have been as strong had we been lovers.

Because lovers cannot remain friends once the relationship falls apart?

There is always an undercurrent of tension in such situations, whether it is acknowledged or not.

She bit her lip, expression clearly troubled. He could tell her thoughts without having to read her mind or taste the uncertainty in the link. Her fears were evident enough in her eyes.

What hope does that offer us, then? she asked eventually. *We are lovers, and we are friends. Are you saying it's inevitable that we'll eventually drift apart?*

He sighed. *No. We are far more than just lovers, Nikki. We are two minds, two souls, one heart.*

But—

No buts. Simply trust in the fact that what I feel is every bit as strong as what you feel.

Tears washed through her dark amber eyes. She bit her lip, blinking as she looked away. But emotion surged through the link, a wash of love that almost drowned his senses. It was a drowning he could have endured forever.

Jake stepped through the doorway as the police began making moves to leave. "I've arranged for you to be moved back into the other suite. This room won't be useable for a few days yet."

Though his words were addressed to Nikki, his

gaze sought the shadows still haunting the bedroom. Looking for a vampire, Michael thought with a smile.

She nodded. "And what about Mr. Harris?"

"Expecting us as soon as the police will let you go."

"She can go now," an officer said. "We know where to find you both if we have any more questions."

Nikki glanced his way. *How are you going to get out of the room?*

I am the wind, remember?

Amusement swam around him. *So you're going to fart your way free?*

Vampires don't get wind.

Her eyebrows raised. *Really?*

Really. My diet does not lead to an excess of gases. And here I was thinking you were simply being polite these past four months. She rose. *I'll call the elevator and wait for you there.*

Good.

She and Jake left. Michael waited until he heard the ding of the elevator arriving, then pushed away from the wall. He glanced at each of the police officers, focusing their attention on whatever it was they were working on. Then he ran for the door, the room little more than a blur as he moved through.

"We have a problem we have to deal with before we head over to Harris' place," he said, reappearing beside Nikki as the elevator doors closed.

Jake jumped. "I wish you wouldn't do that. Not good for the old heart." He paused, then added, "What problem?"

He hesitated. "Mary. I'm afraid she could be on the killer's list."

What?" Nikki stared at him, face suddenly pale. "Why would you think that?

"Because the kidnapped women all had one thing in common—everyone but Dale were in the same year at Boston High."

Jake punched the button for the sixth floor. "So were a couple of hundred other people." Though his voice was flat, the acrid smell of his fear hung heavy in the air. He believed, even if he didn't want to.

"True. But there are other links among these women."

"Who says these attacks aren't random?" Jake said. "This guy obviously isn't sane. He may not have—or need—a motive."

"But he *has* got a motive—revenge." Nikki's gaze was thoughtful, distant. "For what they did to him in school. For what they did to him at the prom. Dale was one of those who taunted, even though she wasn't in the same year as the other ladies.

A chill ran through Michael. She was reading the killer's mind—or at least, his memories—as easily as she breathed. He touched her back, and she jumped, her gaze leaping to his.

"It's getting stronger," she said.

"It is." Both her clairvoyant abilities, and this odd link between the killer and her. "Seline's making a charm, which she'll courier over by morning. It'll stop him using the connection between you to track us."

Her eyes widened as the implications of his words sunk in. "Meaning, when we go down to rescue Harris' wife, he'll know?"

"And more than likely be waiting. Which is why—"

"No," she cut in. "Don't say it. Don't even think it."

"What about Mary?" Jake cut in harshly. "What are we going to do with her? We can't protect her twenty-four hours a day—not from this madman, and not if we want to save the other woman."

"No. Which is why I suggest you send her away. She's one of four other women currently living or visiting San Francisco who attended the same year of school as the first four kidnap victims. If Mary disappears, the killer will simply turn his attention to the remaining three." And if Seline was right—and she usually was—it was all going to end here in San Francisco, anyway. Mary should be safe just about anywhere else in the country.

Jake swore softly. "She's going to assume this is some sort of scheme I've come up with to get her out of San Francisco."

"I'll talk to her," Michael said.

Nikki's glance was sharp. "Just talk?"

He hesitated again. "No."

"Damn it, you know—"

"And you know," Michael cut in, anger touching his voice, "That it could be the fastest and easiest way of discovering what is going on."

"Would someone like to tell me what the hell is going on?" Jake cut in impatiently. "There's a whole level of conversation I'm missing out on here."

"Michael's intending to probe Mary's memories," Nikki said.

Jake's gaze met his. "You can do that? To anyone?"

"Anyone I choose. And most times, they're not even aware of it."

Jake's gaze widened a little. "Would Mary be aware?"

"No."

"Then do it." Jake glanced at Nikki. "If Mary's in the firing line, then we need to do everything we can."

The elevator doors slid open. Jake strode down the corridor and swiped his key card through the slot at the last of the half dozen doors.

Mary turned around as they entered, relief etched on her drawn features. "Nikki, Michael, are you all right?"

Nikki walked over and gave the older woman a hug. "Just a little wet," she said softly.

Jake took his wife's hand and led her towards the sofa. "We need to ask you a few questions."

Mary's gaze jumped from person to person, finally coming to rest on Michael. "Something's wrong."

He nodded and sat down on the coffee table beside Nikki. "You remember when we were talking earlier, you mentioned Boston?"

Mary nodded. "What has that got to do with what happened this morning?"

He touched her thoughts, pushing deep into her memories. Controlling, but not intruding any more than necessary. "You were telling me about the prom where the two girls died."

"Yes." Mary's voice was flat, remote.

Jake, who'd never really seen him in action like this before, stared at him, a touch of fear in his eyes.

"Did you know them?" Michael said softly.

"Yes."

"They were your friends?"

"Yes."

"Did you see them drinking alcohol anytime during the night?"

129

"No."

"Was anyone else drinking alcohol?"

"Not that I know of."

"Did anything unusual happen during the night?" He'd asked that question before, but this time his control was deeper.

She hesitated. "No."

The mere fact she hesitated suggested something *had* happened. "So what did you do that night?"

"We teased Billie."

"Billie?" He glanced at Jake, wondering if it was a name he knew. Jake shrugged. "Who's Billie?"

"Local nerd, and a bit of a loner. He turned up in his dad's blue suit."

"And you taunted him?"

"Yes."

"Is it something you often did?"

"Yes."

"How many of you were there in this group?"

"Twelve."

No real surprise there. "Who were the main instigators?"

"Rachel and Monica."

"And they were the two who jumped off the roof?"

"Yes."

"What was Billie doing at the time?"

"I don't know. I never saw him again after he ran off."

"Did anyone see him again that night?"

"The police interviewed him, apparently, but nothing came of it."

"Does Billie have a last name?"

"Farmer."

"The name of the guy who attacked us last night,"

Nikki murmured, glancing at Jake. "Lord, how bad could their teasing have been for him to seek revenge forty years later?"

"Just think back to your own teenager years," Jake said, voice grim. "And multiply that by twelve."

"I never had a normal teenage life."

"No, but you were certainly a normal teenager, just carrying a bit more angst than usual. Just ask our favorite police detective."

"Never thought I'd say this, but I wish we had MacEwan with us now. The man has a knack for being in the right place at the right time." She hesitated and nodded towards Mary. "What are we going to do?"

"I can put a compulsion on her." Michael ignored the rush of irritation through the link and held Jake's gaze. Not quite compelling. "Make her leave right now, without fighting."

"Will she remember it?"

"You can't do this, Jake," Nikki said. "It's wrong to control another's behavior like this." *Damn it, Michael, don't do this to her.*

Stop letting your own fears override common sense. You agree Mary has to leave San Francisco, don't you?

Yes, but—

You agree that she won't go willingly, don't you?

She didn't reply, just glared at him. He was right, and she knew it.

He looked back at Jake. "No, she won't feel the compulsion. Where do you want me to send her?"

"Not to Boston, that's for sure." Jake hesitated. "What about Long Beach? She has a friend down there—a recent friend, not one from Boston. Mary said some time ago she'd like to see her again."

"This friend's name?"

"Anna."

"Then that's where we'll send her. You want to go call the friend and make arrangements? I'll hold Mary until you come back."

Jake walked into the bedroom. Michael glanced at Nikki. She'd crossed her arms and was carefully holding herself away from him. The anger he could feel in the link was evident in the glitter in her eyes.

"This is part of what I do," he said, keeping his voice even, unapologetic. "It's also probably the least of my sins when it comes to getting a job done. It's not something I intend to stop just because it bruises your sensibilities."

"Damn it, she has a right to choose her own destiny."

"So you'd rather she stay here and die?"

"No, and that's not—"

He touched a hand to the warmth of her lips, stopping her words. "The point is, I'm trying to stop a killer, and I will do whatever it takes to achieve that goal. I don't care whether you like it or not. It's what I do. Accept it and get past it."

She took a deep breath and released it slowly. "Fine," she muttered. "I'll say no more about it."

The stubborn look on her face suggested that while she might not say anything more, she'd definitely be thinking it. He smiled and touched her chin, gently directing her gaze back to his. "One of the things I love about you," he said softly, "is the ungracious way you give in when you know you're wrong."

He brushed a kiss across her lips. Her mouth was warm and pliant under his, and the kiss deepened. Heat simmered through the link, a yearning that could not be quenched for some time yet. Eventually she sighed and wrapped her arms around his neck.

"And one of the things I love about you," she said, eyes dancing with amusement and desire, "is the way you make me want you, even when I'm so damn mad at you I could spit fire."

Jake came back into the room. "All arranged," he said. "I've booked Mary onto the eleven o'clock flight."

Michael nodded and began rebuilding Mary's memories, imprinting on her mind the exuberance of her seeing her friend again and making sure there were no doubts about the trip and leaving Jake for the next week. Then he released her.

"You'd better be getting ready if you want to make the plane," he said, prompting her.

Mary glanced at her watch and surged to her feet. "Ohmigod, you're right. Jake are you going to take me to the airport or not?"

"The limo has been booked, but I'll be escorting you out there." He hesitated, waiting until Mary had left the room, then added, "I'll meet you two at Harris's later."

Nikki rose. "I'll just go say good-bye, then we can get going."

Michael nodded and glanced at Jake. "You got the address?"

Jake handed him a card. "From what he said, she was snatched from her bedroom last night."

He frowned. "Were they at a hotel or a bed and breakfast?"

"No. Private residence."

His frown deepened. "It can't be vamps snatching these women then."

"Well, it isn't human, that's for sure. Harris took a

swing at the man and said he simply stepped back into shadow. If that doesn't sound like a vamp, then what the hell is it?"

It certainly sounded like a vampire. The question was, how were they getting into the house in the first place? One of the few myths about them that was true was their inability to step into a private home unless invited. It couldn't be forced, but had to be freely given.

It was doubtful if any man or woman would give such permission in the early hours of the morning.

So how were these vamps getting in?

Ten

Nikki stepped onto the sidewalk and stared up at the beautiful old Victorian house. Painted blue and yellow, it was a cheerful sight that belied the deep sense of sorrow and anger she could feel coming from inside the old house.

She shivered and rubbed her arms. Emotions were not something she'd ever been able to feel before now—not unless she was linked through psychometry to the mind of another. It was not something she wanted to feel *now*.

Michael climbed out of the cab and touched a hand to her back. "Let's get inside."

She glanced up at him. His face had gone pink. Sunburn. "You pushing your limits?"

"It's past ten, so very definitely." He opened the gate and ushered her through.

Worry slithered through her. "It could be midday before we finished. What are you going to do then?"

"Let's worry about it then."

He climbed the steps and pressed the doorbell. A cop answered. Nikki all but groaned. It was hard enough to focus her gifts—harder still to control them, especially given the way they were currently changing. To try to do so in a room filled with disbelieving police officers would be next to impossible.

"Could you please tell Mr. Harris that Nikki James and Michael Kelly are here to see him?" Power caressed the air as Michael spoke. For a heartbeat, the cop's eyes went blank. She clenched her fists and bit back her instinctive comment.

The cop nodded and disappeared. A second later, a small, bearded man appeared, his brown eyes red-rimmed, face haggard. "Come in, come in, both of you," he said and offered Michael his hand. "Jeff Harris."

Nikki shook his hand in turn. His fingers were clammy, feeling oddly like wet parchment against her own. She had to resist the temptation to wipe his touch away afterwards.

"The cops aren't too happy about me inviting you here," he continued, voice raspy, almost harsh. "But I told them they could stick it. You found the other woman, and found her alive, and I'm not about to turn my back on any chance, no matter how remote."

He led them into the living room. Besides the cops, there were several suited men inside—Feds, she presumed. They were hovering around the phone, waiting for a call she knew would never come.

Michael glanced at her sharply. *Why not?*

She hesitated, examining the distant, shadowy thoughts. *Because he fears us. Or me. And he cares more about the revenge now than the money itself.*

Which means we may not have much time to play with to rescue this woman.

We don't. She rubbed her arms and tried to ignore the bitter fury that swam around her. Billie Farmer, if that was this killer's true name, had already begun to take his revenge on Anne Harris.

"So, what do you need?" Harris said, coming to a stop in the center of the room.

"Something she wore all the time. A favorite necklace or bra are usually good."

He nodded and left the room again, leaving them under the watching eye of the silent police officers.

Michael twined his fingers through hers, his touch furnace hot.

Jeff Harris returned with a jewelry box and a handful of bras. "Take your pick," he said, dumping them all on the coffee table.

She skimmed her hand over the top of them. Muted rushes of color and heat ran across her senses, but there was nothing she would have deemed truly promising—until she reached the heart-shaped pendant that had fallen from the box. Fear practically swamped her.

She swallowed heavily and glanced up at Harris. "Do you have a plastic bag?"

He frowned, but disappeared into the kitchen to get one. Michael took it from him and carefully swept the necklace into the bag before handing it to her.

Though she held it by the plastic and wasn't actually touching the metal, flashes of fear and darkness still pulled at her mind. If she went in uncontrolled, as she normally did, it could be very bad indeed. She met Michael's gaze. "How do you want to do this?"

He pushed the coffee table back against the sofa. "Sit on the carpet and relax."

She did. Michael sat cross-legged in front of her and took hold of her free hand. The heat of his touch burned through her flesh, warming the ice formed by her apprehension.

"Now relax and close your eyes."

She closed her eyes, but the awareness of all those watching them burned deep, tearing at her concentration.

He gently squeezed her fingers. "Listen to the sound of my voice. Concentrate on it. On me."

She took a deep breath and released it slowly. *Why not use the link?*

Because the link and your talents seem to work on two entirely different levels, and I don't think they're truly compatible for what we are about to try. Aloud, he murmured, "Breathe deeply and relax."

She listened to the rhythmic flow of his breathing and tried to match it. Gradually, the tension began to leave her limbs.

"Relax, relax."

His voice was a whisper that soothed her soul. Gradually, the tension, the awareness of everyone else, began to ease away. All she could hear was Michael. All she could feel was the necklace burning into her palm, the gold almost molten against her skin. But she ignored the images pushing at the edges of her mind, knowing she dare not follow them yet.

"Open your mind to me. Let our thoughts become one."

She lowered her barriers. Felt him do the same. Heat danced through her, a warmth that burst like an explosion through every fiber of her being and left her tingling with awareness. His mind flowed around her, separate yet united with her own. His thoughts, his emotions, were a blaze of color that almost left her blind. She could see areas he wished kept hidden, vast tracks of forbidding darkness. Knew there would be identical areas in her own mind—memories she had no wish to share yet, even with him.

It was similar, and yet so very different from the first time they'd tried this. Then, they'd been wary strangers—lovers, but still strangers, distrusting of each other, distrusting the strength of the emotions that swirled between them.

Concentrate. The cool breeze of his thoughts whispered through her. *Now, reach for Anne Harris. Let our thoughts become hers, separate but one.*

She wrapped her fingers around the necklace, pressing the plastic wrapped metal into her palm. It had grown suddenly cold against her skin, but her fingers twitched, burned by the images rushing from the jewelry. Her senses leaped away, following the trail that led to Anne Harris. Shapes began to form. Fear trembled through her fear, but Michael chased it away.

Concentrate on Anne, Nikki. Reach for her. See her. Feel her. Let her thoughts, her mind, touch ours without ever overriding us.

She reached—and was swept into Anne Harris' thoughts and actions. Became an observer who did not feel or fear . . .

. . . Darkness surrounded her, but she was not alone. She could hear them—their breathing was rapid gasps that spoke of fear. Or excitement.

She knew they watched her. Their gazes caressed her skin, heated touches that were not real, and yet they seemed to sear so very deep. She thought the watchers were probably waiting for her to break under the strain of her terror. But she wouldn't. Even though fear trembled through every limb, even though she was so damn nervous—so afraid—it felt like she was going to throw up, she wasn't going to beg them to leave her alone. She refused to give them that satisfaction, no matter what they did to her.

A chill ran across her flesh. She swallowed back bile and let her gaze roam around the darkness. The newspapers said the third victim had been found in the sewers. Though this place was dark, she didn't think it was the sewers. Though there was a slight fishy odor in the air, it didn't smell as bad as she imagined any sewer would. Nor was it damp.

"Do you wonder why you are here?" The voice swam out of the darkness—cold, deep and vaguely familiar.

She jumped, her heart beating so loudly it seemed to echo like a drum. The darkness around her stirred, as if in hunger.

"I know why I'm here. You're going to kill me." Her voice was high, almost childlike. She cleared her throat, determined to face the disembodied voice with courage. Jeff had often said the only thing we truly have control over in this life is the manner in which we accept death. It wasn't until now that she really understood what he meant.

Tears stung her eyes. She wouldn't see him again. Would never get the chance to tell him she loved him—something she hadn't said in such a very long time. Moisture rolled past her chin and dripped onto her hands, clenched tightly in her lap.

"Interesting." The voice was behind her now. "There is a strength in you lacking in the others."

"Maybe the others didn't know what you intended to do. Or maybe they thought begging would save their lives."

"And you don't think it will?"

"No. Begging makes no difference to a sick mind."

The disembodied voice laughed softly. The sound sent another chill across her flesh. There was nothing remotely human in that laugh.

"If I have a sick mind, then you are partially responsible for it."

She frowned, then wondered why she was even

bothering to take anything this man said seriously. "What do you mean?"

He didn't answer. The beat of her heart seemed to reverberate through the silence, a sound that was oddly, briefly, accompanied by a more metallic-sounding beat and a rushing sigh of wind that stirred her hair and caressed her skin with momentary warmth.

"I guess I shouldn't be surprised you don't remember me," he said eventually. "None of the others did. Until later."

She swallowed back the rush of bile. "Given what you did to them, do you really think it was memory? Or was it just the frantic need to agree with anything you said in the hope you'd stop?"

He chuckled again. "You are very clever."

"Not clever enough, obviously. I have no idea why I'm here."

"Revenge. You will suffer, as you made me suffer, all those years ago."

"We've never met."

"Yes, we have. And when you remember, I'll savor the taste of fear in your thoughts."

The darkness around her stirred as if restless. The breathing was heavier, almost needy. Her mouth was dry, her throat aching, and her heart drumming a million miles an hour.

"In the meantime," he continued, "I do believe you are overdressed for what we intend next. Mike, Ray, remedy that please."

Figures emerged from the darkness, bloody hands reaching for her. Despite her vow, she screamed . . .

. . . Nikki scrambled to her feet and ran for the kitchen. For the next few minutes, she leaned over the sink, throwing up the coffee and doughnut she'd eaten in the cab on the way over.

Warm hands touched her shoulders, squeezing gently, then Michael leaned past her and turned on the tap. He wet his hands and gently patted moisture across the back of her neck, then her forehead.

"Are you all right?"

She nodded and reached for a cup, filling it with water. She rinsed her mouth, then turned around and rested her cheek against his chest. He wrapped his arms around her and simply held her.

I'm glad you kept the full impact of that from me. It would have been bad, otherwise.

It may be the way we have to proceed with this gift of yours—at least until you gain some semblance of control over it.

I'm not sure if it's something I'll ever be able to fully control. Those images were coming at me before I'd even touched that necklace. I didn't even have to really reach.

Which is a worrying aspect. He brushed a kiss across the top of her head. *Our client grows restless.*

She lifted her cheek from his chest and leaned back against the sink. *He'd be more than restless if he knew what was happening to his wife right now.*

I know. He smoothed the hair from her eyes, fingers still hot against her skin. The caring in his gaze almost liquefied her insides. *If you're not up to talking to them yet, I can sidetrack their thoughts.*

Annoyance swirled softly, but she ignored it and touched a hand to his cheek. *No, I'm fine.*

Harris came into the kitchen. His hands were thrust into his pockets, and his expression was a mix of anger and hope. "Well, did anything happen?"

She sighed and dropped her hand. "Yes. I found her."

Her words seemed to galvanize everyone in the room.

"What?" one of the blue suits said. "Where?"

She grimaced. "I can't pinpoint it exactly without leading you there. But she's in a tunnel of some sort."

"Lady," the Fed said dryly, "between the Bart and Muni tunnels, the sewers and storm drains, this city is a labyrinth of tunnels. Care to be a little more specific?"

A train ran past. Ten minutes ago. Michael twined his fingers through hers.

"It's near a train tunnel, I think, because one went past when I made contact—about ten minutes ago."

"Well, gee, that narrows the search area."

"And you were searching where, precisely, before now?" she asked.

The Fed smiled reluctantly, blue eyes crinkling near the corners. "Okay, so you show us. Boys, make arrangements."

The police began making frantic calls. Harris thrust a hand through his hair. "Was she ... is she. ...?"

"She's alive, Mr. Harris. She hasn't been hurt yet." The lie tasted bitter on her tongue. She swallowed heavily and looked away.

Michael squeezed her fingers lightly and turned. "Tell me, Mr. Harris, just how did those men get in here this morning to kidnap your wife?"

Harris shrugged. "I'm not sure. Anne apparently left a window open in the dining room, and the police think they may have climbed through there."

Michael didn't glance at her, but she knew he was thinking the same thing she was: Vampires couldn't

143

enter a private residence unless asked, so there was no way in hell they could have climbed through that window to kidnap her.

"Did you have any odd callers during the week? A salesman, perhaps, that insisted you invite him in?" she asked.

Harris shook his head. "Though we did have to call the plumber during the week because our hot water heater stopped working."

She shared a glance with Michael. "What time of day did the plumber arrive?"

Harris frowned. "Evening. We were both out during the day, and it was dark by the time we got back."

"And he was the only stranger you let into the house?"

"Yes."

"Do you keep your hot water heater in the house or the garage?" Michael asked.

"The house. Why?"

"Do you mind if I take a look?"

Harris' frown deepened, though he shrugged. "Sure. It's through that door there." He pointed towards a door to their right.

Michael squeezed Nikki's fingers then released her hand and headed for the door.

"Hey," a police officer said, "Where are—"

Power slithered through the air. The officer's words died, and he turned and walked to the window, staring outside. Michael's gaze met hers, almost challengingly. She didn't say anything, and after a moment he disappeared through the door Harris had indicated.

A blue suit approached. If he noticed Michael's absence, he made no mention of it. Maybe Michael had touched his mind, too. She crossed her arms and tried to ignore the rising tide of annoyance. He was right. There were times, like this, when it was simply easier to control everyone's thoughts. It sure beat answering difficult questions.

"There's no way you could define the search area?" the Fed asked.

"As I said, not unless I take you there—and I'll need the necklace as a guide. I feel her vibes through it." She glanced at Harris as the older man looked set to protest. "I'll return it, of course."

He shut his mouth and nodded. She looked away, disgusted. God, what did he think she was going to do? Run away with the stupid thing? How idiotic would that be, especially when she was going to be surrounded by Feds and cops?

There's no entrance into the room with the water heater, Michael said. *Though I'd bet the plumber was a vampire.*

"Miss James, are you able to try locating the tunnel for us now?"

"Yeah, sure." She pushed away from the sink and headed into the living room to retrieve the plastic bag she'd dropped earlier. *Michael? What are you going to do?*

I think I saw a sewer grate just up the street. When you go outside, lift the lid. I'll dive into the sewers and try to navigate my way to wherever you end up.

What about the police?

I'll move too fast for them to see me.

And the sun?

He hesitated. *You'll have to treat me gently tonight. I'll be sunburned.*

What about using sun block?

Sun block?

Yeah, you know, that greasy white stuff we

human's smear all over our skin to prevent sunburn. Harris is bound to have some in his bathroom.

I'm on my way to check.

She smiled. *You mean to say that in over three hundred years of existence, you've never thought to use sun block?*

Sun block has not been around for three hundred years.

Well, no, but it's got to have been around for at least fifty. I would have thought you'd have experimented by now.

I've had no need to before now. Besides, running around in the sun to test the feasibility of sun block is not something I'm inclined to risk without reason.

Couldn't argue with that logic, she supposed. She picked up the bagged necklace and followed the suits out the door. She went down the steps slowly, studying the street either way. The sewer grate was several houses up to her right.

Power surged, tingling across her fingertips. One of the Feds took her arm, guiding her towards a car parked just down from the grate. *You ready?*

Yes.

The Fed opened the door. She climbed into the car and studied the grate through slightly narrowed eyes. As the two agents climbed into the car and started the engine, she reached out kinetically and lifted the grate. It was heavier than she's expected, and she had to reach for a little more energy. She slid the lid toward the shadows of the car in front of them.

Go.

Nothing happened for a heartbeat, then a shadow flowed into the sewer hole and disappeared. She slid the grate back into place quickly to ensure any stray beams of sunlight couldn't touch him in the sewer's darkness.

You okay? No answer came and fear stirred. *Michael?*

I'm okay.

His words were a sigh in her mind, and she closed her eyes in relief. *Are you badly burned?*

Not as burned as I could have been. The sun block did take some of the sting off the sun.

But . . .?

But it's nearly eleven, Nikki. A deadly time for me, no matter how many layers I wear.

Can you move? She'd been burned badly herself once or twice and knew how painful it could be.

Yes. The vampires came down this way. I can smell the scent of their evil.

So you should be able to find the tunnel easily enough?

Hopefully. I'll meet you there.

Don't go out in the sun again.

His smile spun through her mind, a liquid caress that stirred her senses and made her body ache. *Never fear, my love. I have no intention of getting a tan deeper than the one I already have.*

She wrapped her fingers lightly around the necklace. "Head downtown," she said. "Towards the Civic Center area."

They pulled away from the curb and joined the slow crawl of traffic. They were past the Federal building and closing in on Market Street by the time the necklace began to burn white-hot in her hand. "Pull over and stop," she said.

"Thought they were in a train tunnel," one of the Feds said as he opened the car door for her.

"No." She climbed out and for a moment wished

she could simply relax under the cool canopy of trees in the nearby gardens. "They're in an underground room of some sort, accessed through the sewers. It's close to a train tunnel, though."

"Sewer rats," one of the cops muttered. "There are hundreds of them down there, and hundreds of places they can run."

"I doubt if we're after homeless folk," the blue-eyed FBI agent said. "This is too well organized for them." He handed her a flashlight, then added, "Which way?"

She took a deep breath and fought the pull of the images pulsing from the necklace. One little push, one tiny reach, and she'd be with Anne Harris, sharing her pain, sharing her fear. She swallowed back bile and nodded up the street. "That way."

They were close to a hall of some kind when she stopped. "Here," she said, pointing to a grate. "We need to go down here."

Several cops glanced at each other, then bent and levered free the grate. A ladder led down into deeper darkness.

"Down there?" The cop pointed his flashlight at the rusty-looking ladder.

"Yep. You want me to lead the way?"

"I'll lead the way," Blue Eyes said. "Mitch, Davidson, you follow me down. When we know it's safe, the rest of you follow."

They disappeared into the darkness. She shifted her weight from one foot to the other, needing to move, needing to chase the images flashing through her mind. She crossed her arms and reached out to Michael instead.

You near?

Close. I'm not alone, though.

Fear tripped through her heart. *What do you mean?*

I mean there's a Loop of vamps nearby.

What in hell is a Loop?

It's a term for fledglings who were all basically created around the same time. They tend to flock together.

I thought fledglings couldn't control their blood-lust enough to hang around with anyone but their master?

The newly risen can't. But these have a few years on them and, while the bloodlust still reigns, common sense is beginning to reassert itself. There is safety in numbers.

What sort of numbers are we talking about?

Five.

We've already destroyed six of his vampires. How many of these so called Loops has he made?

Quite a few, by the look of it. Our boy appears to like his harems.

Bile rose in her throat. *What are we going to do?*

Nothing much we can do. I doubt if the police will be too pleased if you suddenly lose direction.

Besides which, we have to free Anne Harris.

Yes. He hesitated. *She lives. I can hear the frantic sound of her pulse.*

So could she, through the necklace. Only the sensation came with flashes of horror—fragmented memories of what the vamps had done to her. Repeatedly.

She closed her eyes and took a deep breath. *Could you go rescue her before we get there?*

I could—but I prefer not to. I don't think Farmer has realized you're not working alone. I prefer to keep it that way for as long as possible.

Why?

Because he'll undoubtedly change his method of attack once he realizes you have a vampire protecting you.

"All clear down here," a distant voice said. "Start climbing down. You first, Miss James."

She did. She stepped off the ladder and into inch-thick muck. The air had a slightly damp, fishy smell, and the darkness was lifted only by the lonely flashlight beams. She clicked hers on and swung it around. Graffiti greeted her—angry scrawls and disjointed pictures—representing God knew what.

"Where now?" the Fed said once the last of the officers was down.

"That way." She pointed to the darkness on her left.

In single file, they began moving through the darkness. Some of the tunnels were so damn small they had to almost bend over double. Others seemed to soar high above them.

And all the while the pulsing got stronger, until the agitated beat of Anne's heart was a rhythm that matched her own.

Michael?

Here. His mind voice was a whisper that breathed warmth past her ear. Darkness brushed across her fingers, searing heat deep.

And the vamps?

Up ahead.

Energy surged to her fingertips. She flexed her hands, trying to relax.

They're not going to attack?

No. I think they plan to await discovery then attack.

Why? It didn't make any sense to give up the

advantage like that, though they were talking vampires. She guessed it didn't really matter if they *did* give up the benefit of surprise. Fledglings or not, they'd still beat the crap out of most of the officers here.

I suspect Farmer intends to let the police finally know what they are up against. His mind voice was grim.

Thank God there are no reporters down here with us. It'd cause a panic if people knew vamps were real and living in the sewers.

His smile spun around her, a touch of sunshine through the darkness. *This is a city renowned for both its tolerance and its diversity. Somehow, I don't think people would be all that surprised.*

The necklace burned into her hand. She held it by the top of the plastic instead, but it made very little difference to the images assaulting her mind. Anne was alive but in a bad way. She might not have had a heart attack like Dale Wainwright had, but the vamps had assaulted her and fed off her, and she was struggling to survive.

We're approaching the large chamber where the Loop waits, Michael said. *You'd better try to warn the police.*

She cleared her throat. "We're nearing where Anne is, but there's something waiting just ahead." As she spoke, fog seemed to stir the darkness. It wasn't the vampires, wasn't anything threatening. Yet it came with an almost overwhelming feeling of fear.

The Fed with the blue eyes hesitated and looked over his shoulder. "What do you mean by some*thing?*"

The ethereal form disappeared as quickly as it had appeared. Maybe it had been nothing more than a puff of colder air drifting in from the vent ahead.

She dragged her gaze back to the agent's. She couldn't tell him it was vampires, because he wasn't likely to believe her until he saw them himself. And maybe not even then.

"Just that. There are five 'somethings', actually."

"Probably homeless folk." Even so, she heard the sound of a safety clicking off.

They proceeded more cautiously. The flashlight beams bit through the darkness, spotlights that somehow left the greater darkness looking more ominous. They came into a chamber— a fact evident only by the bigger feeling of space. The Feds in front of her stopped, making her do a quick sidestep to avoid running into them.

Then she saw why they'd stopped.

The vampires were spotlighted by the flashlights as they stood in the middle of the chamber. All of them had the same disdainful expression, their arms crossed and stances casual. They were all wearing leather jackets, faded denims and black biker boots.

All of them were blood-smeared.

Guns came out of holsters. The vamps' sneers became more noticeable, revealing bloody canines.

"F.B.I.," Agent Blue Eyes stated. "Slowly drop any weapons you might be holding and raise your hands."

The vamp in the middle chortled. "Know what F.B.I. stands for?" His voice was guttural, like that of a man who'd spent too many years smoking. "Fuckin' bloody idiots."

"Raise your hands," Blue Eyes repeated stonily.

"Yeah right," the vamp said. "Boys, let's show 'em."

Night stole the vampires from sight, and all hell broke loose.

Eleven

Nikki ducked to her right and ran forward. The night stirred in front of her, something she felt more than saw. She flung out her hand. Kinetic energy caressed the night, and something heavy hit the distant wall with a grunt.

She ran on. The necklace was a ribbon of fire, burning with fear. Anne was very close. A booming of a gun cut across the tense silence, followed quickly by another. Laughter spun through the night, a harsh, sarcastic sound.

A man screamed—a sound that quickly became a gurgling cry. She closed her ears to the noise, knowing it was more important to get to Anne than to help the cops right now. The harsh laughter stopped, and the scuff of flesh hitting flesh filled the night. Michael had joined the fray.

Goose bumps ran across her skin, a chill sensation that warned of danger. She slid to a stop but was flung backwards as the night found form. She hit the ground with a grunt, her flashlight slipping from her hand and scuttling away into the darkness. The vampire was heavy, smelling of blood and sweat and sex. He snarled, canines extended and dripping wet, dark moisture.

Blood.

Her stomach rolled, and energy surged through her body, the sheer force of it making every muscle shake. "Burn in hell," she muttered and thrust her hand in his face.

But what came out was a mix of kinetic energy and

fire. It ripped the vampire from her body and flung him across the room like a flaming comet. He hit the far wall with a splat and slipped to the floor, the high-pitched sound of his screams stinging the night as he rolled in a futile attempt to put out the inferno consuming him.

For several heartbeats she could only stare. Despite her words, she hadn't intended to burn him. While she felt no sympathy for the vampire, fear caught her heart and squeezed it tight. This was only one more piece of evidence that suggested she was changing faster—and in more ways—than she'd feared.

But now was not the time to dwell on such fears. She thrust to her feet then reached for the nearby wall, leaning against it heavily as the darkness swam around her. She felt drained, weak, her legs shaking and barely supporting her weight.

The back of her neck prickled in warning. She looked up, saw the slight blur of movement across the darkness. Knew another vampire was coming at her.

She reached again for kinetic energy. Pain slithered through her body, arrowed into her brain and became hot lances of fire that had her blinking back tears. She'd barely used her abilities, and yet she was close to reaching her limits. The flames, whatever they were, obviously took a lot more strength than kinetic energy.

The unseen vampire screamed, and the wind of his approach stroked cold air across her skin. She raised her hand, energy dancing like weakened fireflies across her fingers and pain booming through her brain. But suddenly Michael was in front of her, flowing into being from the inky gloom.

He grabbed the vampire with one hand, then twisted him around and snapped his neck in one smooth, vicious movement. He tossed the body to one side and turned, gently touching her cheek.

Are you okay?

She nodded, a little chilled by his ruthless efficiency. *Go help the cops.*

He flowed back into the darkness. She took a deep breath, then pushed away from the wall and retrieved her flashlight. Clenching her fingers around the bagged necklace, she continued. The frantic pulsing led her past an entrance that had been smashed into being through bricks and into a smaller room. There, on a soiled, sorry-looking mattress, she found Anne.

She lay on the mattress, curled up in a fetal position, her skin marred by bruises and bloody nips. Her eyes were closed, and even when Nikki kneeled beside her, they didn't open.

She touched a hand to Anne's shoulder. Her skin felt like ice. "Anne?"

The older woman didn't respond. Nikki felt for a pulse, which was rapid, unsteady. It was the rhythm she could feel in the necklace. She gently lifted the older woman's eyelids—her pupils were huge. She'd been drugged, undoubtedly to stop her running.

"Miss James?"

The sharp voice bit through the darkness, and she jumped. "In here."

The FBI agent with the blue eyes appeared in the doorway. The beam of his flashlight hit her square in the eyes, and she threw up her hand to cut the glare.

"Sorry," he said, moving the light to one side. "You found her?"

She nodded. "She's been drugged and assaulted. You'd better get the paramedics down here quickly."

He stopped by her side, his expression grim as he

stripped off his coat and placed it carefully over Anne. It wouldn't have offered much in the way of warmth, but at least it offered a little more dignity.

"They've already been called. We've got one man dead out there and another with half his neck ripped apart." He hesitated. "What were those things?"

"What did they look like?" she hedged, wary of telling him the truth.

"Well, they certainly fit the image of every damn vampire I've seen on the silver screen. But vampires just can't exist."

"Why can't they? Vlad the Impaler was certainly real."

He stared at her for a second. "Yeah, but he was a sicko human."

"So were those men, once."

He continued to stare at her. It was hard to read his expression, hard to know his thoughts.

After what he has seen, he believes, Michael said softly. *He just doesn't want to.*

The heat of his unseen presence pressed warmth into her back. She resisted the urge to lean back against him and offered the agent the bagged necklace. "You want to take care of this from now on? I don't think Harris trusted me with it all that much."

"Yeah, I noticed that myself." His slight grin suggested he was relieved to be moving on to safer subjects. He looked past her as several more officers walked into the smaller room. "Davidson, those paramedics here yet?"

"On the way down now."

"You want to direct them here the minute they arrive? And keep an eye out in case any more of those . . . men . . . decide to attack."

"Will do."

The officer moved away, and the big man's gaze came back to her. "That's some talent you have there. We would never have been able to find Mrs. Harris so quickly ourselves."

She rubbed her arms. "I just hope we're fast enough to save her."

"So do I." He hesitated. "Would you like an escort back to the hotel?"

"Just back to the sewer cover will be fine." The vampires wouldn't attack her once she was out in the sunshine. Which was some place she desperately needed to be, just to warm the ice beginning to form in the pit of her stomach.

The agent nodded and called to another of his men. "You're not intending to leave San Francisco for the next few days, are you? We may need to talk to you a bit more."

"I'm staying at the Diamond Grand."

He smiled. "Yes, I know. We did a thorough check on you when Mr. Harris requested your help."

She raised her eyebrows in surprise. "Why?"

He shrugged. "Wouldn't be the first time a supposed psychic has worked a kidnapping scam."

"Do you really think anyone human could have done what was done to those first two women?"

He studied her for a moment, gaze calculating. "And how do you know what was done to them?"

"The same way I knew where to find Anne and Dale. It's not a very pleasant gift to have, you know. I'd much rather do without knowing the gruesome details." She hesitated. "I have something else for you, too. The name of a possible suspect."

"Who?" He grabbed a notebook and pen out of his pocket.

"Billie Farmer. Apparently he was taunted in high school by a gang of twelve women."

He raised his eyebrows. "And I suppose the four victims so far were a part of that gang?"

"You catch on rather fast."

"That's what they pay me for. We'll check it out. In the meantime, don't leave the city. We may need to talk to you again."

"I have no intention of going anywhere." Not until this fiend was caught. Killed.

He nodded. A second agent made an appearance and motioned her to follow him.

I dare not risk the sun again, Michael said as they began the walk back to the sewer entrance. *I'll have to meet you back at the hotel.*

And perhaps do a little exploring along the way?

He hesitated. *Yes. But don't ask to come with me. Not when Farmer is aware of your every movement.*

Don't worry. I have no intention of invading your work space right now.

Nikki—

She flung up a hand. *Yeah, I know. It's for my own safety.* Which was a load of crap. She was probably safer with him than being alone at the hotel. Especially when Farmer and his gang had no apparent trouble getting into that building.

Which is why I don't want you to go immediately back to the hotel. Walk around and do some sightseeing. I'll contact you when I'm heading back myself.

Like hell she'd be doing the touristy thing while there was a madman running around underground. *I have to call Jake and let him know what's going on.*

Then do so. Just don't go back to our room until it's safe.

Fine. I'll play it your way. For now.

158

Warmth flowed through the link, a tender caress that made her toes tingle. *Keep safe. I'll see you soon.*

She blew him a mental kiss, and the heat of his presence disappeared. The cop stopped and motioned her up the rusting ladder. She climbed, blinking as she reentered the bright sunshine. Two cops helped her out, another helping her escort a second later.

"You want a ride back to the hotel, Miss James?" he said.

She shook her head. "It's a nice day. I think I'll walk."

They let her go. She dragged her cell phone from her pocket and dialed Jake's number.

"About time," he grumbled. "What's happening?"

She gave him an update, and he swore softly. "We need to catch this bastard fast."

"The problem being we have no idea where he is, while he has every idea where I am." And until Seline came through with this charm Michael was talking about, there wasn't much they could do to alter that situation.

"Wish there was some way we could make that work for us," Jake muttered.

She bit her lip for a moment, mind racing. "Maybe there is," she said slowly.

"What?"

"How's Dale?" she said, by way of answer.

"Not good. She's still in intensive care, and the doctors are not saying much."

"Is she conscious?"

"Apparently not. Why?"

"Do you think you could convince Mark to get us in there?"

"I'm not sure we'd be allowed. He could try I suppose. Why?"

"Because going to the hospital is not likely to raise any major alarms in Farmer's mind. And if we can get in to see Dale, I might be able to touch her mind and see if she's retained any memories of how she was snatched, and how she arrived at her cell."

Jake was silent for a minute. "I don't think Michael will be too pleased about you trying something like that."

Annoyance surged through her, and she struggled to keep her voice even as she said, "Right now, I don't really care what Michael would or wouldn't be pleased with. And since when did it matter to you if it means solving the case?"

"He said it's dangerous, Nikki."

"So you'd rather sit on your hands doing nothing while this madman runs loose?"

He sighed. "No. But I don't want anything to happen to you, either."

"I'll be fine. Really." She forced her voice to be positive, even though she was far from certain. "I'm walking up Hyde Street now. You want to talk to Mark, then zoom by and pick me up?" She hesitated and glanced at the street sign. "I'll wait near the corner of Ellis."

"I'll be there as soon as I can."

She hung up, then sat down on the nearest fence to wait.

The scent of evil was distant but powerful. Michael ran swiftly through the darkness, keeping the shadows locked around him. It wasn't Farmer he was following, but rather his fledglings. The scent wasn't evil enough or strong enough to belong to a master vampire.

Though why he thought of Farmer as a master when the vampire was obviously a lot younger than he himself, Michael wasn't entirely sure. But only masters could control the minds of other vampires— or a very strong telepath.

Farmer certainly wasn't what he'd term strong when it came to psychic gifts—at least not when compared to Nikki or himself.

So how could one so young become a master?

He wasn't sure. Even he, despite his years and experience, could barely be classed as one. Elizabeth had been a master, though. She'd been comfortable with what she was, comfortably aware of her strengths and weaknesses. Had he wished, he could have taken that knowledge, that skill, from her mind when he'd killed her. It was his right as victor.

And perhaps that was his answer. Perhaps Farmer had killed the vampire who'd turned him and sucked all the knowledge from his mind. But he was still too young in vampire years to process all that information and use it to full advantage.

For which they could be extremely grateful.

He slowed as the scent of evil grew stronger. Night stirred ahead, and the languorous beat of half a dozen hearts filled his ears. He'd found a nest that contained yet another loop. Farmer himself was nowhere near—which wasn't unusual. Fledglings could never be entirely trusted, even those mostly over the initial blood frenzy. It usually took ten to twenty years before true sanity returned—if the turning hadn't made them completely crazy.

He slowed and switched to the infrared of his vampire vision. The vampires were blurs of red heat in

161

the small chamber just ahead. They were all asleep—the sun was high, and vampires this young had no choice but to slumber during the day.

If he killed them, Farmer would know. But if he didn't, these six would kill again and again and again. Their evil stained the very air. There was no goodness left in them—if there had been any in life. He had no choice but to destroy them.

He moved into the chamber and began his bloody task. It didn't take long. Once he'd finished, he carried their bodies to the nearest sewer cover, piling them underneath it. Then he kinetically lifted the cover, stepping back quickly so no stray rays of sunlight caught him. He'd been burned enough for one day. The fledglings flamed instantly, and the smell of burning flesh stung the dank air.

He watched until they were nothing more than ash then stepped back into a small chamber to wait. Farmer would have felt them burn. It would be interesting to see if he came to investigate. He crossed his arms and leaned back against the cold brick wall.

Seline?

Here. Her mind voice was decidedly cheerful. *You'll never guess what has happened—Jon and Maddie have finally set a wedding date. The invitation just arrived in the mail. They've sent one for you, too.*

He raised his eyebrows. *I thought Jon had a thing about commitment?*

Seline's unladylike snort rattled the mental lines. *No. Like you, he feared to make a commitment because he feared his enemies taking revenge on those he loved.*

I don't fear making commitment. Though, like

Jon, he *did* fear enemies being motivated enough to take revenge on those he loved.

Perhaps not. But you have every intention of compartmentalizing your life.

There's nothing wrong with wanting to keep her safe.

Unless it's something that will kill her emotionally. She's not the type to play mother at home, Michael. If she was, I seriously doubt you'd still be together.

Her words reminded him of the pain Nikki had revealed at never being able to have kids. He briefly closed his eyes. Seline was wrong about one thing—he could have easily played family man with Nikki. Could imagine nothing better than coming home from a normal day and relaxing with her and their kids. But he'd given up any sense of normality long ago, and there was no point in wishing for what could never be.

I can't risk her working with me, Seline. Couldn't risk losing her. She was his heart, his soul. He couldn't imagine life without her now. Didn't want life without her.

It won't work, I'm telling you that now. You can't ever hope to keep Nikki and what you do separate. Nikki is a part of your life because of your work, and you're just going to have to accept the fact that she will forever be a part of it.

He rubbed a hand across his eyes. *I didn't open this line of communication to get a tongue lashing, you know.*

I know. It's just a bonus.

One I can do without, thank you very much. Especially when he was hearing much the same words from Nikki herself. *What did you find out about Billie Farmer?*

Not much. He dropped out of sight just after graduation and wasn't seen for a good ten to fifteen years. He was spotted a couple of times in the years since then, but the first reliable sighting we have of him is in Albuquerque two and a half years ago.

Six months before the first killing.

Yes. We're reasonably sure he was turned shortly after he dropped out of sight, because by the time he was spotted in Albuquerque, he was well past the fledgling stage.

Don't suppose there's any chance of finding out who turned him?

You know how difficult a task something like that is. We haven't enough researchers to keep those sorts of records.

But you're still keeping records of master vampires?

Yes. Her mind voice was suddenly cautious. She knew, as he knew, that a master was serious trouble. *Why?*

Was there one around Boston around the time of Farmer's turning?

I could certainly check. You think Farmer was turned by one?

Yes. I also think he somehow killed the master and sucked in his knowledge. Fortunately for us, he's too young yet to assimilate all that knowledge.

Thank the stars. A master is not what we need in this sort of situation.

No. Especially with Nikki and Jake involved.

Are you still intending to meet him tonight?

Yes. But I've just killed his nest of fledglings, and he'll know it could only have been done by another vampire. He won't walk into that meeting without some form of insurance now.

Then why tip him off that way?

Because he's obviously created more than one loop, and the number—combined with an inept master—would test even my capabilities.

True. She paused. *Just watch Nikki over the next few hours. He may make a grab for her.*

He'll probably try. Which is why I told her to stay in the sunshine. Master or not, he hasn't the years behind him to walk out in sunlight. He hesitated. *Speaking of which, it appears sharing my life force with Nikki has had some unexpected side benefits.*

What do you mean?

I mean, I was out in the sunlight for several seconds after eleven in the morning, and I didn't instantly flame. I did have sunscreen on but, given the hour, it wouldn't have made that much difference.

Concern flooded the link. *Michael, you could have died.*

I know, but my only other choice was letting Nikki enter the sewers alone, and that wasn't going to happen.

How badly were you burned?

He glanced down at his hands. Originally, they'd been a red so fierce they practically glowed, but the color and the heat were beginning to fade. *Bad. But that's not the point. It was after eleven. I should have died.*

Your merging with Nikki has improved your immunity.

So it would seem. Either that, or sunscreen offers vampires better protection than it does humans.

Not that much more, I'd wager. She paused. *Has anything else happened?*

I think you were right about me developing pre-

cognition—and I'd like to know how my merging with Nikki has brought all this about.

Until we find out more about thralls, we won't really know. But I've got a feeling this has more to do with your compatibility with each other.

He frowned. *What do you mean?*

She hesitated. *Do you remember the night we stood watching Hartwood burn?*

Yes. How could he forget? That night had signaled the end of a sorcerer's bitter reign. The end of a twenty-year battle for revenge and justice. But it was also the beginning of what had become the Circle.

Do you remember what I asked that night?

He frowned. *Not really.* Though he could remember what he'd been feeling. Not elation, despite the fact his quest of twenty years had finally reached fruition. Just an odd sense of . . . emptiness.

I asked what you intended to devote your life to now. You said perhaps finding the other half of yourself.

He smiled, remembering. *I was being flippant, Seline.*

But in many a jest there lies a truth. I think in Nikki you have found your other half. What is happening to you both now is merely the end result of locking two highly compatible pieces together—which is what you've done by sharing your life force with her.

That doesn't explain either of us developing new skills.

It does if the skills are not new but latent. By combining life forces, you've forced those skills into the light.

If he'd had latent skills, surely they would have made some sort of appearance by now. After all, he'd been on this earth for more than three hundred and sixty years. *This is all nothing more than theory.*

True—at least until you come into headquarters so we can run tests.

It isn't going to happen. You know I hate those damn tests of yours. Her sigh was overly dramatic, and he smiled as he added, *And you can cut the theatrics, as well.*

She didn't answer, and the link between them suddenly hummed with tension—became a whirlwind of color that was oddly electric. He knew instantly what was happening—she was having a vision.

No good will come from you putting these tests off, she warned. *It will only throw you into greater danger when he comes.*

Her mind voice had become abstracted, vague. He held back his questions, knowing from experience that talking at the wrong moment could shatter the dream.

He seeks revenge. He seeks our destruction. Not the Circle itself, but you and me. For what we did to his brother so long ago. And he will start with you. Silence swirled through the link, thick with fear, then she added, *Nikki could be our savior or our destruction. It very much depends on your actions.*

What actions? And who was this 'he' Seline was talking about? It could have been any one of hundreds—between the two of them and the Circle itself, they'd been responsible for a fair number of dispatches back to hell.

And if what Seline was seeing was indeed the future he faced, then in many ways, it only ratified his determination to keep his life with Nikki truly separate from his work.

He is a brother who has kissed the night goodbye,

she continued absently. *If he cannot steal your heart, he will steal you then destroy you. But only after he has destroyed all you care for.*

A cold sensation crawled through his gut. Seline's visions were vary rarely wrong. The ending often varied, but never the initial facts. If she saw this madman taking vengeance on them both, then it would happen. Lord, he had to walk away from Nikki. He couldn't risk dragging her into something like this . . . .

No. Michael, no. Seline's mind voice was suddenly clear again, but filled with fear. *I sense it is already too late for that.*

I won't have her involved—

She's already involved. This man has been planning his revenge for a very long time. And there's nothing either of us can do to stop him until he comes out of the shadows and actually attacks.

He took a deep breath and released it slowly. *Do you have any sense of time?*

No. It could be next week, next year, or ten years from now.

Do a search, he said. *Backtrack over every case you and I have handled. See which of them had brothers who turned. I want this madman found before he finds us.*

Will do. In the meantime, be wary of Farmer. If he has stolen the knowledge of the master who turned him, then he may prove very dangerous indeed.

I'll be careful. Just make sure you are from now on, too.

I rarely leave headquarters nowadays. I am as safe here as I would be anywhere.

Then make sure you don't leave at all. Not for anybody.

I won't. By the way, I've couriered that charm you wanted. You should be getting it late tonight or early in the morning.

Thanks, Seline.

He cut the link and pushed away from the wall. Farmer obviously wasn't that attached to his fledglings, because it certainly didn't look as if he was coming down to check what had happened to them.

Time to get back to Nikki. Before she did something stupid—like try to track Farmer's whereabouts. He stopped suddenly, a cold sensation running down his spine.

Or try to enter a dying woman's mind to search for clues.

He swore softly and blurred his form, running for the hospital.

Nikki took a deep breath, trying to calm the butterflies battering the walls of her stomach. Though they felt more like condors than butterflies.

A steady bleeping filled the silence. Dale's heartbeat, stable for the moment. Dale herself lay on the bed, her face as white as her sterile surroundings. She hadn't yet woken. Nikki suspected she never would.

"Five minutes is all you have," Jake prompted softly.

She took another deep breath and released it slowly, gathering her courage. Then she glanced past Jake and met Mark's red-rimmed gaze. In his brown eyes she saw a mix of emptiness, despair and deep, dark fury. The sort of fury that fired the bitter quest for revenge.

"I can't promise this won't hurt her," she said. "I've never tried anything like this before."

His nod was tight. Angry. "The doctors said she might never ..." he hesitated, his gaze moving back to his wife as he took a deep, shuddering breath. "If she doesn't, I want the bastard that did this to her. I want him dead. You understand me? *Dead*."

Jake placed a comforting hand on his friend's arm. Mark shook it off. "Just tell me you'll try. Tell me you won't hand this bastard over to the cops. He doesn't deserve justice. All he deserves is death. A long and lingering death."

"We'll do all we can." Jake glanced at her. "You sure you want to do this?"

She nodded. "It's our only chance of finding out where Farmer might be hiding."

"Then do it now, because we're running out of time."

She walked over to the bed and stared down at Dale's still features. Goose bumps chased their way across her skin, and the sensation of evil stirred through her mind.

Imagination, she thought. She flexed her fingers then raised her hands, lightly touching Dale's temples.

She closed her eyes, trying to ignore the condors making such a mess of her stomach, and gingerly reached with her mind.

And met not the thoughts of a sick woman, but the trap of a vampire.

Twelve

For a second, Nikki froze, like a deer caught in the glare of headlights. Farmer's laughter spun around her, cold and victorious. Her first instinct was to pull away and break the connection between them, but she resisted the urge. If they were going to stop this man, they needed to know more about him, and that might only be achieved by actually talking to him.

I know how your mind works, remember, he said, his mind voice devoid of any emotion, yet somehow chilling. *It was not hard to guess you'd try something like this.*

Haven't you done enough to her? she spat back. *Leave her some dignity in death, at least.*

Why should I? They gave me no dignity in life.

School children are notoriously cruel. That's a fact of life. Something we all had to live with at one time or another.

But these twelve were not children. They were adults. There were no excuses for what they did.

Just as there was no excuse for taking over the minds of those two young women, forcing them to get drunk then jump off the roof. Though it was a guess, she knew it was a fairly safe one. There was really no other sensible explanation for what had happened—not that the authorities would ever consider *that* a sensible explanation.

An easy death, compared to the hell they gave me. Or the death you're now giving the remaining ten.

His laughter spun around her, a flat sound that

chilled her very soul. *You are very clever—but not clever enough.*

Malevolence swirled, and the sense of impending doom hit her like a punch in the stomach. Winded, chilled, she somehow wrenched her hands away from Dale's forehead and opened her eyes. And saw the other woman open hers. But there was no life in her blue gaze. No humanity. Only an evil colder than hell.

"Mine," she said. It was a feminine voice, yet somehow it was also Farmer's.

Silver flashed through the air. With a cry of fear, Nikki stumbled back. Heat seared along her arm.

"Where the hell did that come from?" Jake shouted, rushing for the bed along with Mark.

Dale's fist flew, knocking them both away, her strength seemingly inhuman. She wrenched the wires and sensors from her body, then thrust the sheet aside. Nikki flung out her hand and stopped her kinetically. Blood dripped from the wound on Nikki's arm, pooling at her feet. Another chill ran across her skin. It was an omen, but of what she wasn't sure.

Dale screamed and twisted, her movements furious, her face turning a mottled sort of red.

Nurses and doctors appeared from everywhere. "What's going on here?" one said. He took one look at Dale and swore under his breath. "All of you— out. Now."

"I wouldn't advise that," Jake said, climbing to his feet and rubbing his chin.

The doctor glared at him. "Nurse, get security. I want these people out of here." He grabbed a needle from the trolley one of the nurses had pushed in and walked toward the bed.

A second nurse grabbed Nikki's arm and wrenched

her away. She broke the woman's grip with a sharp twist, but by then her kinetic hold had slipped. Dale screamed. She kicked the needle from the doctor's hand then smashed him sideways with a clenched fist. Nurses ran to help him but were just as easily swatted away. Dale rose on the bed and launched herself across the room—the knife a deadly point at the end of her human arrow.

Nikki hit her again with kinetic energy, holding her still and high above the floor. Sweat trickled down the side of her face, and pain as sharp as the knife aimed at her heart slithered through her brain.

"Jake," she groaned out, ignoring the gasps around her. "Grab the knife off her."

She lowered Dale several feet. Jake pushed past the nurses and pried the knife from Dale's stiff fingers. She screamed in rage, fighting Nikki's hold on her. The arrowheads of pain became a landslide, and she knew she wouldn't be able to hold her for much longer. Not after her efforts in the sewers.

"Now, grab a bandage or something to tie her hands and feet."

He found a bandage on the trolley and quickly did as she asked. "Now, doctor," she ground out. "When I place Dale back on the bed, you be ready with that sedative, because I'm not going to be able to hold her much longer."

He climbed to his feet and readied another sedative. Nikki thrust Dale towards the bed, dumping her none too gently on top of the twisted sheets. Nurses jumped on her, holding her down as the doctor injected her. Within minutes, the fight went out of her.

"God almighty, what on earth happened there?" Mark stared at her, a mix of confusion and fear in his gaze.

Knowing she was psychic and actually seeing those skills in action were obviously two very different realities. "The man who attacked your wife is a powerful telepath. He was controlling your wife's actions just now."

"But—" His voice faded as he ran a hand across his bald head. "Remember what I said. Justice is no answer here."

Jake placed a hand on Mark's arm. "He'll get what's coming to him, never fear."

The back of Nikki's neck tingled in warning. She turned. Michael was close—and the very lack of emotion in the link told her he was furious.

He stepped into the room a moment later. His dark gaze stabbed towards her, and she met it defiantly. She'd done nothing truly wrong. Granted, attempting to read Dale's memories while he wasn't there was a bit foolish. But he wasn't always going to be around, and she really did have to learn to control her growing gifts. No matter how dangerous that might be.

Power swept the room. Everyone froze but Jake and her. "Out, both of you," Michael said, his soft voice holding no hint of the anger she could feel in him.

She shared a glance with Jake, then walked from the room. Jake swiped an antiseptic swab and another bandage from the medical cart, grabbing her arm as they entered the corridor.

"What's he doing?" he asked, as he began to patch the wound on her forearm.

"As a guess, wiping everyone's memory of what just happened." She hesitated as Michael walked over to Dale. "And probably forming some sort of block in Dale's mind so that Farmer can't use her like that again."

"Well, at least something good will have come from this whole mess." He finished bandaging her arm, then added, "You want me to hang around when we get back to the hotel?"

She smiled and leaned forward to kiss his leathery cheek. "Thanks, but I don't need a protector. What I need is a piece of two-by-four to knock some sense into Michael's thick skull."

Jake hesitated. "That's a two-way street, you know. You can't expect him to compromise his beliefs when you're not willing to do the same."

Oh, great. Now Jake was stepping towards Michael's side of the fence as well. Or maybe Michael had simply rearranged Jake's thoughts. She scowled at him. "What do you mean?"

Jake waved a hand towards Michael. "I can understand your need to be a part of what he does. But you've also got to take into account that there *will* be cases you simply can't get involved in—for whatever reason."

"Don't you think I know that?" she said, trying to curb her irritation. "The whole problem I have is the fact that he won't let me get involved in *any* way. He won't tell me anything about the Circle, or Seline, or his missions. Everything I know I've dragged out of him. He has a whole separate life I know nothing about. We don't talk about it, ever."

Jake raised his eyebrows. "Sounds like there's a little jealousy happening there."

She blinked. Was she jealous? Maybe. In many ways, the Circle and Seline demanded—and got—as much of his attention as she did. "Put yourself in my shoes—or better yet, remember back to when you and Mary had just met. How would you have felt if Mary had a whole separate career you knew nothing about? One that involved lots of other men and took her away from your side a good half of the year?"

"I'd have been as pissed as hell."

"Exactly."

"You can trust Michael, though. He doesn't seem the straying type."

She waved the comment away. She did trust Michael and certainly wasn't worried about him straying sexually. "The point is, wouldn't you have at least wanted to find out more about Mary's other life?"

"Yes." He paused. "But that's not all you're asking for, is it?"

No. But was it asking too much to become a part of that other life—even if it was only a minor part? She didn't think so.

Especially when he knew just about everything there was to know about her.

"What are you going to do if he continues to refuse?" Jake added softly.

She thrust a hand through her hair. "I don't know." Her gaze drifted back to Michael. "I just don't know."

But she had a horrible feeling that unless things changed dramatically in the next week or so, she might have to carry through with her threat to leave him. Because as much as leaving would break her heart, it was better than the slow death she suffered every time he went away.

She couldn't survive that happening time and again. Not for the next ten years, let alone the next fifty. Or one hundred.

Maybe she *was* being selfish. Maybe she should just shut up and be thankful she'd found a man who loved her as much as he did.

But she just wasn't built that way. She couldn't be part-time. And part of the reason was her memories of her parents' relationship. They did everything together—even die—and right to the end they'd been extremely happy. Maybe she was fantasizing it a little—after all, they'd died when she was barely a teenager. Maybe it all wasn't as rosy as she remembered. But to this day she could still recall the looks they'd shared, the way they'd touched, the way they'd talked over every decision—and she'd always wanted *that* sort of relationship. The sort that lasted through thick and thin. The sort that shared good times and bad.

And if Michael wasn't willing to shift from his comfortable plane of existence and include her more fully in his life, then the love they shared would mean little in the end.

Because she knew from bitter experience love just wasn't enough.

Michael leaned against the wall and watched the elevator numbers rise. When he'd finally calmed down enough to open the link between them, he found it locked down just as tight from her end. Nor had she argued when he'd curtly ordered her back to the hotel. Which undoubtedly meant she was furious, though why, he had no idea. *She* was the one risking her life with acts of stupidity.

He took a deep breath, crossing his arms as the elevator came to a halt on their floor. Nikki stepped out alone, which surprised him. He'd half expected her to drag Jake along to help argue her case.

She hesitated when her gaze met his, and anger singed the air between them. Then her gaze slithered away, and the anger disappeared. Or rather, was re-shuttered.

"You had a key," she snapped. "You didn't have to wait for me."

"I know I didn't," he replied evenly. "I wanted to."

"Didn't trust me to do as ordered, huh?" She swiped her key card through the slot then shoved open the door.

"I just wanted to make sure you got here safely."

"Likely story." She threw off her coat and stalked over to the minibar. "Can't have the little woman straying too far off the leash now, can we?"

His own anger rose again. "Damn it, Nikki, I had every right to be furious. What you were trying to do was stupid and dangerous, and you *know* it."

"What I was trying to do was my job!" She grabbed a soda out of the fridge and slammed the door shut. "I *am* a private investigator, in case you've conveniently forgotten that."

"You also know how dangerous it is trying to enter someone's mind like that. Especially when the man who attacked that person has a psychic connection to both of you."

She popped the top off the soda. Froth bubbled over the lip and dripped onto her shoes. She didn't seem to notice. Or maybe she just didn't care.

"So I should just sit around and do nothing?"

He clenched his fists, then flexed them when he realized what he was doing. "I'm not saying—"

"Yes, you are," she bit back. "You don't want me using my talents if you're not there. You don't want me and Jake investigating without you coming along. So tell me, what else am I supposed to do?"

"What you're *not* supposed to do is run off and try some stupid stunt without me!" His voice had risen slightly, despite his efforts to keep calm. "Do you realize your actions have basically destroyed any chance we have of getting information from Dale's memories? Farmer made sure he blurred them into an indecipherable mess. If there was ever a chance of finding a clue, it's gone now."

Tears touched her eyes and were just as quickly blinked away. He half reached out to comfort her, despite the fury that still chased through him, but she spun away, moving to the other side of the room.

"Don't," she said flatly.

He raised an eyebrow, confused. "Don't what?"

"Don't touch me, don't kiss me. I won't be side-tracked, not this time."

Exasperation rose. "I wasn't trying—"

"Like hell. It's a ploy you've used many times before when the conversation turns to a topic you don't like."

He stared at her for a minute then strode across to the refrigerator to get a drink himself—but something far stronger than a soda.

"I have no intention of sidetracking the conversation today, believe me." He poured himself a bourbon and added a few ice cubes.

"At least we've reached agreement on something, then.

He took a drink and turned to her again. "Farmer is a vampire," he said, keeping his voice flat. "He's not a fledgling, and he could overpower you in a second flat. Especially when you've overextended your abilities, as you did today."

She returned his gaze defiantly. "Jasper took longer than a minute to overpower me, and I'd certainly extended my abilities that day."

Yes, she had. And she'd damn near died because of it. "It was nearing dawn when Jasper attacked. It had weakened him."

"Yet it still took the two of us to take him down." She hesitated, glaring at him. "It was teamwork that killed Jasper that day. You do know what teamwork is, don't you?"

He clenched the glass so hard his hand was shaking, and liquid splashed over his fingers. "Sarcasm will get you nowhere."

"Neither will trying to talk sanely and rationally on this matter, apparently."

"Damn it, are you trying to get yourself killed?" His voice rose several notches.

"No!"

"Then why insist on joining me on Circle missions? You're not a killer, Nikki, and that is what I do. I kill. I murder them in cold blood, and then I walk away. Is that what you're so anxious to become a part of?"

Her face paled, but her chin still rose. "If that's all you do, then why did you save my life in that old house near the park? We hadn't even met then, so I meant nothing to you. It would have been easy to kill Jasper if he'd been distracted by feeding off my body. And why did you agree to send Rachel to the Circle to see if she could be saved if all you ever do is kill the bad things and walk away?"

"Neither of those were exactly normal cases."

"How would I know when you won't even discuss what you do with me?"

"I have spent too many years in darkness. I don't want to bring that into what we have."

"All we have is great sex," she shot back. "And you know what? It's a good foundation, but it's not enough to build a lasting relationship on. *That* takes trust, honesty and a willingness to compromise occasionally."

"So you're saying you don't trust me?"

"No, I'm saying *you* don't trust *me*. Nor are you honest with me. Not completely, not ever. And just where in the hell have you met me halfway of late?"

"Just where in the hell have *you* met *me* halfway? This is a two-way street, Nikki. You can't keep demanding I consider your wants if you're not willing to do the same."

She studied him for a moment, then looked away. "You know, Jake said much the same thing to me this afternoon."

Michael raised an eyebrow. That was surprising, given Jake was fiercely protective of Nikki. The two were more like father and daughter than boss and employee.

"And?"

"And you're both right. To a degree, I am being unreasonable. But so are you."

Which put them right back to square one. They were arguing in circles and getting nowhere. "Nikki—"

She held up her hand. "For once, will you just shut up and listen to me?"

He downed his drink and slammed the empty glass down on the nearby shelf. "Why should I, when you refuse to offer me the same courtesy?"

"I've heard all your arguments!" Anger sparked her eyes, roughened her voice. "That's all I *ever* hear whenever I bring this subject up. 'What I do is too dangerous', or, 'I don't want the darkness in my life to touch you', et cetera, et cetera. Well, guess what?

The darkness is not just something you do, it's a part of who you are."

"A part that nearly killed you not so long ago." And the nightmare of waking with her blood on his lips and her close to death was not something he wanted to relive.

"But—"

"No buts, Nikki." He was as aware of her fury as he was his own, despite the fact the link was still shut down tight. "You asked me to compromise? Fine. I will. Ask anything you like about Seline, the Circle, or my past, and I'll answer you. Just don't ask to accompany me on missions, because the answer is still no. It's far too dangerous for both of us." If only because worry about her safety would take his attention from what he was supposed to do and possibly lead to mistakes. Or death.

"Damn it, I know I could never go on all your missions, but surely there are some—"

"There are none. Jasper is the least of the fiends that I have hunted, believe me."

"But I found Jasper and Cordell all by myself. Keeping me locked away from what you do is no guarantee that I'll keep safe."

"Maybe. But the chances of you remaining safe are a lot higher."

She considered him for a moment. Something in her amber gaze sent a shiver through his soul. If he wasn't very careful, she'd walk away. The resolution was there in her eyes.

"So, when you told me yesterday you'd consider the matter, it was nothing more than another lie," she said softly.

"No, it wasn't. I did consider. I just didn't change my mind."

"So how is a willingness to share some of your history with me compromising? I thought that was something all couples did."

"Perhaps it is. Remember, I've never been part of a couple before."

"I was. You know, for all that Tommy tried to control my abilities—and by default, me—he let me in. I knew Tommy. Knew everything there was to know about him. There were no secrets between us."

Her voice was still remote, flat. The chill running through him intensified. It wasn't supposed to be going like this. For the first time in his life, it felt like he was on a train running full bore out of control, and he didn't like the sensation one bit. "Tommy was only sixteen. He didn't have many years behind him to gather secrets."

"But he'd lived on the streets since he was eight. He'd seen the worst life could throw at someone that young. He was a thief, a prostitute, and in the end, a murderer. Yet he wasn't afraid to let me see the darkness in his soul. Why are you?"

"Right now, it's not the darkness in me that I fear might hurt you. It's the darkness in others." Though that in itself wasn't entirely the truth. He would always fear the darkness in him. He knew what it— *he*—was capable of doing when that darkness was allowed free rein.

"I know that." She hesitated, taking a sip of her drink. "And I've considered what I'd be stepping into, as you asked me to. I've thought about Jasper and Cordell and Farmer."

The link between them was still shut, leaving him with no avenue to judge her thoughts beyond her expression, body language and the odd flicker of emotion that swirled between them. And those three things were scaring the hell out of him.

"And it strikes me that maybe I have something to offer this Circle of yours," she continued softly. "You defeated Jasper and Cordell with my help, remember. You certainly wouldn't have found Dale or Anne Harris alive had it not been for my gifts. In cases like this, where there are lives at risk, I can help you."

Yes, she could. There was no doubt about that. But the risks she'd be facing were enormous, and there was no way on Earth he'd place her safety on the line to save the life of another.

"Nikki, I love you—"

"That's not the damn point! I'm tired of only being told half-truths. I'm tired of having to fight for every bit of information about Seline and the Circle. But most of all, I'm tired of only being part-time."

"You're not—"

She made a chopping motion with her hand, spilling soda again. "I am. In the four months we've been living together, you've been away nearly two of those months. And half that time, you couldn't even remain in contact with me."

"You knew from the start that was a possibility."

She acknowledged his words with a nod. "What I didn't know was just how much I'd wanted a relationship like the one my parents had. They were equals in every sense of the word. All risks, all decisions, were shared. Granted, the risks in our case are *way* higher, but the fact is, we haven't got that sort of relationship, Michael. You order, I do. No discussion, end of story." She hesitated and took a deep breath. "Well, it will be the end of the story, unless you're willing to change your stance a little."

He stared at her. He couldn't do anything else

when it felt like a fist of ice had formed around his heart and squeezed it tight. "That's blackmail." Emotional blackmail.

"Maybe it is. Or maybe it's just self-preservation." She shrugged. "Four months ago, you were willing to walk away from us because you truly believed I would be better off without you in my life. Well, I truly believe that unless you let me into your life—your *whole* life—you're going to destroy us both. And I won't let that happen. I'd rather walk away now."

Though her face was as impassive as ever, her dark amber eyes glittered with unshed tears. And determination. She would do this, of that he had no doubt.

He wouldn't give in to blackmail, but by the same token, he didn't want to lose her. She was his sunshine, his heart. His soul. If she walked away, he'd have nothing left but the darkness.

But he had to keep on arguing, even though he sensed the futility. "Nikki, you can't possibly cope with what I have to deal with day in and day out."

"How do either of us know that unless you let me try? I'm not asking to be involved in every case—just some."

Some would lead to all, and they both knew it. "Even one might be one too many.'

The tears in her eyes threatened to well over. The fist around his heart clenched tighter, threatening to splinter it into a million jagged pieces.

"So you're not willing to even consider it?" she asked softly.

No, he wasn't. God, he should have followed his instincts and just walked away four months ago . . . but he hadn't. He'd let his heart rule his mind and, despite everything, he didn't regret it. "I'm not willing to lose you, either."

"Then where does that leave us?"

At an impasse. One that seemed to have no through tunnel. "I won't be blackmailed, Nikki." The bitterness he was feeling, the anger at what she was trying to force, crept into his voice. And he knew that *this* might destroy them just as easily as anything else.

A solitary tear broke the dam in her eyes and rolled down her cheek. He clenched his fist and stared at her, willing her to see what she was doing to them. Willing her to revoke her ultimatum and just let things be.

Neither moved. He wished he could read her thoughts, wished he could force the link open and taste the rainbow of her emotions. But he couldn't, simply because doing either would truly spell the end for them.

After several seconds, she placed the soda on the coffee table and walked towards him. She stopped so close that all he could smell was cinnamon, vanilla and desire. Her gaze searched his, then she rose on her toes and brushed a kiss across his lips. It felt like he'd been touched by fire—a fire that seared down to his soul and set his body alight.

He groaned and clasped his arms around her, pulling her close. He deepened the kiss, tasting her mouth, her neck. She sighed, a sound that was more a groan, then her fingers were on his shirt, impatiently pulling it free of his jeans before tugging at the buttons. It was an urgency he understood only too well. He needed her in a way he'd never needed her before. Needed to taste and touch and feel her, imprint every pore of her in his mind. Needed to lose himself deep inside her.

He pulled off her sweater, then nipped at the hard

buds of her breasts through the lace of her bra. She shuddered, arching into him as her hand slipped down his stomach and undid his jeans. Too fast, he thought, as she touched him. But right then, he could no more stop himself than he could that runaway train.

He ripped loose her bra, then pushed down her jeans. She stepped free quickly, taking her panties with them. He kicked out of his jeans, then wrapped an arm around her waist and picked her up, kissing her hard as he carried her over to the table. He moved his mouth down the long line of her neck, kissing and nipping, blazing a trail downwards. His blood beat a tattoo of urgency through his body, and every muscle quivered with the need to sheath himself deep inside her. But not yet. Not just yet.

He thrust his tongue into her moistness, tasting her, teasing her, until her breath began to quicken and the shudders took hold.

Only then did he pull her close and thrust deep inside her. Her soft moan was a sound he echoed. He pushed harder, wanting, needing, to claim every inch of her. Her breathless cries washed across him, sharpening his urgency, urging him to greater heights. Her muscles contracted against him, enveloping him in heat, bringing him closer to the edge. He claimed her mouth and kissed her ferociously. Their tongues duelled, the rhythm resonant of his thrusting hips.

The red tide rose, becoming a wall of pleasure he could not deny. His movements quickened. Her gasps reached a second crescendo, and her cries echoed in his ears as her body bucked against his. He came—a hot, torrential release whose force tore her name from his lips and sent his body rigid.

This was more than just great sex. More than just

love. It was a completeness. A wholeness. Surely she had to see that. He leaned against her, breathing in the warm scent of her and listening to the rapid pounding of their hearts. His body stirred.

It wasn't enough. Not yet.

Without a word, he picked her up and carried her into the bedroom. They made love through the rest of the afternoon, speaking with actions not words, until their bodies could take no more and they fell asleep.

It was only when he woke and saw he was alone in the bed that he realized she had, in her own way, just said good-bye.

Thirteen

Nikki walked. Numbly. Aimlessly.

Dusk crowded the sky and fingers of fog drifted in around her, precursors to the thick, white blanket beginning to roll off the bay. People bustled past her, so full of energy and life they made her feel old. Lights blazed through the streets, lending a warmth to the oncoming night.

Not that *she'd* ever feel warm again. It felt as if someone had ripped out her heart and left an empty block of ice in its place. She felt dead—not just her heart but her mind as well. And she wished, for perhaps the thousandth time since she'd woken, that she could just take back the words and leave things as they'd been.

But she couldn't. She'd said what she'd said and, in the process, had probably destroyed the best thing that had ever happened to her. But better death by her own words than a slow and painful one over the next few years. They couldn't have kept going as they were. Couldn't have.

She pushed away the doubts that crowded her mind. She couldn't allow doubts, or she just might break down and cry. She blinked back the tears that crowded her eyes anyway, then rubbed her arms. The night was getting colder, the fog thicker. She looked around, wondering for the first time where she was. She didn't recognize any of the buildings. But then, what she knew of San Francisco came from watching the various TV shows set here over the years.

In the distance a light twinkled, catching her eye.

She frowned at it for several seconds and it gradually became a cross. A church, she thought. Though she'd never entered a church in her life, there was something about that cross that seemed to draw her.

She walked towards it. Wet fingers of mist played across her skin, and the darkness seemed to close in. The noisy rush of traffic began to fade away until all that remained in the night was the rasp of her breathing, and the steady, glowing light of that cross. A light that was oddly visible, no matter what turn she took or what building rose in front of her.

A chill raced across her skin. Magic swirled through the night, so strong she could almost taste it. She licked dry lips but kept on walking. She could sense no evil in the magic that danced around her, but that didn't mean there wasn't any. Sparks danced across her fingers, lighting the night like tiny fireflies.

She rounded another corner. A cathedral loomed in front of her—large, Gothic, and beautiful. The cross was as dark as the church itself, but the sense of magic still stung the air.

Her steps slowed, then stopped. She listened to the night, watching the fog drift through the trees. Waiting, but for what she didn't know.

A sound invaded the odd silence. A soft tapping, like that of wood against concrete. She frowned, then jumped as her phone rang. Heart pounding somewhere in her throat, she dug the phone out of her pocket.

"Yes?"

The tapping stopped. The night seemed to be holding its breath, as if waiting.

"Jeez, Nikki, where the hell are you?" Jake said. "We've been worried sick here."

"If Michael was worried sick, he would have come

looking for me." And he would have undoubtedly found her, too. Even though she still had her end of the link shut down tight, there was still something between them that would always allow one to find the other.

"He said you needed the space. That make any sense to you?"

She snorted despite the cold ache in her heart. Part of her *had* hoped he'd come after her. "He's probably hoping I'll come to my senses."

Jake paused. "What do you mean?"

"It means I'm leaving him. Once we finish this job, it's over between us. He won't compromise in any way, and I'm sick of being second best."

Jake blew out his breath, the sound almost a sigh over the phone. "Nikki, at least think about it a while longer. It's nearly Christmas, for God's sake."

"Won't be the first Christmas I've spent alone."

And it certainly wouldn't be the last. She had an eternity of them to look forward to. No sharing kisses under the mistletoe. No drinking eggnog and stealing a look at the presents under the tree on Christmas Eve. She bit her lip and blinked away the sting in her eyes.

"Nikki, you and Michael were made for each other. I'm sure this could all be sorted out if you just sit down and talk."

She closed her eyes, holding on to her determination by the slenderest of margins. "We have talked. And talked."

"This is stupid and you know it."

"Ask Mary how stupid I'm being. I bet she'd understand exactly why I'm doing this." After all, she'd been second best to Jake's true passion—his job—for the last thirty years. Something Nikki had only just begun to see and understand in the last couple of days.

Jake swore softly. "Look, Michael has to go meet Farmer soon. He wants us to keep out of the hotel and to keep moving around."

"I'm out of the hotel and moving around."

"Together, Nikki. Not separately."

Anger flicked through her. He was still ordering. Still not trusting her to be able to look after herself. She studied the night for a moment and knew there was something here, something instinct suggested she needed to see.

"I have to do something first," she said. "Take a phone with you, and I'll call you when I'm finished."

"Nikki—"

"And if they use real silverware in that fancy hotel of yours," she cut in, "I'd grab a couple of knives. Just to be on the safe side."

She hit the "end" button then turned off the phone and shoved it back into her pocket. The soft tapping resumed almost immediately.

The night grew colder, its touch almost icy. A breeze swirled around her, tangling her hair and chasing chills down her back. Yet ten feet away, the fog stirred sluggishly through the still limbs of a tree.

An old woman became visible, tapping a cane against the sidewalk in front of her with every step. She was small and gnarled, with clothes that were as gray as the fog and just as flimsy.

The taste of magic increased, tingling across her skin. Sparks skittered across her fingers, sending flickers of red and gold dancing through the damp darkness.

"You'll not be needing that weapon against the likes of me."

The old woman's voice was melodious, soft and yet somehow powerful. She stopped and, though a bare five feet separated them, Nikki couldn't see her eyes. It was almost as if she didn't have any—and yet, if that were the case, how could she know about the energy dancing across Nikki's fingers? Surely it wasn't caressing the night *that* strongly.

"Why have you called me here?" Nikki had no doubt the magic she sensed was coming from this woman. And she had no intention of dropping her guard, no matter how safe her instincts were suggesting that would be.

The old woman smiled, revealing stained teeth and black gaps. "I am not the one who summoned you. I have merely been chosen to escort and explain. Come along, young woman."

She turned, tapping towards the church. Nikki's hesitation was brief. She had no idea who was crazier—the old woman, or her for following—but it didn't matter. The scent of magic was so strong it practically crawled across her skin, and it was obvious something was about to happen. Oddly enough, she felt no fear. No sense of approaching doom. Maybe her instincts had finally given up and gone away, as she'd once wished.

The old woman didn't enter the church but walked around the left side of it. Nikki followed her. The fog seemed thicker here, slapping her with wet fingers and dribbling moisture down her skin. The silence was so thick she could almost taste it, and her skin tingled as if she was walking through a wall of energy.

"Come, come," the old woman said, almost impatiently. Her form was lost to the fog. It was almost as if she'd become a part of it.

The tingling increased, crawling like electricity across her skin. The fog was dense and cold. It felt like ice, and every step became an effort. It was almost as if she were moving through a force of some kind.

But as quickly as it had appeared, the sensation was gone. She stumbled forward several steps but quickly regained her balance and looked around for the old woman. The thickness of the fog eased but it still swirled sluggishly, touching her with fingers that now seemed oddly warm. She spied the stranger on the top of a small hill just in front of her and made her way towards her. The fog parted, as if it were stepping aside. Nikki stopped suddenly, her stomach plummeting as she realized the fog *was* stepping aside.

Only it wasn't fog.

It was ghosts.

Music thumped from the interior of the café. Michael stopped under the awning, eyeing the building in distaste. He'd never been a fan of rock music—in any of its configurations. Though he'd certainly heard a lot of it since Nikki had come to live with him.

Nikki . . . God, what was he going to do with her?

He was only certain of one thing—he loved her, and he'd be damned if he was going to let her walk away from him when this case was over. Jake was right. There had to be a common ground somewhere. Had to be some compromise that would make them both happy. All they had to do was find it.

And find it they would—even if he had to tie her to the bed to keep her in his life and talking to him.

He took a deep breath and tried to push all

thoughts of her aside as he entered the noise-laden building. His senses tingled with awareness—the fiend was inside, waiting.

"Table for Farmer," he said, as a waiter walked up to greet him.

The young man smiled. "Sure. This way."

Michael's gaze swept across the room and met the blue eyes of his foe. Farmer was everything he'd imagined—short, stocky, and balding. His face was hard, and tattoos covered what little skin there was to be seen. He was wearing a black leather jacket, a sleeveless jean jacket over that. Michael had no doubt his club's colors would adorn the back of the jacket— everything about this man said biker. Except, perhaps, his eyes. They were the eyes of a man lost in the wonder of his own little world.

Which was odd, because Farmer had certainly seemed sane enough when he'd talked to him earlier.

The younger vampire rose as he approached the table. "You would be the man I spoke to last night," he said, offering his hand.

He was wearing fingerless leather gloves, the leather oddly damp against his palm as they shook hands. Farmer was as strong as the muscles bulging against the restriction of his jacket suggested.

"Michael." He pulled out a chair and sat down.

"Bill." Farmer motioned to the bottle of wine that sat on the table, the movement almost feminine. "Drink?"

Michael shook his head and ordered a bourbon from a passing waiter. Farmer poured himself a glass then raised it, sniffing the aroma. His behavior was so at odds with his appearance, Michael was hard-pressed to hold back his smile.

"How long have you been in the city?" He reached

out psychically, carefully testing the other vampire's defenses. They were locked down tight, as he'd expected. He had no doubt he could breach them but was reluctant to do so here. There were too many innocents Farmer could use as weapons. And despite what he'd said to Nikki, he didn't simply walk in and kill. Not in crowded situations like this, especially when the target was ready and watchful for tricks.

Farmer leaned back in his chair and idly sipped his wine. "Two months. I like this place. Might settle here for a while."

"You living in the Castro area?"

He was careful to keep his voice neutral, and though Farmer's gaze narrowed slightly, Michael could sense no anger. Which again was odd, given the young vampire's history of retaliation when the suggestion of being gay was raised.

"No. But I might, if I decide to stay here."

Michael nodded. "And you were the maker of the fledglings down in the sewer?"

"Yes." Farmer paused. "Why did you kill them?"

Michael snorted. "You have no need for a harem in a city this size. You start killing too many people, and the cops will begin to notice. We survive by being unnoticed.

Farmer's sudden smile was derisive. "We survive by being stronger and faster. The cops are no threat to the likes of you and me."

"Don't ever underestimate humans. They'll do the unexpected every time." Like walk out the door rather than settle for part-time happiness.

"I disagree. From what I've seen, humans are all predictable." Farmer took another sip of his drink. "Take that witch I'm chasing. I can tell you now, she'll do whatever she can to rescue her loved ones."

Michael's gut clenched. He was suddenly glad Nikki was out wandering the night. Farmer's minions—if he had any left—would not be able to track her down. Even Farmer himself might have trouble, despite the odd connection he seemed to have with her.

"I think we all tend to do that, human or not." His palm began to tingle, and he scratched it idly. "Have you managed to track her down yet?"

"No. But I won't have to. She'll come to me."

Michael didn't like the confidence in the younger vampire's voice or the smirk beginning to twitch his thin lips. He raised his eyebrow. "You sound extremely confident of that.

"That's because I am. I have someone she loves."

The itching was getting stronger, creeping up his arm. Michael frowned and looked down. His hand was red, as if burned. For a moment, his vision blurred. He blinked, but as he looked up, the room spun around him. The glove, he thought. There'd been something on the glove.

He thrust upwards and hit the smirking younger vampire with every ounce of psychic strength he had. Farmer's eyes went wide with fear an instant before Michael surged into his mind and took control. He forced the younger vampire to rise and walk out the door, then he threw some money on the table and followed. He didn't have much time left. There was an odd buzzing beginning to run though his mind, and the room seemed to be drifting in and out of focus. He had to take care of Farmer before whatever it was that had been on that glove took full effect.

They walked out onto the street then down towards the Aquatic Park. The buzzing in his head was getting stronger, until it felt like there were hundreds of bees swarming through his mind. He gritted his teeth, battling to keep control as he marched Farmer in front of him. All the while he searched the buildings around them, looking for some place that was empty. Looking for some place were he could quickly and safely destroy Farmer without the risk of involving others.

But every step pushed the drug further into his system.

Every breath became harder.

And though he was a vampire and didn't really need to breathe, his body still seemed to crave air. He blinked sweat away from his eyes and forced Farmer to the right. His gaze swept the buildings on both sides of the street until he found one that showed no life—a restaurant in the process of being renovated, by the look of it. He hurried them both towards it.

He thrust psychic energy at the door. It flew inwards, shattering as it hit the floor. People around them stopped and briefly stared, but none saw them enter. He had enough strength left to ensure that.

The interior shadows wrapped around them. Michael stumbled as he came through the door, his feet suddenly blocks of ice that refused to obey his commands. His psychic hold slipped, and Farmer swung around, lashing out with a booted foot. Michael avoided the blow, but only just. His reactions were slow. Far too slow. It felt like he was moving through glue while Farmer danced around him at high speed.

He tried to reach out and recapture his hold on Farmer's mind, but the bees were buzzing so loudly he could barely even think let alone control his psychic abilities. Farmer danced in close, fist swinging. Michael ducked again then lashed out with his fist, connecting with flesh with a satisfying thump. He stumbled forward, reaching for the younger vampire, trying to get a grip on his neck. He needed to break it. Needed to kill.

His fingers slipped across leather, then cloth, but oddly could find no purchase. The darkness had closed in, and he realized he couldn't see. He blinked, switching to his infrared vampire vision. Farmer was a red haze who laughed insanely several feet in front of him.

He dove forward, knocking the younger vampire down, dragging them both to the ground. Farmer hit hard, his head smacking against the rough tiles. Curses flew from his lips, singing through the night. Michael ignored them, wrapped his arm around the younger vampire's neck and twisted hard.

Realized in that instant he didn't have the strength required to complete the act. Anger rushed through him—anger and fear. Not for himself. For Nikki.

As the bees grew more frenzied and the night began to blur into nothingness, he knew he had to do something, anything, to at least maim Farmer and give her a chance.

He moved his grip from the fiend's neck to his elbow and snapped it back as hard as he could. There was an unmistakable pop of bone and sinew, and relief swept through him. It was something. Not much, but something. Farmer's howl filled the night, a dog baying at the moon neither of them could see.

The buzzing got louder and louder, all but consuming his mind. Farmer's face loomed into focus, his expression contemptuous as his fingers brushed the chain at Michael's neck. Realizing what he intended, Michael reached up, trying to stop him from wrenching the cross free. But his strength had slithered away. The smell of burning flesh briefly stung the air, followed by a sharp curse. Then the warmth of the cross was gone. A second later, it hit the floor with a gentle ting.

The night blurred, and he found himself on the floor, his body shuddering with blows he couldn't even feel. He scraped his hand across the tiles, trying to find the cross. Tried to reach for Nikki, to warn her not to come after him, but that only made the bees react in fury. After a while, he stopped trying to do either.

Yet it seemed an extraordinarily long time before the night became a smudge of blackness and consciousness receded.

"They will not hurt you." The old woman's melodious voice was far from reassuring. Nikki flexed her hands, battling the urge to use the energy that danced across her fingertips. Would energy even hurt ghosts? Somehow she doubted it.

The ethereal faces that surrounded her were none she knew. Yet she felt their sorrow, their pain and anger, as if it were her own. It stabbed deep inside, settled like a weight in her stomach.

She tore her gaze away from them and looked back up the hill. The old woman was just as flimsy as the ghosts around her, but for some reason, she held color while these others did not.

"What's going on here?"

Her voice jarred uneasily against the strange hush surrounding them. The ghosts stirred, the delicate gowns that were their bodies dissipating then gathering close again.

"That is what I am here to explain." The old

woman motioned her forward with a quick wave of her cane. "Come. Sit in front of me on the grass, and we shall talk."

Nikki's hesitation was only brief. She had a feeling choice was something she'd left behind when she'd followed this woman through the oddly thick fog that had surrounded the church.

She walked up the hill and sat down cross-legged in front of the old woman. The grass wasn't really grass, but a smoky echo that felt oddly warm. "What's going on?" she repeated softly.

"Consequences."

"Consequences?"

The old woman nodded, the black holes that were her eyes seeming to bore right through Nikki's soul. She shivered, but resisted the temptation to rub her arms.

"Consequences of actions taken," the old one continued." Sometimes they are not apparent right away. Sometimes they must wait before they can be revealed."

This old woman and Michael had one thing in common—neither of them could speak plain English. "What do you mean?"

"You were dead," the woman said. "Your soul had consigned itself to the light, had it not?"

Fear pulsed through her. Nikki closed her eyes, remembering the light. Remembering the feeling of joy and peace as she bathed in its warmth. *Oh Lord, Michael, what have you done. . .?*

"Yes," she somehow managed to croak.

"He pulled you back. He gave you part of his energy, made you as eternal as the night and himself."

She nodded. Fear had become a fist squeezing her heart tight. She could barely even breathe.

"But he could not fully undo what had already been decided."

Her breath stuttered to a halt for several seconds. She stared at the old woman, not sure what she meant. Not sure she even wanted to know. The silence seemed to stretch until it sawed at her nerves. The ghosts around them stirred, restless slivers of fog that brushed warmth across her icy skin.

They were waiting for her to speak, she realized. She licked dry lips and somehow found her voice, "What do you mean?"

"He gave you new life. But a small portion of you will always remain on this plane. That cannot be undone. Death is a part of you as much as he is now."

Oh God . . . "Meaning?"

"Meaning you can walk this plane almost as easily as you walk the other. Meaning you can call forth those whose untimely deaths forced them to remain rather than move on."

She stared at the woman for several seconds, mulling over the implications. Wondering if this was real. Maybe she was tucked safely in bed, with Michael's arms wrapped around her. Maybe—hopefully—this was nothing more than some strange nightmare.

"This is real, young woman. As we are real."

"You're a ghost. As are those who surround us."

"That doesn't make us any less real."

No, she supposed it didn't. And considering what she'd seen over the past four months, ghosts were way down on the list when it came to ghoulies to be wary of.

She took a deep breath and released it slowly. It didn't do much to ease the grip of fear squeezing her heart tight.

"So you're saying I can now see ghosts?" Just like the movie. Great.

"Yes." The melodious voice was soft. Sympathetic.

"And you're saying I can talk to these ghosts if I choose to?"

"I'm saying you can call them and bring them into being. Give them the power to react with your world."

She wasn't sure she understood what that meant. And right now, she really didn't want to know. "It's been eleven months since Michael brought me back from the dead. Why have you come to me now and not before?"

"On this plane, time is meaningless. A breath can take a second or a century. It matters not."

"That's not much of an answer," she grumbled.

The old woman's toothless smile flashed. "No. But until now, the results of his actions had not begun to appear."

She remembered the whispers she'd heard down in the sewers. The nebula cloud that had briefly appeared before the vampires attacked. Ghosts? Or the imaginings of a fearful mind? Despite what the old woman was saying, she wasn't entirely sure she could believe it was the whispers of the dead she'd heard.

"So how am I supposed to empower these ghosts of yours?"

"Reach out psychically. They will connect with you and draw on your strength to gain substance."

"That sounds dangerous."

The old woman's smile was wry. "So is taking a walk across the park these days."

True. But muggers she could cope with. She wasn't so sure she could handle nebular bits of mist sucking at her energy to gain form. It reminded her too much of vampires.

The old woman climbed to her feet. "I must take you back," she said. "You cannot remain long on this plane. Remember that in the future when you roam this world."

Nikki frowned as she rose. "What do you mean?"

"I mean your soul was never destined to stay on this plane. You were meant for the light. The longer you remain here, the more it sucks your strength. The more it sucks his strength."

She stared at the old woman as the implications of her words sank in. "What? How is that possible?"

"Your energies are linked. He is your strength, and you are his. You are two halves of a whole and function as such."

Oh God ... Michael was meeting with Farmer. And she was here. Sucking his strength when he needed it most. "You have to get me back. Quickly."

The old woman nodded and walked down the hill. The ghosts parted, an unearthly wave that made no sound and yet whose whispering filled her mind.

Then their presence gave way to the damp touch of real fog. The tingling hit her, burning across her skin, through her mind. Then she was stumbling forward, landing on her hands and knees, her fingers sliding against grass that was real and wet rather than ghostly.

She looked around quickly but couldn't see the old woman. But Nikki had a feeling she would be there, on the other side, if and when she chose to go back.

She thrust upwards, but at that moment, pain hit her, so thick and fast it snatched her breath and drove her face-first back to the ground.

Not hers.

Michael's.

Fourteen

For several seconds Nikki could do nothing more than lie there. The simple act of breathing had become a struggle, and fire burned through every fiber of her being. Her muscles thumped and quivered, as if someone was kicking and punching her. And she knew what she was feeling was merely an echo of what was actually happening to him.

Michael? She thrust the link wide and called with every ounce of strength she had.

There was no response. His mind wasn't shuttered, simply lost in a fog she could not traverse. A fog she'd felt once before—when Jasper had drugged her to stop her using her talents to contact Michael.

If she'd sucked away his strength, if he couldn't use his talents because his mind was warped by drugs, he couldn't protect himself—not in any way.

Panic tore through her heart. He couldn't die . . . not now, not when there were so many things left unsaid between them.

Tears stung her eyes. She took a deep breath and tried to regain some sense of control. *Don't think. Don't feel. React.*

She pushed to her knees and grabbed the cell phone from her pocket, quickly dialing Jake.

"Where are you?" she asked, the minute he answered.

"Down at Fisherman's Wharf." He hesitated, and concern touched his voice as he continued. "Why?"

"Because Michael's in trouble. Meet me near the Hard Rock on Van Ness Avenue."

She hung up and climbed to her feet. She thought briefly about catching a cab but knew it was probably faster to run, even though the peak of rush hour had come and gone. So she ran. The fog slapped wetly against her skin, soaking her hair and dribbling down her face. Or maybe that was tears. She didn't know. Didn't care. Her heart pounded a rhythm that was as fast and fearful as every step, yet deep inside she knew no matter how fast she was, it was never going to be enough. Not to save Michael from the damage Farmer was inflicting.

Maybe not even to save his life.

A sob escaped her lips. She put a hand to her mouth and kept on running. The streets, the lights, the people still out and about, blurred around her. All she wanted—all she could think about—was Michael.

She swung onto Van Ness. Heard rather than saw the Hard Rock. Did see Jake, pacing impatiently out front. She slowed, then stopped.

He took one look at her face and swore softly. "Where is he?"

"Not here." She bent, leaning her hands against her knees, her entire being shuddering as she sucked in great gasps of air. "But close."

"If there's any hope of rescuing him, we have to hurry, Nik."

They didn't have a hope of finding him let alone rescuing him. Not right now. She knew that without a doubt. But they had to try. She'd never forgive herself if she didn't at least try.

She pushed upright and studied the night. The pull of his presence came from up ahead. "This way," she said.

"What's happened?" Jake's quick steps seemed to

echo against the sidewalk while hers made no sound at all. It was almost as if she were part of the night, as silent as the breeze.

Or Michael.

Her breath caught somewhere in her throat. *Don't think. Don't feel.* Not yet. "I don't know exactly. I just know I can't touch his mind, and that Farmer has beaten the crap out of him."

"Drugged?"

She nodded tightly and wondered how in hell something like that had happened. He was usually so careful . . . but then, maybe it was a little hard to concentrate when someone you loved had just threatened to walk out of your life. Guilt swirled, but she pushed that away, too. She had no time for guilt or fear or anything else beyond determination.

She'd save him from Farmer. Find him, save him, and somehow kill Farmer in the process. She swung right and made her way down a smaller street. An old restaurant came into sight, its windows boarded up but the door gone.

This was it. This was where they'd been. Where they no longer were.

Jake stopped beside her. "Anyone there?"

She shook her head, her gaze searching the street, trying to catch some sense of where Farmer had taken Michael. Instinct suggested they were heading northwest. But it also suggested they shouldn't follow. Not yet.

Jake looked around, then stepped past the shattered doorway into the old restaurant. She followed him inside.

He bent and studied several dark smudges on the floor. "Blood." His voice was as grim as his expression when he looked up.

She swallowed bile and somehow managed to say, "He's alive, Jake. Farmer wants to use him as bait."

"So what the hell are we going to do? The two of us are pretty much next to useless when it comes to fighting a vampire and his horde."

"Maybe." She moved past him into the deeper darkness. There was something here that teased the outer reaches of her psychic senses. Something she had to find. "There are ways we can protect ourselves, at least."

"I thought garlic and holy water didn't work."

She edged forward and held out her hand. Energy tingled across her fingertips, warning she was close. "It doesn't. But silver does. Wooden stakes do."

"So does shooting the bastard's head off," Jake said. "I'd rather be armed with a gun any day."

"Gun's don't frighten vampires. They tend to think they're beyond them." She knelt and brushed her fingers against the old tiles, touching a sliver of metal.

It was the cross she'd given Michael when they first met. Farmer must have torn it from his neck, because Michael would never have left this here willingly. Michael knew she'd use it to follow him—and that was something he'd never want.

She wrapped her fingers around it. Though her palm tingled, no images rushed from the cross's silver heart. He was still unconscious, and there was no telling yet just how badly he'd been hurt.

But if the muted ache pounding through her brain was anything to go by, his wounds were serious. Maybe not enough to kill, but certainly enough to be more serious than any he'd suffered before Farmer's attack.

She walked back to Jake. "We should go back to the hotel and plan what we're going to do next."

Jake's expression was shocked. "You're not going after him?"

She held out her hand and showed him the cross. "Michael would never have left it. We both know he wouldn't want me to follow him, no matter how deadly his situation. Farmer took it off. He's the one who wants us to follow."

"And if we don't, he might just kill Michael."

She took a deep breath. It didn't calm the churning in her stomach or the fear pounding through her heart. "He won't until he gets his hands on me. So we keep away until we have a surefire way of killing the bastard."

"That's not going to be easy. For a start, we don't even know what he looks like."

"I'll know him when I see him." If only because the scent of evil was never easily disguised.

Jake nodded. "Then let's get back."

He led the way out the door. They walked quickly through the damp night, and while she could find no scent of evil in the darkness that swirled damply around them, it was a huge relief when the warm lights of the hotel finally came into sight.

The woman manning the reception desk looked up as they entered. "Miss James? A parcel has arrived for you."

Jake raised an eyebrow. "You expecting anything?"

She shook her head. "But Michael was. Seline was sending him a charm of some sort."

"Ah, the mystery lady who runs the Circle. We ever going to get to meet her?"

Nikki gave him a dirty look as she picked up the small, wrapped box. "I can't even get him to talk about her—which is one of the things we were arguing about."

"Ah. Sorry, Nik."

She shrugged. Their argument wasn't what mattered right now. Getting Michael back safely was.

"You want something to eat?" Jake continued as they made their way across to the elevators.

She shook her head. "I very much suspect if I eat anything right now, I might just throw up."

He looked at her, then touched her elbow and drew her into his embrace. "He'll be okay," he said softly. "Michael's survived for more than three centuries. It'll take more than a psycho like Farmer to destroy him."

She closed her eyes, fighting tears. She couldn't cry. Wouldn't cry. Not until Michael was safe. A bell chimed into the silence, announcing the elevator's arrival. She didn't move and neither did Jake, and for that she was glad. In many ways, he'd become almost a father to her, and right now, she needed a father's comforting. Needed to be held. Needed to be told it would turn out all right—even if the words were nothing more than a lie.

It was several minutes before she sniffed and pulled away. Forcing a smile, she said, "Thanks."

He nodded, thumbing a tear from her cheek. "Michael's a survivor. Remember that, if nothing else. And there's no way on this Earth he's going to give up life until he's had a chance to tell you off for walking out on him like you did."

Her smile became warmer, but no less strained. "You're probably right."

"There's no probably about it. I was with the man. Believe me, annoyed doesn't begin to cover it." He hit the elevator button again and the door slid open. "You going up to your room?"

She shook her head and followed him in. "Neither of us is going anywhere alone from now on. If you want something to eat, I'll follow you into the dining room. I can grab a coffee, if nothing else."

"Nik, you can't fuel you talents on nothing but coffee, you know."

"You've been hanging around Michael *far* too much."

He smiled. "He's only echoing what I've been saying for years."

She snorted softly. "This from the man who didn't believe in my talents for how many years?"

"I didn't *dis*believe, you know."

The doors slid open again, and Jake led the way into the dining room. She waited until the waiter had taken Jake's order then placed the box on the table and began unwrapping it. Inside was a single braided rope bracelet, similar to the one she'd worn to stop Cordell's magic from touching her. Only this one had several tarnished charms woven through the thick red, yellow and blue cords.

"What is it?" Jake said, when she held it up.

"From what Michael said, it's supposed to break the link Farmer has with me." She slipped it over her wrist and up under her sweater. The rope was slightly scratchy against her skin and oddly warm.

"A piece of rope and a couple of old coins are supposed to do that?" Disbelief edged his voice.

She grinned. "Yeah, I know. But her charm worked the last time I tried one, and I'm not about to discount this one. We need all the breaks we can get."

"Amen to that."

Her coffee was brought to the table, then his meal. Jake thanked the waiter then attacked his steak with a gusto that made her look away. She might have to eat to fuel her talents, but right now just watching him was almost more than she could bear.

"So is it?" he asked, waving his knife at the charm hidden under her sweater.

"I don't know." She leaned back in the chair, frowning as she searched for internal changes. The bracelet's pleasant warmth was beginning to flush through her, and for the first time since she'd arrived in San Francisco, she felt an odd sort of peace. It was as if she'd stepped into a cone of silence, without having realized before then just how much noise there was around her. "Maybe."

"Will that thing affect your ability to find Michael?"

She wrapped her fingers around the cross in her pocket. Warmth pulsed through her fingers and shadows crowded her mind. He was regaining consciousness—but if those ghostly, distant images were anything to go by, he was still heavily drugged.

"No, it won't." If only because their connection went far deeper—and was far stronger—than any of her talents. She would have been able to find him even without the aid of the cross and her psychometry skills.

"So what's the game plan?"

She sighed and rubbed a hand across her eyes. "I don't know. I just know we can't rush in and try to rescue him because that's what Farmer wants."

"And if he doesn't get what he wants, he'll try something else."

"I know."

Jake finished his steak then pushed the remaining vegetables away and leaned back in his chair. "First things first. Weapons?"

"You've got your gun, and we've got that rifle we confiscated."

He nodded. "I also took several knives from the kitchen, but I won't guarantee how much silver there is in them."

"Probably not a lot, but Farmer's younger in vampire years than Jasper, and a silver kitchen knife certainly helped do him in." She frowned, trying to remember everything Michael had said about vampires over the past few months—which was not a lot, in reality. "What about wood?"

"As in stakes?"

She nodded. Wood in any form was supposedly deadly to vampires—not that she really wanted to confront Farmer armed only with a sharpened piece of wood. That would be nothing short of foolishness.

"I can get some."

"Good."

A waiter approached and refilled their coffee cups. Jake waited until he'd left then said, "You know he's not going to be alone."

"I know." And she didn't know how they were going to handle a harem of fledglings plus Farmer. "I wish we were back in Lyndhurst. At least we could call in MacEwan."

Jake's smile was wry. "Bet you never thought there'd come a day when you'd be saying that."

"No." MacEwan had been the bane of her existence as a teenager, and one of the biggest decriers of her talents on the police force. Yet, oddly enough, he was one of the few cops they could go to for help, no matter what the situation, simply because he'd known them long enough to trust them. Up to a point, anyway.

"We could call him," Jake said. "Ask if he's got

free time. At the very least, he might get us some credibility with the cops here in San Francisco."

"I've got a feeling we haven't that sort of time." Which was not exactly the truth. What she was really feeling was that, as of five minutes ago, they'd *totally* run out of time.

Her gaze drifted to the maître d', and a chill ran down her spine. Something had happened. Something more than Michael. The phone rang shrilly, and her heart lodged somewhere in her throat. The maître d' answered it then glanced their way.

"Oh great. Just what we need right now—another of your little feelings." Jake's voice seemed to be coming from the end of a great hollow.

She couldn't answer. Could only watch as a waiter bought the phone over to their table.

"Mr. Morgan? Phone call for you, sir."

Jake accepted the phone with a nod of thanks then said, "Hello?"

There was a long silence, and in that brief moment, Jake seemed to age twenty years.

She closed her eyes. Knew without being told what had happened.

Jake hung up the phone and placed it on the table. For several minutes there was nothing but silence. It was as if the whole world had faded away, leaving an echoing void with only them in it.

His chair creaked as he slumped back. She bit her lip, fighting tears.

"That was Anna." His voice was remote. Empty. "Mary never made it to Long Beach."

Voices whispered. Sharp, excited voices, heated by lust, spiked with desperation. At first, Michael wasn't sure whether they were real or just a result of the feverish pain pounding through him.

More cries touched the night—the sound of fear mingled with ecstasy and lust and hunger. The darkness in him stirred and his canines lengthened. Anticipating. Wanting.

He tried to force his eyes open, but they seemed glued shut. Tried to move his arms, only to have a red wall of pain rise up his left arm and knock him back into unconsciousness.

When he stirred a second time, the voices were gone, replaced by the stink of evil.

"So the dead awakens." Farmer's amused tones seemed to be coming from a great distance. "And here I was thinking I might have been a little too harsh with the boots."

His voice was coming from the far left. Michael turned his head that way. Beyond the stink came the tantalizing aroma of fresh blood. The darkness in him came to life again. He needed to feed. Needed the sweet strength of human life to help him heal . . .

No, he thought. Not human. He could kill Nikki if he drank from her again . . .

Nikki. Her image jumped into focus through the fogginess enshrouding his brain, and fear swelled. But she wasn't here. It wasn't her whose death he could smell. Wasn't her blood Farmer had all over him.

Relief washed through him, a river that cleared some of the confusion from his brain. How much time had passed since Farmer had kicked him unconscious and dragged him down here? And where, exactly, was here?

"I'd offer you some sustenance," Farmer continued. "But I'm afraid my fledglings and I overindulged, and there's not much left of the poor girl."

The smell of death mixed with a damp, slightly fishy odor, indicating they were in the sewers again. But beyond that, there was a seaweedy, salty sort of tang. In the distance came a continuous, thumping roar, like that of ocean pounding against rocks. They had to be near an old outlet to the sea, even though those had been blocked many years ago.

But why here? Especially when it was such a long way from where they'd found the other two victims? What was Farmer up to this time?

"I know you're awake," Farmer continued, his tone less jocular. "Feigning unconsciousness in the hope of getting me closer will achieve nothing. You're chained, in case you didn't realize it."

He shifted his right arm carefully. Heard the clink of metal. Normally, chains wouldn't hold him. Farmer knew that and so did he. Which meant he was hurt far more than the pain pounding through his body would suggest.

"This won't—" The words came out a cracked, almost unintelligible whisper. He stopped and ran his tongue around his mouth. Three teeth were chipped, his top lip was split, and the bottom half of his face seemed horribly swollen. Farmer obviously hadn't been overly careful on where he'd placed his boots. It hurt to breathe, let alone talk. "—get you any-where," he finished.

"Interesting you should say that, because I really did expect the witch to come rushing to your rescue. She hasn't, and I'm wondering why."

Because she's smarter than you think. Smarter than I think. "Argument," he ground out.

"Well, that's just downright inconsiderate of you. How bad?"

"Split up." It hurt to say those words. Hurt more than any of the wounds Farmer had inflicted on him. And if he got out of this situation alive, he was going to ensure she stayed in his life. There had to be a compromise that suited both of them. Had to be.

And if there wasn't?

Then he'd do what it took—even if that meant walking away from the Circle, from everything and everyone else he loved. Her leaving him this afternoon had allowed him to glimpse the future, and it was as he'd long suspected. Life without her was a long, dark tunnel. He'd been through that tunnel once. He had no intention of going back.

Farmer tsked. "Very inconsiderate. Still, maybe she has no idea yet that you're my captive. Maybe she failed to find that damn cross of yours."

She would have found it. Of that, Michael had no doubt. But why she hadn't yet tried to rescue him he couldn't honestly say. Maybe all the arguing they'd been doing over the past few days had actually done some good. Maybe she was thinking instead of simply reacting.

Which wasn't really a fair thought. Especially when it was part of what he loved about her.

"Perhaps I shall send her a little souvenir and let her know."

Over *his* dead body. "Great . . . idea."

The silence seemed to stretch. He could feel Farmer's confusion, even if he couldn't yet see it.

"It worries me that you so readily agree with me," the younger vampire said eventually.

It was supposed to. Obviously, Farmer wasn't the sharpest tool in the shed, and at least that gave

Michael himself some advantage. Right now, he needed every little bit of help he could get. He shifted his right hand and carefully rubbed his face. Blood crusted both his eyes. He wiped it away and opened his eyes—or eye. The left one remained swollen shut.

Farmer was a blur of red heat fifteen feet away. Farmer's left arm was heavily bandaged, indicating Michael had been successful in at least one aim. Behind the younger vampire were four others—the fledglings he'd heard feeding earlier.

"Why do you want me to send her such a reminder when it is your flesh I'll be taking?" Farmer continued.

"How . . ." His voice faded, and he coughed. The action sent pain slicing through him, and the metallic taste of blood filled his mouth. He swallowed it. Blood was blood, and right now, he could not afford to lose any more than he already had. " . . . would you react?"

"I'd be hysterical. Then I'd want revenge." Farmer paused again. "Which is exactly the reaction I want."

"Go for it."

Farmer crossed his arms, expression wary. Puzzled. "You're just trying to psyche me out of it, aren't you?"

"Yes."

The puzzlement on Farmer's face deepened. "And now you're just agreeing with everything I say and trying to confuse me."

"Yes." At this stage, there wasn't much else he could do. Not until the pain ebbed a little.

"Perhaps I should try to contact her first. Give her a little taste of what I intend if she doesn't come to your rescue." Farmer glanced at his watch. "In the meantime, I have a pressing engagement with another prisoner." He turned, then hesitated. "And don't bother trying to escape. My boys will be more than a match for you in your current condition."

The boys in question stirred restlessly. None of them were particularly old, three of the four probably little more than eighteen or nineteen. The taste for young flesh was something he had never been able to understand. Even in the darkest days of his early years as one of Elizabeth's fledglings, he had always chosen older victims to feast on. The destruction of such young life was something he'd always abhorred.

As Elizabeth had often said, he never did make much of a 'proper' vampire.

Farmer left. The Loop milled uncertainly for several seconds, then followed their creator. But they didn't go far. Their restless movements and hungry, blood-crazed thoughts stirred the darkness from just around the corner.

If Farmer wasn't careful, these four would soon slip the leash. They were too new to their condition, too crazed by the urgency pounding through their veins. And that could lead to a bloodbath on the streets above. Not that Farmer would particularly care, except for the fact it might put a dent in his plans for revenge.

Plans Michael still had every intention of stopping. He closed his eyes, breathing deeply and taking stock. The pain was centered in three areas—his ribs, his left arm and his stomach. His legs were undoubtedly bruised and battered, but he could move them without great walls of agony hitting him, so nothing was broken. His arm *was* broken—every twitch sent hot lances arrowing into his brain. His ribs and stomach were almost as painful, but neither of those would hamper his escape as much as his useless left arm.

He reached out to the link and tried to contact Nikki. Nothing but a haze of gray came back to him. It was something he'd felt once before—when Jasper had kidnapped and drugged her. Farmer had undoubtedly done something similar to him. He'd felt the full force of Michael's mind strength in the cafe. He wouldn't risk being captured like that again.

Michael glanced at the metal cuff around his right wrist and tried to kinetically pry the attached links apart. The fog swirled sluggishly, and the metal links remained stubbornly locked together.

No relying on his psychic skills, then.

He edged carefully onto his back, but the movement still jarred his arm. Sweat broke out across his brow, and he hissed, battling waves of nausea and the threatening tide of unconsciousness.

He couldn't slip back. He didn't trust the fledglings not to attack him. And he needed to get out of here, away from Farmer, before Nikki *did* come looking for him.

He continued to breathe deeply until the pain had subsided once again, then turned to study what held the chains. It wasn't the wall he'd expected, but a rusting metal ladder. His gaze followed it up into the darkness. The cover looked as if it hadn't been moved in some time, but that didn't mean it *couldn't* be moved. It was certainly worth a try.

But first, he had to do something about his arm.

He looked down at the limb in question. Bone gleamed whitely in the darkness. One break, close to his elbow. It would heal with time but, right now, time was the one thing he didn't have much of. He looked back at the ladder. Muck and silt had built up over the years, and the bottom rung was half buried and looked rustier than the rest of the ladder. If he could break it off, it would make a good splint.

He wrapped his fingers around it, took a deep breath, then pulled with all his strength. It came away with a snap that jarred every part of him. A scream tore up his throat, but became nothing more than another hiss of air through clenched teeth. Sweat stung his eyes, and for several seconds, everything went red. He wasn't sure if it was blood or pain.

Gradually his vision cleared, and he saw he was clenching a one-foot section of the rung. What in hell was he going to tie it with?

He stared into the darkness and listened to the restless stirrings of the fledgling's. They'd attack soon. Farmer had obviously stepped past the distance from which he could control them—or perhaps he wasn't even aware there were such limits. Either way, the blood-craze was stirring the 'boys' into a frenzy of lust and wanting. And he was fresh meat all too close, all too tempting.

He slipped off his shoes then edged off his socks. Hooked them, one at a time, between his toes and held them up so he could grab them with his good hand. He positioned the rung on his chest then carefully took hold of his broken arm and eased it towards the pipe. He knew it would hurt and it did.

When the red haze had once more cleared, he clumsily secured his socks around both his arm and the rung. Then pulled the bottom of his shirt from his jeans, undid the bottom button and pulled it up over his arm, reattaching it to one of the top buttons. As slings went, it wasn't the best. But it was the best he could do.

He turned his attention to the chain holding him captive. It was thick and strong, but the ladder to which it was attached wasn't. He carefully edged into a sitting position, thrust his bare feet against the ladder, grabbed a fist full of chain and pulled back hard.

Against the strength of his desperation, the ladder had little hope. The rusted side gave way with a snap that sent him sprawling backwards. Through a haze of pain he heard the sudden silence, felt the surge of panic and lust.

Saw the red glazed eyes of the fledglings as they rushed towards him.

Fifteen

Nikki stared at Jake, not wanting to believe his words even though she knew them to be true. "Maybe she just missed the flight."

"She didn't even check in." Jake scrubbed a hand across his face. "God, I should have gone into the airport with her. Should have escorted her to that plane."

"None of us thought Farmer would go after her in the daylight," Nikki said, trying to ease her own guilt as much as his. Lord, if only she hadn't been so consumed with her own problems, maybe she would have seen this coming . . .

"We have to find her. Now. Tonight."

"Yes." And there was only one way they were going to do that—with her psychometry skills. But finding strangers and finding someone she knew and loved were two entirely different propositions. She wasn't sure she was strong enough to handle what Farmer might be doing to Mary . . .

Farmer. He'd want them to know. Want them—or her—to choose. She quickly stood. "I have to get back to my room."

Jake looked up. His expression—a mix of fear, guilt and confusion—wrenched her heart. "Why?"

"Because Farmer will try to contact us. Go get something of Mary's then meet me upstairs." She hesitated. "If she's okay when we rescue her, we'll need some place safe to hide her. You able to arrange that?"

He nodded and rose. Rather than waste precious

time waiting for an elevator, she ran up the stairs to her room. Energy tingled across her skin the minute she entered. She kicked the door shut and walked into the bedroom. A man stood there, his image rippling, as if it were a pond in which a stone had just been thrown. She hesitated in the doorway, but the image gave no indication he'd sensed her.

Farmer was just as she'd pictured—short, thickset in a powerful sort of way, and balding. He wore dirty looking jeans, heavy black boots, a zipped leather jacket that struggled to hold in his stomach, and over that, a sleeveless jean jacket.

She slowly walked around him. On the back of his jean jacket were his gang colors—*The Shadows*. A somewhat appropriate name for a vampire gang. She finished her tour and stopped in front of him. His eyes were small and mean looking, his mouth thin and petulant.

He showed no sign of realizing she was there. She frowned, wondering why—then remembered she was wearing Seline's charm. She retreated, took it off, then went back into the bedroom. His image came to life almost immediately.

"So." His voice didn't match his tough appearance, tending to be high, almost feminine. "We finally meet."

"We're not exactly meeting."

His smile revealed bloodied canines. A chill ran down her back. *God, don't let that blood be Mary's . . . or Michael's.*

"I suppose, technically, you're right. But we will meet in person soon, have no fear of that."

She had plenty of fears about that. She crossed her arms, suddenly glad this image wasn't real. At least

Farmer couldn't taste her apprehension. Couldn't hear the rapid pounding of her pulse.

"What do you want, Farmer?"

"I suppose you know I have your lover?"

She nodded tightly.

"What you probably don't know is that I also have the woman you consider your second mother."

She kept her face stony. Disbelieving. They needed to buy time. Needed to make Farmer believe they *didn't* believe. "Bullshit. We sent her away on a plane this morning."

"I'm afraid I just couldn't let that happen. Not when I had so many delicious plans for her."

God, if Mary had been a captive of this madman since this morning, there was no saying what sort of condition they'd find her in now. He may have been taking his time with his earlier victims, but time was the one thing running out on him now. He may have decided to just do her quick ... Bile rose in her throat, and she swallowed heavily.

"I don't believe you," she said, forcing her voice to remain flat. "It was daylight. Neither you nor your fledglings can move around in the sun."

Farmer chuckled. It was a cold sound that churned her already agitated stomach.

"Ah, but I didn't have to breach the sun's barrier. I just took over the mind of another and had him kidnap her for me."

She clenched her fists, fighting the urge to smack the image's smug smile from his face. "You're just playing mind games, you bastard."

"Actually, no. Both my parents were married." He snorted softly at his own joke. His image wavered as he shifted his stance, and electricity stirred the tiny hairs along her arms. "However, perhaps you should call her friend in Long Beach and check. And call the airlines while you're at it, just to see that she didn't board another flight."

"I will, believe me."

His smile widened. His canines were wicked points that dug past his bottom lip. She rubbed her arms, but it didn't stop the goose bumps fleeing across her skin.

"Good. Then think about the decision you must make. I will let you save one. The other I will destroy. You will have an hour to decide, then I'll reappear to hear your decision."

His image faded a little, then flickered back to full strength. "Oh, and remember, I know everything you do, so don't think you can mount a rescue attempt for either of them without me knowing. You move from that hotel room, and I'll kill them both. Clear?"

"Clear," she murmured between clenched teeth.

His image disappeared just as Jake walked into the room. "What was that?"

"Message from Farmer. We've got an hour, then he's going to kill either Mary or Michael." Though she seriously doubted Farmer had *any* intention of letting her save even one.

Jake took a deep, shuddering breath. "At least that means they're both currently alive."

"Hopefully. Did you manage to find some sort of safe house?"

He nodded. "Friend of mine owns a boat. It's ours for the next couple of days." He handed her a business card with all the details scrawled on the back.

She slipped it into her pocket. "Did you find something of Mary's?"

"Bra."

He placed the white garment in her hand. Almost instantly images assaulted her, hitting her mind so hard she staggered back several steps.

Jake grabbed her arm. "What's wrong?"

"Nothing." She flicked the bra out of her palm, holding it by her fingertips near the catch. The flood slowed to a trickle of shadows that, at least, she could cope with.

"Is there a problem with the bra?"

"No. I was just caught off guard by the sheer power of the images." She moved out into the living room and sat down on one of the sofas. Placing the bra on the coffee table, she grimly met Jake's look. "This is going to be extremely dangerous. If the images I got just then were any indication, the minute I try to find where she is, I'm going to link right into her mind. Which means I'll be seeing and feeling everything she does."

Jake stared at her, face paler than before. "Dear God . . ."

"Exactly. I could lose myself in her, especially with Michael not here to pull me out."

"If you think it's too dangerous . . ."

"No." Besides, a little thing like losing her mind was nothing when Mary's life was at stake. She had to at least try. *Had* to. "But you'll have to keep close watch on me. If I start looking too stressed, you pull me out, any way you can."

He didn't ask how he was supposed to do that. He obviously knew she had as little idea as he did.

"When I nod, place the bra in my hand." She edged back on the sofa and crossed her legs. Closing her eyes, she breathed, slow and deep, trying to follow the process Michael had shown her. Only he'd been there to help her, guard her . . .

Fear rose. She chased it away. She had no time for that now.

Breathe in, breathe out. Slow. Rhythmic. Gradually, the tension began to leave her limbs and her mind. She lowered her barriers, felt the buzz of expectation run through her psychic senses.

She opened her hand and nodded. The minute the bra touched her hand, images burned through her soul. She wrapped her fingers around the material, pressing it into her palm.

Her senses leaped away, following the trail that led to Mary. Shapes began to form. Fear trembled through her.

She thrust it from her again and concentrated on Mary. Imagined their thoughts as two separate streams that ran side by side, touching but not merging.

Then she reached—and was swept into Mary's thoughts . . .

. . . The darkness moved. Breathed. Fear shuddered through her, so strong it caught in her throat, making it difficult to catch her breath. She tried to shift back. The bed rocked underneath her, creaking loudly— but not loudly enough to cover the rattle of the chains that held her. They were tight, biting into her wrists and ankles.

Two blue lights appeared in the night. Eyes, she realized. Eyes ringed by bloody red. Teeth gleamed at her. Sharp, bloody canines.

Oh God . . .

She'd heard Jake talking about vampires. She'd never truly believed him.

Until now.

She whimpered, her breath a shudder her heart

228

pounding so loud it seemed to echo not only in her ears but through the night itself.

The eyes moved closer. Became a man. A man whose teeth were extending even further.

She couldn't scream. Couldn't do anything. Simply stared in horror at the thickset man approaching her. Her heart raced so hard it hurt, and she couldn't seem to breathe fast enough.

"Do you know who I am?"

He was the devil come to life. She could think of nothing more apt for the man who stood in front of her. An odd sort of mewling sound rose up her throat, and she edged away.

He clamped a hand around her ankle. She kicked at him, but her feet were bare and had little impact. Her blow drew little response beyond a chuckle.

"I'm gathering you don't, so allow me to introduce myself. I am Billie Farmer, the man whose high school years were hell thanks to you and your upmarket cronies."

Her eyes widened at the name. Beads of sweat rolled down her face, even though she felt so cold she was shivering.

His hands were like fire as they slipped up her legs and forced them apart. His fingers stroked her thigh, his touch bruising. *Oh God, oh God* . . . She began to struggle, desperate to get away from his touch, his intentions.

"And now I shall return the favor." His voice was still conversational. Almost friendly. The chill in her body increased as he continued, "Your final hours here on Earth will make hell seem like a holiday resort."

His teeth dripped blood onto her thigh. It was a liquid heat that seemed to burn like acid. Her breath caught and her heart seemed to stutter to a halt. Then he lowered his head and his teeth sank into her flesh, tearing and sucking, and all she could do was try to scream . . .

. . . Cold water slapped her face, all but drowning her. Nikki blinked, shuddering, as the link between her and Mary snapped. For several seconds she did nothing more than breathe deeply, trying to ease the fierce churning in her stomach. Trying to ignore the horror and fear pounding through her.

God, Mary didn't deserve what this monster was about to do to her. *None* of these women had. He had to be stopped. *She* had to stop him. Tonight. No matter what.

She wiped her sleeve across her face then looked around. She was at the opposite end of the sofa and no longer held Mary's bra—it was on the floor under the coffee table. She doubted if she'd thrown it there—Jake must have wrenched it free to help break the connection between her and Mary.

He moved across the room, a glass of water held in one hand. He squatted in front of her, his fingers shaking as he touched her forehead. "Are you okay?"

She nodded and grabbed the glass he held, drinking it quickly. And noted her hands were shaking almost as much as his.

His gaze continued to search hers. "And Mary?"

She couldn't lie to him, as much as she wanted to. He would never forgive her is she was anything less than honest with him. "He's feeding off her." She hesitated, fighting the tears that stung her eyes. "I think he intends to suck her dry."

He didn't move, didn't blink. Just continued to

stare at her in that remote, angry way of his. "Is she still alive at this moment?"

"Yes."

"How long has she got?"

She hesitated. "I don't know." But it wouldn't be long, if what she'd seen was any indication. Her spirit might already be walking that foggy plane.

He thrust to his feet. "Then the sooner we get to her the better. You ready to move?"

Even if she wasn't, she would. Time was of the essence. She rubbed her forehead then looked at the clock. "We have fifty minutes to get in, get her and get back here."

He nodded and swept up the bra, shoving it in a plastic bag before handing it to her. "Where is she?"

"Not in the sewers this time, though I'd guess he's still using them to get around."

"Where then?"

She glanced down at the bag in her hand, contemplating the stirring shadows. Trying not to think too much about the distant but powerful images that spoke more of death than life. "We'll head towards the Castro area. I'll know more once we get there."

"Will we need weapons?"

"I don't know. Maybe."

"Then let's go get some, then go rescue my wife."

He spun and stalked from the room. Nikki grabbed her coat and Seline's charm and ran after him. But even as she closed the door, she knew they were going to be too late.

Michael barely had time to jump to his feet before the fledglings were on him. He staggered back until he hit the wall, but they still tore at him, using hands and teeth, greedily sucking where they cut. Their desperation stung the air, making it difficult to breathe. His head swam with pain, and the room was drifting in and out of focus. But he couldn't let go. If he did, he was dead. Not because they'd suck him dry, but because in their desperation they'd tear him apart.

One fledgling ripped into his broken arm. Pain flashed white-hot and a scream tore up his throat. Gritting his teeth, his breath little more than a hiss, he rolled the chain around his knuckles then punched the youngster in the face. The blow wasn't full strength—couldn't be, given the amount of blood he'd lost—but the chain still shattered the fledgling's nose. Gore flew, spraying across his face. His mouth watered as the darkness in him rose, eager to taste the sweet offering. He swallowed heavily and hit the young vampire again. This time the blow was hard enough to make the fledgling stagger backwards. The minute he did he was dead. The smell of his blood stung the air, and two of his loop mates swooped down on him, too consumed by the need raging in their blood to consider who or what they were killing.

Which left him with only one. He wrapped the chain around the youngster's neck and pulled it tight. The fledgling didn't notice, just continued to suck greedily at his flesh. Michael took a deep breath, gathering strength, then ripped the youngster free and smashed him against the wall.

There was a sound similar to wet meat splattering, then the fledgling slumped to the ground. Not dead yet. But certainly more bait for his loop mates, which would buy *him* more time. But he had to get going. Had to move while he still could.

He pushed away from the wall. The night swam around him, unfocused and blurry. He blinked, but it didn't seem to help. Weakness crept through his limbs until it felt as if every muscle trembled. Too much blood lost. Too much pain.

Nothing he could do about either.

He edged closer to the ladder and stared up at the sewer plate. It looked pretty grimy, as if it hadn't been moved in ages. Even if he had the strength to climb the half-shattered ladder, it was doubtful if he'd be able to move the cover. He'd have to find an easier way out.

He stepped past the remaining two fledglings. They didn't even look up, too busy consuming their loop mate. The aroma of blood wrapped around him, and his canines lengthened. He stumbled away, battling the need, the desire, to take what his body so desperately craved.

He stopped at the intersection, swaying slightly as he considered his options. But really, he didn't have any. Farmer had gone left, so he had to go right. The last thing he wanted right now was to run into the fiend. He was in no fit state to battle a mouse, let alone a monster.

He half ran, half stumbled through the darkness, splashing through puddles of muck and God only knew what else. The smell of the sea increased, indicating he was heading towards it rather than away. Sewer plates appeared at regular intervals, but he kept on running, wanting to put some distance between him and the remaining fledglings before he stopped.

Eventually, exhaustion caught up with him. He collapsed against the wall, body bathed in sweat and muscles so weak they almost felt liquid. Had he been human, he'd probably be suffering a heart attack right about now. His pulse rate was unbearably high, even for a vampire. He leaned the back of his head against the wall and closed his eyes, listening to the darkness as he gulped in air. Air he didn't really need but his body seemed to crave.

Footsteps whispered, distant but urgent. The fledglings were coming after him. They were obviously sated, or the second fledgling wasn't as badly injured as he first thought, because there was no way they could have consumed their two loop mates in such a short space of time.

Either that or Farmer was returning and had ordered them away from their feed and after him. He had to get out of these sewers—now.

He staggered on to the next cover. Climbing the ladder was an awkward and painful process. He lurched from one rung to the next, pulling himself up one-handed, jarring his broken arm with every movement. By the time he reached the top his muscles burned and his vision was so blurred he couldn't see his arms.

Hooking one leg through a rung to hold himself steady, he pressed his hand against the cover and pushed with every ounce of strength he had left. For several seconds nothing happened. Sweat dripped in a steady stream down his face, stinging his eyes. Something popped, as if a seal had broken, then the cover disappeared with a suddenness that almost had him falling backwards.

Fog swirled through the darkness above. Obviously, he hadn't been unconscious for as long as he'd feared. He gripped the rim and pulled himself up, then rolled onto his back as he breathed deep the salty tang.

As the rasp of his breath eased, sounds encroached. The gentle roar of traffic mixed with the pounding of waves. Beyond that, the trumpeting of an elephant.

He blinked. Was there a zoo in San Francisco, or was he imagining things?

He hoped it was the former rather than the latter. A zoo would be the perfect place to sate his hunger without endangering anyone—or anything. And while an elephant's hide was far too tough for his teeth to pierce, a zoo would undoubtedly have giraffes or bison or even zebras.

The trembling eased. He found the sewer cover and slipped it back into place, then sniffed the night air, searching for the scent of hay, dung and animals. It came from up ahead. He looped the chain into his hand and staggered forward.

Farmer would undoubtedly come looking for him. He had to revive his system, had to be alert and free of these chains. Had to be ready to fight and kill the fiend. Before Nikki came to do it for him.

Nikki. He longed to call her, let her know he was okay and free. But he couldn't. Until Seline's charm arrived, Farmer was still connected to her. If *he* called, she'd undoubtedly come rushing to help him—and lead Farmer straight to them both.

Besides, calling her to his rescue would be far too dangerous. In his current condition he doubted if he'd be able to resist the lure of her blood. She was the first human he'd tasted in well over a hundred years, and while he had the urge to drink from her well under control in normal circumstances, not enough time had slipped by yet to make him forget the taste. If she found him like this, he'd kill her. He had no doubt of that.

Maybe that was what Farmer had been intending. Maybe that was why they'd fed off that woman in his presence—to work his need into a fever pitch so he'd attack when the slightest chance came.

He shuffled on, his steps becoming shorter as his weakness grew. A huge fence came into sight. He found a gate but could sense no guards, though he knew, logically, they'd have to be here somewhere. He raised a hand and dredged up kinetic energy from God knew where. The gates flew open, and he entered, finding himself in a courtyard. A type of shop lay just ahead, and other smaller buildings to his left, containing smaller animals if the patter of their hearts was anything to go by. He switched to the infrared of his vampire vision. And saw the alarm on the gate. Security would undoubtedly be on their way.

He swore softly and blurred into the night. And not a moment too soon. Twin beams of lights cut across the darkness, and with it came the red blur of human heat.

His canines lengthened in anticipation. His body was so desperate for blood it was getting ready to feed on anything—and if he wasn't very careful, that's exactly what would happen. Swearing softly again, he retreated in search of zebra.

Nikki climbed out of the car. For a minute, everything whirled and her knees felt like water. She grabbed the door for support and took several deep breaths. The sensation slithered away, but unease rose in its place. The strange old blind woman had suggested that she and Michael were capable of sharing energy. Was he so badly hurt he was beginning to siphon her reserves?

God, she hoped not. She couldn't survive losing him.

She took another deep breath then turned to study

the building in front of her. Though it made no sense, the sensations emanating from the bra were coming from an empty shop in the middle of a busy shopping strip.

Why would Farmer choose a place like this? It wasn't what she'd call safe, particularly if his victim tried to scream. . . .

Mary had tried to scream. No sound had come out—maybe because her voice was lost to the horror of her situation. Nikki's stomach churned, and a chill crept down her spine. She didn't want to think about that chill. Didn't want to think about the instinct that suggested there could be other reasons why Mary hadn't screamed.

Jake told the driver to wait then joined her on the sidewalk. "This the place?"

She rubbed her arms. She didn't want to go inside. Didn't want to find what she suspected she might find. Tears stung her eyes, but she tried to ignore them. "Yes."

"Not exactly what I expected."

"No."

She looked to her left then right. No one sitting at the nearby café tables was paying any particular attention. And they wouldn't, as long as both of them looked as if they had every right to be here.

She strode up to the door and raised her hand, as if inserting a key. Instead, she pushed kinetically at the lock and opened the door.

She stepped through but stopped just inside the doorway, listening to the silence. Searching the darkness with her psychic senses, trying to find the scent of evil. Farmer wasn't here at the moment.

Jake closed the door behind them then flicked on the flashlight. The bright light cut across the shadows, highlighting old bits of furniture and lots of dust. "Where do we go?"

"Up. She was chained to a bed, and the darkness had an airy feel. It certainly wasn't a basement or anything like that."

"There's some comfort in that, I guess."

It was no comfort—not to Mary, not to her and certainly not to him, if the crack in his voice was anything to go by. She walked to the other end of the narrow shop and found a set of stairs behind a half wall. Jake handed her a flashlight, and she shone the light upwards. Nothing but shadows and cobwebs. If Mary was up there, she was making no sound.

Because she couldn't . . .

Bile rose in Nikki's throat. She swallowed heavily and edged up the stairs, pausing between each step, listening to the silence and testing the air for the approach of evil.

Three steps from the landing she paused and carefully peered through the railings. The room beyond was dark and quiet. No sound of breathing. No sound of life.

Not that she had truly expected any.

She swallowed a sob. Holding back guilt, holding back pain, she forced her feet up those final three steps. The beam of her flashlight cut across the darkness and centered on the bed.

Mary lay on it. Naked, chained and bloody.

Dead.

Sixteen

Nikki didn't say anything. Couldn't say anything. For several seconds she just stared, taking in the bloody evidence of horror. Taking in the open, screaming mouth and the stump that had once been a tongue.

A sob escaped. She raised a hand to her mouth and put out her other hand to stop Jake. He pushed past angrily then froze. For several seconds neither of them moved. Then with a sound that was half groan, half anguished denial, he rushed towards his wife. Dropping to his knees, he touched her neck, feeling for the pulse Nikki knew he would never find.

He made another broken sound and gathered Mary's lifeless body in his arms. Nikki bit her lip, battling for control. She couldn't give in to anguish just yet. She had to stay alert in case Farmer returned.

She glanced at her watch and saw they had less than forty minutes to get back to the hotel. Or *she* did. She doubted if Jake would leave Mary's body so soon.

Tears trickled down her face. She took a deep, shuddering breath, then dragged her phone out of her pocket and called the ambulance and the cops.

"Jake?"

He didn't answer. Just continued to sob and cradle Mary.

"Jake, I have to go. I can't be here when the cops get here, or I won't get back in time to catch Farmer's message. He can't know . . ." Her voice broke. She swiped at her eyes and continued, "He can't know we know."

"I'm going to kill that bastard," Jake muttered.

"We'll get him, don't worry."

"Not we. Me." He looked up. His face was ravaged, eyes bloodshot. "Promise me you won't go after him without me."

"Jake—"

"Promise me!" His voice was savage, his eyes intense.

"Jake, I don't want to lose you, too."

"You won't. I'll kill him for this. And nothing, or nobody, is going to stop me from doing it."

She hesitated, then said, "Okay. I promise."

He nodded and went back to his grieving. From a distance came the sound of sirens. She had to get out while she could. She swiped at her eyes then walked forward. Jake didn't move, just continued to gently rock Mary back and forth. She brushed a kiss across Mary's head and bid her a silent good-bye.

A wispy cloud swirled past Jake, catching her eye. She frowned, wondering how the fog had gotten inside the room when there were no windows open. The mist drifted past again, briefly forming something almost human. Nikki's stomach dropped. It wasn't fog. It was a spirit—a ghost.

Mouth dry, she watched the thing, wondering if it was Mary's spirit or someone else's. She could find out . . . but was either she or Jake really ready to confront Mary if it was?

"Jake?"

He looked up. "What?"

"I think Mary's spirit may be in this room."

He didn't react in any way, simply stared at her. She raised her hands. "Don't ask me to explain how or why, but it appears I'm developing the talent to see ghosts."

"Like the movie?"

"Not as graphic or as clear as the movie, but yeah."

"And she's here?" His voice was an odd mix of hope and apprehension.

"It may be her, or it maybe someone else." The mist swirled in the one spot, as if listening to what she was saying. "I can't say for sure until I empower it."

"Then do it."

She met his gaze. "You sure?"

He nodded. "At the very least, it gives me the chance to apologize. To say good-bye."

It would give them both the chance to do that. She looked back to the misty form and took a deep breath. Its movements had quickened, as if in excitement. Closing her eyes, Nikki reached out. With her hand and with her psychic gifts.

Fog caressed her fingers, but it was warm rather than cold and damp. Something latched on to her psychic probe—she could feel the drain of energy flowing through her fingertips, though it was more a trickle than the rush that happened whenever she used her kinetic skills.

Jake made an odd, strangled sort of noise in the back of his throat. She opened her eyes. It was Mary who touched her fingers.

"I'm sorry," Jake whispered brokenly. "I'm so sorry."

Mary brushed a hand across his head. His hair stirred, as if touched by electricity rather than flesh. "You did what you thought was best. It's not your fault this happened."

241

"But I could've—"

"No." Her voice was gentle and somehow ethereal. Though her skin seemed to hold color, there was little substance to her flesh. "It was my time. Destiny cannot be changed. Only the location."

Michael had changed Nikki's destiny. He'd loved her enough to snatch her from death's arms, and yet here she was, ready to walk away because he refused to share one part of his life. Tears rolled down her cheeks. She was a fool. After everything he'd been through, after everything he'd done for her, he deserved far more consideration than that.

Deserved far better than her.

"You asked for revenge." Mary looked Nikki's way. "That is what I also wish. Let us be a part of this monster's death."

Fragile wisps of vapor stirred the darkness beyond Mary. More ghosts, probably. Nikki had no doubt it was the other women Farmer had killed here in San Francisco.

"I'm new to all this. I don't know if I can handle more than one. Especially if I have to touch you all." Not to mention the fact that standing still when someone like Farmer was around could be extremely dangerous.

"You don't have to touch us."

Nikki glanced down at their joined hands. "Then why do you hold my hand?"

Mary's smile was wistful. "Because you needed it. Because I can."

The tears spilling down her cheeks became a flood. Nikki drew another deep breath and somehow managed to say, "I'm sorry we weren't here sooner."

"So am I." Mary brushed a gossamer finger across

Jake's damp cheek. "Take care, my love. I'll be waiting for you when it's your turn to cross."

"No, don't—"

Mary faded. Jake made an anguished sound and hugged his wife's body fiercely. The sound of sirens was perilously close.

"Jake, I have to go."

He nodded. Her gaze swept the darkness, seeing mist shimmer in the corner. He wasn't alone, and of that she was glad. She turned and made her way down the stairs.

Police cars rounded the corner as she stepped onto the sidewalk. She walked down a couple of shops then stopped, watching the three cars screech to a halt and the officers pile out. The F.B.I. agents were among those who entered the shop. At least Jake would be relatively safe now.

She headed to the limo and asked the driver to take her back to the hotel. She'd barely entered her room when electricity shimmered across her skin. Farmer was early. Or maybe he was just checking whether she was still here.

She slipped off the charm and walked into the bedroom. "If you've hurt them, you bastard, I'll kill you."

He snorted. "Isn't that what you intended anyway?"

"Yeah, but I'd intended it to be quick. You'll have no such luxury if you've hurt either one of them."

"I haven't hurt them. Just played with them a little."

Liar, liar ... God, she hoped Michael was still alive—surely she would have felt it if he'd died? He was a part of her, she a part of him. The two of them were bound together forever, so surely she *would* feel his passing ... and the very fact she wasn't sure scared the hell out of her. Farmer had already gone back on his word once. There was nothing to say he hadn't done it twice.

"Let them go."

He gave her a Cheshire cat sort of smile. "Have you chosen?"

She crossed her arms. There was only one choice now, but he wasn't to know she was aware of that. "No. And I have no intention of doing so."

"Then they both die."

"No!"

"Then choose."

"How will I know you'll keep your word?"

He gave her that smile again. "You don't."

"Bastard."

"Choose."

She took a deep breath. "Michael."

"Obviously, the fight he mentioned wasn't as deep as he'd feared."

If Michael had mentioned their relationship to Farmer, then he was in a *bad* way. He wouldn't talk to her about it, so why would he do so with a stranger—an enemy?

"Where is he, Farmer?"

"Somewhere safe. You'll have to come and get him, of course."

She snorted. "Yeah, that would be real wise, wouldn't it?"

Farmer raised an eyebrow. "If you don't, he's dead."

They were all dead anyway, unless she was very careful. And very lucky. "Where and when?"

He considered the question for several seconds, though she had no doubt he had this all planned to the very last detail.

"You'll find a park on the corner of Vincente and Twenty-eighth Avenue in Sunset. Meet me there just before dawn."

Why dawn? That was nearly six hours away. "Why not meet now?"

"Because that is what I wish, and that is what you will do."

He was a cocky bastard, that was for sure. She was going to enjoy wiping that smug smile off his face. "Michael had better be alive."

"He will be."

She didn't trust the light in his eyes. Didn't trust the smile that played about his mouth. He was up to something, though she had no idea what—beyond the fact that it boded no good for her.

Farmer's image faded. She retrieved the charm and slipped it back on, then made herself some coffee. Cup in hand, she walked across to the window and stared out on the foggy night.

She had to rescue Michael before that meeting. She didn't trust Farmer one iota, and if they could get Michael out and hidden before dawn, the advantage would fall on their side. They could walk in and confront him without having to worry about anyone's safety but their own.

The trick was finding Michael and getting him out. She placed the cup on the sill and reached into her pocket, drawing out the silver cross.

Warmth pulsed through her palm. She clenched her fingers around the cross and closed her eyes, reaching for any images that might lie within the cross's heart. Nothing. Michael was alive, but he was still mind dead. She couldn't connect with him, not through the cross and not through the link.

She opened her eyes, her gaze drawn to the southwest. He was there. And in need of help.

She grabbed a pen, scrawled a note to Jake then grabbed her coat and ran out into the night.

Michael eased over the enclosure wall and padded quietly toward the exit. Though his thirst was finally sated, he felt no more energetic. His body had taken a pounding over the last few hours, and it had pushed his natural healing capabilities to the extreme. It would be days before he regained full strength.

And they certainly didn't have days left. Farmer had to be killed long before then.

The guards were still near the exit. He wrapped the shadows around himself, but even that small task had sweat running down his face. Once outside and beyond the sight of the two men, he stopped and leaned back against the fence, sucking in great gulps of air.

Everything still hurt, his arm most of all. It would have to be reset, and soon, before the bone began to knit in its current position. He closed his eyes, listening to the sounds washing across the darkness as he tasted the flavors of the cold night.

The slight scent of antiseptic told him there was a hospital close by somewhere, but between him and it came the smell of evil. The remaining fledglings were on the prowl and closing in. He'd never be able to outrun them. He didn't have the strength, and once they'd caught his scent, they'd be on him quicker than dogs on a bone.

He'd have to make a stand here. At least he could keep his back to the fence. He reached up, gripping one of the branches that dipped over the top of the fence and broke it off. Snapping it in two, he pulled off all the leaves and twigs until two jagged stakes were left. All he could do now was wait.

The seconds ticked by. His eyelids began to droop, and he forced them open again. But it was a battle he was bound to lose. A vampire healed mainly in sleep. Now that his hunger was sated, his body demanded rest. He shifted his stance and listened again to the sounds of the night. Footsteps whispered, drawing ever closer.

He gripped the stakes tighter and switched to his vampire vision. The shadows retreated, and three fiery figures came into view. The fledglings, moving in fast.

Sweat rolled down his face. Under normal circumstances, these three would be little more than nuisances easily swatted away. But given his current condition, the pendulum had certainly swung their way.

Two went high, one went low. He stabbed wildly, striking one in the stomach rather than the heart. The fledgling screamed in agony, his flesh smoking where it touched the wood. White ash was best, but any wood was dangerous to vampires as young as these.

One tore into his good arm, the second into his leg. He kicked it away, almost unbalancing in the process, then thrust his arm backwards, smacking the fledgling feeding on it against the fence. It did little more than ripple the chain links. It certainly didn't dislodge the fledgling. Pain became a wall threatening to topple him. He hissed, flipped the stake, and thrust it into the youngster's chin and up, through flesh and bone and brain. The fledgling was dead before he fell.

Which still left two others. He grabbed the hair of one and flung him away, but the second grabbed

247

his broken arm and twisted it. White-hot lances of fire flashed through his brain, and a scream was ripped from his throat. He dropped to his knees, unable to stand, unable to do anything. Barely even conscious.

The fledgling's touch disappeared. This is it, he thought. This is the end. Nikki's image swam through his mind, and a bitter taste invaded his mouth. After three hundred years of emptiness, fate could have allowed him a little more time for happiness . . .

No attack came. Through the haze of agony he thought he heard the sound of fighting, but it might have just been the roaring in his ears. He stayed on his knees for what seemed like hours, fighting unconsciousness and waiting for death.

Hands touched him. Hands that were warm and smelled vaguely of cinnamon and vanilla. Wishful thinking, surely. With the link out of action and his psychic gifts blocked by drugs, she had no way of finding him so quickly.

"Michael?" Her voice was soft, edgy, as if she were crying. "Can you hear me?"

God, was there a sweeter sound on this Earth? He wanted to wake up to those tones for the rest of his days . . .

"You have to stay with me," she pleaded. "I'm here alone, and you're too heavy to lift."

"Why?" His voice came out little more than a hoarse whisper, and even the effort of that one word had his head swimming.

Her laugh had a brittle sound to it. "Always questioning my decisions, even at a time like this."

It wasn't his intention to question her actions. He'd just wanted to know where Jake was. He couldn't force his eyes open, but he reached out, running his fingers down her cheek. It was as wet as his.

She leaned into his touch for a second, then her lips pressed into his palm. "No time for details," she continued softly. Power surged, and the chains rattled as they dropped from his wrists. "We have to get you somewhere safe. You ready to move?"

He wouldn't be ready to move for at least several hours. But he couldn't stay here, either. Farmer would find him all too easily.

Might even be searching for him now. He would have felt the fledglings die.

"Not ... hotel," he said. It was the second place Farmer would come looking for him.

"No." She shifted, her arm slipping under his. "Ready?"

He nodded. There was little else he could do. She counted to three then thrust upwards. He helped the best he could, but the pain became a wall of agony that rushed through his body. His breath left in a hiss of air, and sweat rolled down his spine and legs. More drips ran past his fingers. Or maybe that was blood. The fledglings had torn into his battered flesh, so anything was possible.

"The limo isn't far away. You think you can walk?"

What other choice did he have? She couldn't carry him kinetically—it would drain her energy to a point where she'd be defenseless should Farmer attack. She shifted her grip, her shoulder sliding under his good arm. Together, they stumbled forward.

But her version of not very far away and his seemed to be vastly different. They'd barely moved ten feet, and the night was little more than a dizzy blur. His breath was a desperate gasp of air and his muscles were liquid heat, barely able to support his weight. If it wasn't for Nikki, he would have fallen.

Her breathing was as sharp as his, and the smell of her sweat and fear stung the night air. He wanted to comfort her, to tell her he'd be all right after an hour or so of sleep. But the words stuck in his mouth, refusing to pass his battered lips. Footsteps hurriedly approached, then another set of hands grabbed him, carefully easing him into the car.

"You'll have to take him to the hospital, Miss."

The voice was male, one he didn't recognize.

"No. It's not safe there for him at the moment."

"But his arm will need attention, and he's lost a lot of blood—"

"I'm a nurse." Her voice held a steely determination, indicating she was barely controlling her anger. "I can take care of him. Please, just get us to the boat as quickly as you can."

The driver's grunt wasn't exactly a sound of agreement. A door slammed shut, then Nikki's scent surround him. He breathed deeply the sweet smell and allowed himself to relax a little. The need to sleep was almost overwhelming, but he refused to give in to it just yet. A moist cloth touched his face, gently wiping the muck and blood away. He forced open his good eye.

Her amber eyes were bright with tears. "You're a goddamn mess."

He would have smiled if it didn't hurt so much. "Yeah." Even that one word hurt, but he couldn't leave it there when there were questions that had to be answered. "Jake?"

Tears washed her amber eyes, trickled down her cheeks. He raised a hand, thumbing them gently away. Something bad had obviously happened in his absence—though surely not to Jake. She'd be in a worse state than this if it was.

She dunked the cloth into water and gently wiped his mouth. "Mary's dead." Her voice was flat, but the drugs blocking his psychic abilities had to be fading because her pain was a tide of agony that overwhelmed anything he was feeling.

He wrapped his arm around her and pulled her close. She buried her face against his chest, her tears searing his skin. He held her while she sobbed, offering her no words of comfort simply because there were none that could ever erase such pain. Only time could dim it.

After a few minutes, he croaked, "How?"

She sniffed and pulled away from his touch. "He snatched her from the airport. I guess we have to be thankful it was relatively quick. He cut out her tongue so she couldn't scream, then he drank her dry." She hesitated, swallowing heavily. "Jake's with the police at the moment. He'll meet us at the boat when he can."

"Why . . . boat?"

She shrugged. "It belongs to a friend of Jake's. And we knew we couldn't risk leaving either of you at the hotel."

He nodded. If Farmer hadn't already discovered his escape, he soon would. And the hotel was the first place he'd look. Unless, of course, he'd reached out to Nikki. He might even now be tracking their movements. "The charm?"

"Arrived earlier this evening." She shoved up her sleeve, revealing the coin-entwined rope charm. "When I'm wearing it, Farmer has no sense of me."

He frowned. "How do you know?"

She hesitated, her gaze suddenly evasive. "Long story. I'll tell you when you regain some strength."

"Nikki—"

She placed a gentle finger against his bruised lips. "Now is not the time for arguments or lectures. Besides, we're here."

Masts rose beyond the tinted window. The car stopped, and a few seconds later the door opened. The smell of the ocean swept in, followed by the gentle sound of lapping waves.

The driver stuck his head in. "I'll give you a hand to the yacht, Miss, then I have to go pick up Mister Morgan."

"Thanks, Henry."

Hands grabbed Michael, hauling him out of the car as gently as possible. The driver was a big man and basically carried him down the jetty to the boat. Nikki moved forward, disappearing briefly from sight. She came back with a key and unlocked the doors.

The driver deposited him onto a bed then straightened. "I'm off, now, Miss."

"Thanks."

The driver nodded, cast a dubious gaze his way, then retreated. Nikki took a deep breath then sat down next to him. "I'm going to have to reset that arm, aren't I?"

"I'll pull it straight, but you're going to have to splint and wrap it, because I'll be close to unconsciousness."

She bit her lip but nodded. "And blood? Your clothes are practically stiff with it. Will you need to feed soon?"

"I have, at the zoo." He touched a hand to her lips, wishing he could kiss them. *I really will be fine.*

Her eyes widened slightly, then a wave of love flooded the link, drowning him in its warmth.

God, I missed this. She brushed a kiss across his fingertips. *I didn't realize until the link was gone just how much I'd grown used to having you so close.*

Nor I. But now was not the time to show her just how much he'd missed it. Missed her. *I'm going to have to sleep soon, so my body can begin to heal itself. We'll have to hurry to set my arm before then.*

She nodded. *What do we need?*

Bandages. Something to splint my arm so it can't move while the bones are knitting.

She nodded again and moved away. He closed his good eye, listening to her searching through cupboards and drawers.

"Okay, got both."

He took a deep breath and looked at her. *Undo the makeshift splint.*

That's certainly a novel use for socks. Though her mind voice held a note of amusement, it was countered by the trembling in her fingers. She didn't want to do this—but then, neither did he.

The socks and the bar supporting his arm slipped away and agony threatened. He took a deep breath, fighting the tide.

"Okay, what next?"

I'll set the bone into place using my vampire vision, then you'll have to quickly splint and wrap it.

She nodded again. He switched to infrared vision and looked at his arm. His flesh disappeared, became instead a glowing beacon of sinew, veins and bone. The break was fairly clean, despite the fact one end of the bone had punctured skin.

He took another deep breath then grabbed his wrist and pulled. A scream tore up his throat. He swallowed the scream and sucked down air, battling the urge to be ill, fighting the darkness and the pain that made his head swim and threatened to sweep him into unconsciousness. Sweat rolled into his eyes. He blinked furiously, staring at his arm, watching the bone slide back through skin and into place.

Now.

She quickly began to splint and bandage his arm. The darkness threatened again, but he forced it away, watching his arm, making sure the bone stayed in place while she worked on it.

But once she'd finished, he finally gave in and let unconsciousness sweep him away.

Footsteps echoed on the deck above them. Nikki rose and walked quietly to the door. The night air was free from the taint of evil, so it couldn't be Farmer or any of his fledglings. Though how they'd find them so quickly she didn't know. Still, she'd learned the hard way never to underestimate the bad guys.

She grabbed the broom handle she'd sharpened to use as a weapon and edged up the ladder. Shoes and jeans came into sight, then a torso. It was Jake.

"You want something to drink?" she said, backing down the ladder again.

He shook his head. He looked haggard, old beyond his years, and just about ready to drop with exhaustion. It was his thirst for vengeance getting him through this, nothing more. "I just want this all over with."

Didn't they all. She sat down at the table and wrapped her hands around the coffee cup. "Did the police say anything?"

He shrugged as he dropped down on the bench

seat. "The usual. The FBI wanted to know where the hell you were."

She raised an eyebrow. "Why?"

"Because I think they suspect we have every intention of going after this madman and administering our own form of justice."

"Their justice wouldn't stop a man like Farmer."

"No. But they don't see it that way."

"No."

Jake leaned back and scrubbed a hand across his bristly chin. It made a sound similar to sandpaper. "How's Michael?"

Her gaze went to the bedroom door. He hadn't stirred, hadn't even twitched, for the last two hours—not even when she'd stripped him down and bathed him. God, she'd never seen so many bruises on one body before . . .

"He's in a bad way. I doubt he'll be awake by dawn."

"So it's just you and me?"

You, me and the ghosts, she thought, and tried to ignore the chill that ran down her spine. "Did you bring the weapons?"

He nodded. "Left them up on the deck."

"What, exactly?"

"A couple of stakes, some silver knives, and my gun."

Not much considering they were going up against a madman. She glanced at her watch. "Dawn's in an hour. I'd suggest we get there early so we can check out the area."

"Get where early?" Michael said from the doorway.

"So much for not waking for a few hours," Jake murmured dryly.

She twisted around in the seat. He was leaning against the door frame, the sheet wrapped around his waist and his face still white and bruised—though the swelling had at least gone down a little.

"What the hell are you doing up? You should still be asleep so your body can heal."

"I heard voices," he said, a touch impatiently. "What sort of meeting have you arranged?"

"We've arranged to meet Farmer at dawn." She threw up her shields even as she replied, knowing his anger would boil down the link at her.

"No. I forbid it."

"You can't forbid me, and you're in no damn shape to stop me."

"He's a vampire. You won't even see him coming."

"No, but I'll feel him coming. Smell him."

"Damn it, Nikki—"

"We've coped with far worse than Farmer," Jake said softly. "Even if they were human."

Michael's gaze flicked briefly to him. "You told me once revenge would kill us all. I think that applies here, too."

"You keep asking Nikki to trust the fact that you can keep yourself safe and alive," Jake said. "Why are you not willing to offer her the same?"

"Because this is different."

"No, it's not. And you keep forgetting one vital thing."

"I'm not forgetting anything."

"Yeah, you are. Nikki's no longer human. And she has skills that are more than a match for the likes of Farmer."

"She may have a vampire's life span, but like us, she can still die."

"But only if she is decapitated, right? How is

Farmer going to know that? How is any villain going to know that?"

Michael took a deep breath, perhaps controlling the anger neither of them could see. Yet. "We don't know all there is to know about thralls. There could be other ways of killing them."

"If you don't know, how the hell would someone like Farmer know?"

"That's not the point." The impatience was more noticeable this time and edged with anger.

"That's *precisely* the point. For Christ's sake, you two have something good going here. Don't let stupidity destroy that."

Nikki wrapped a hand around Jake's. "You couldn't have saved Mary, no matter what you did. As she said, it was her time."

"I know. But it's still too fresh, too hard to accept." Jake's gaze met hers. "At least I had the chance to say good-bye and for that, I thank you."

She nodded and looked back at Michael. "You're the one in no fit state to confront Farmer. You can't even stand up straight."

"Dawn's an hour off yet. I'll be stronger by then."

"But not strong enough. Damn it, Michael, you're always berating me for acting foolishly. What do you call wanting to confront Farmer when your energy levels are so low you couldn't even kill three fledglings?"

He frowned. "What happened to the fledglings?"

"I killed the remaining two. And wasn't it you who told me fledglings were more dangerous than older vamps?"

His expression was as dark as she'd ever seen it. Except perhaps that one time in the warehouse when she'd forbidden him to decapitate Monica Trevgard

257

to stop her becoming a vampire. He might have been right then, but he wasn't now. And he knew it, even if he hadn't yet admitted it.

"If you come with us, Farmer will sense you and disappear back into the sewers. And it'll be a whole lot more dangerous for us to try to corner him there."

"So where is he meeting you?"

"In a park. He offered me a choice—Mary's life or yours. But by then, he'd already killed Mary, and I knew it."

"Farmer knows I've escaped."

"But he doesn't know I know. He'll be there."

"And he'll try to destroy you both."

"Undoubtedly. But we won't be alone. We'll have the dead to help us."

He hesitated. "What are you talking about?"

"I'm reliably informed by a blind old ghost that when you pulled me back from death, one small part of me was left behind. That part allows me to walk death's plane—to see ghosts, and bring them into being."

He frowned. "I've never heard of anything like that happening before."

"How many times have you made a thrall before?"

He didn't answer. Didn't need to.

"That same old woman tells me that in giving me part of your life force, you connected our energies together. So, when I'm walking that plane, I suck energy from you. And when you're seriously hurt, you suck energy from me."

"So that's how—"

"You kept going," she finished. "You were siphoning my energy."

"Did you feel it?"

No, she hadn't—beyond that brief time when everything had swirled. "Did you? I was walking death's plane when you were in that restaurant with Farmer. It's probably why he was able to get the better of you."

He shook his head. "He was wearing a glove with some sort of narcotic on it. It transferred when we shook hands, but I didn't realize it until it was far too late."

Relief swam through her. At least she wasn't wholly responsible for him getting so badly beaten. "My point is, the minute I bring the ghosts into being, I'm going to start sucking your energy. You probably won't be able to stand, let alone walk."

He studied her for several seconds, then crossed his arms. "You asked me a couple of days ago to compromise. I'll offer one now. You and Jake go to that meeting. I'll remain in the limo—far enough away to stop Farmer sensing me, but close enough to help should things go wrong. Fair enough?"

She nodded. It was certainly more than she'd expected—and offered her hope for the future.

"Now that *that's* finally settled," Jake said. "Let's go get the bastard."

Seventeen

Nikki flexed her fingers and tried to ignore the chill creeping down her spine. It was one thing telling Michael she and Jake were capable of taking care of Farmer, quite another to try to do it.

Jake stood beside her, his breathing a harsh rasp, his gaze never still. Not that he'd ever see Farmer approaching—not unless the vampire wished it. The slight bulge in his left sleeve gave away the presence of the charm he now wore. Nikki had taken it off, not only because Farmer needed to know she was here, but because she had a feeling Jake would need its protection far more than she. Farmer wasn't averse to taking over minds, and the last thing she wanted was to have to knock Jake unconscious to stop him from attacking her. While she had no real idea whether the charm would actually help, surely if it had stopped Farmer entering her mind, it would stop him entering Jake's.

She checked to make sure the silver knives were still in place. Michael had helped her make a couple of wrist sheaths, so the blades would slip easily into her hands. They were nowhere near balanced enough and certainly wouldn't throw very well, but they were only meant as a last defense. The gun in Jake's jacket pocket would hopefully do the job—if they could distract Farmer enough to get a clear shot of his head.

The predawn air held an almost icy chill. Beyond the park, the city was beginning to stir, but the sounds were muted, as if heard through a thick pane of glass. A strange hush seemed to dominate the natural amphitheater, as if even the redwoods and eucalypti lining the meadow held their breath in expectation. Fragile slivers of mist moved among their leaves. Ghosts, waiting for their chance of revenge.

She glanced at her watch. It was nearly six. Dawn wasn't that far off—surely Farmer would need to be well underground before the sun warmed the fog from the sky.

"He anywhere close yet?" Jake murmured, shifting his weight from one foot to another.

"Not yet."

"Wish he'd hurry."

She looked up at him. Sweat beaded his forehead. "Are you nervous?"

"Petrified. But that won't stop me from killing the bastard."

"Just remember not to move or take a shot before the ghosts have his attention."

"I know, I know." He hesitated, then added, "What are the chances of this really working?"

Who knew? It was a chance they had to take. If it failed ... Well, they could always run and wait for Michael to get strong again—even if that enforced his belief she was not capable of doing this type of work. "Probably small. Farmer's a born and bred killer. I'm not really sure if being confronted by his victims will make any difference."

"Chances are it won't."

"It's not every day a killer is confronted by those he killed. Maybe the shock of it will hold him long enough."

Jake snorted. "He's a vampire. Why would ghosts scare him?"

"Why wouldn't they? Just because he became a

vampire doesn't mean he lost all his human fears. I think you'll find deep inside that bully exterior is the scared little boy who cowered under the taunts of a dozen women."

"I sure hope you're right. This could get extremely messy otherwise."

It probably would anyway. Nothing had gone right for them so far. Why would it start happening now?

A prickle of warning ran across her skin. Evil stirred the night. Farmer was circling the park, perhaps checking they were here alone. She hoped he didn't sense Michael, who was waiting in the limo a block away.

"Heads up," she said. "He's coming in from the left."

Jake nodded once and shoved his hand into his pocket. Nikki stepped slightly in front of him—half to keep Farmer's attention primarily on her, half to protect Jake. She didn't trust Farmer one ounce and wouldn't put it past him to try to kill Jake first.

But when he arrived, killing seemed to be the last thing on his mind. Or so anyone who couldn't taste his evil would have thought. He walked up the incline towards them at a leisurely pace, an amused smile playing across his thin lips. He obviously thought the game was already his. She hoped he wasn't right.

"That's close enough, Farmer." She flicked one of the knives down into her palm and held the point towards him.

He laughed. "You think I'm afraid of a little pig-sticker like that?"

"Given it's silver, yeah, I think you would be."

His eyes narrowed slightly. "You know a little about vampires, don't you?"

"I've been sleeping with one for months. Why in hell wouldn't I?"

He grunted and shoved his hands into his pockets. His casual stance didn't fool her for a second. His arms and shoulders were tense. He was ready to move, ready to blur into night.

"Where's Michael?" she asked quietly.

His Cheshire-cat smile came back full force. "Safe. Alive."

"He'd better be."

"Or what? You'll stick me with your little knife?" He snorted. "Sweetie, you won't even see me move."

"I don't have to. I'm psychic, remember. I can smell evil."

"Yeah, right."

She raised an eyebrow. "You did a circuit of this park before you walked in here, did you not? Starting from the zoo end and working your way around?"

He sneered. "That's nothing more than a guess."

"No guess. You don't know as much about me as you think, Farmer. And what you don't know will kill you."

"Will it now? Shall we test your little bluff?"

He blurred as he spoke, and the stink of his presence ran around to the left then straight at Jake. She grabbed Jake's arm, yanking him back, then slashed the air with the knife. The darkness howled, and the smell of burnt flesh stung the air.

Farmer reappeared, rubbing a hand at the blackened cut along his forearm. His gaze flicked from her to Jake and narrowed slightly. Energy buzzed the air between them. Jake didn't move, didn't twitch.

Confusion touched Farmer's expression. "Pretty fancy footwork there, missy," he said, as if he hadn't paused to try to take over Jake's mind. "Shame it'll cost you your life."

She shifted the knife slightly, reminding him of its presence. Its danger. "You were going to take it anyway, so why should I worry?"

"So you would give up your life for your lover? Now that's commitment."

"I'm not stupid enough to believe you ever had any intention of letting us go."

"And yet you came here anyway. Why? Surely you do not expect to destroy me with a couple of silver knives and the gun your friend clenches in his pocket."

"No. I actually came here to reintroduce you to some old friends."

She imagined that smoky plane and reached out with a psychic hand, calling the ghosts into being. Gossamer fingers of energy flitted through her mind, then four ghostly figures flowed from the trees and into substance between her and Farmer.

Fear touched the vampire's expression. "What trick is this?"

"No trick." Energy flowed in a steady stream from her to the ghosts, and she knew it wouldn't be long before the pounding in her head began. "I just thought you might be interested in hearing a few final words from your victims."

The ghosts were gaining form, their skin becoming flesh-colored. Pain flicked through her head, the beginnings of the massive headache to come.

"Ghosts can't hurt me." Despite the confidence in his tone, his expression was less than certain.

Mary stepped forward. While she'd gained the most form, her feet were still ethereal trails of smoke that stirred the grass behind her.

"If you are so certain we cannot hurt you, let us touch you."

He stepped back quickly. "No."

Jake moved, edging quietly around the clearing. He had the gun out of his pocket, his finger on the trigger.

"What are you afraid of?" Mary asked. "We're ghosts. Nothing but angry air. As you said, we can't hurt you."

Farmer retreated another step. "This is not real. Ghosts don't exist." His gaze cut to Nikki's. "It's just some sort of mind game you're playing."

"If vampires can exist, why not ghosts?" Mary countered. "What's wrong, Billie? Don't you like the thought of being able to say a final good-bye to your victims?"

Jake edged a little closer then raised the gun. Nikki saw his finger tighten on the trigger, heard the sharp sound of the retort. But in that moment, Farmer wrapped the shadows around himself and spun away. The bullet exploded into the tree where Farmer had been, showering the immediate area with shards of wood. Farmer ran through the flesh-colored figures, scattering their misty forms, his face furious as he headed straight at her.

She hit him kinetically and flung him back towards the ghosts. Hot lances spun through her brain, a warning she was beginning to push her limits—and still the ghosts continued to siphon her energy.

The shadows unraveled, revealing Farmer's horror-filled expression as he stared into the faces of his victims. He jumped to his feet and leaped away, blurring his form as he ran at Jake.

"Nine o'clock left!" She grabbed the vampire kinetically, thrusting him in that direction.

The sharp sound of a gunshot bit through the night, followed by a grunt of pain. Farmer reappeared, blood pouring from a wound to his shoulder as he slid down the trunk of an old redwood. Her psychic grip faded, and he dropped heavily the remaining few feet to the ground. She bit her lip, eyes watering as the pounding in her head sharpened. It felt like there were a dozen heated knives digging into her brain. But it wasn't over yet. Far from it.

There was nothing remotely amused or superior about the young vampire's expression now. His face was mottled, twisted, eyes narrow and sparking blue fire. He disappeared into shadows again, and again his evil rushed at Jake. She ran forward, slashing the night with the knife. Farmer dodged then hit her with an unseen fist, sending her sprawling backwards. She hit the ground with a grunt, her breath leaving in a whoosh of air and the knife flying from her hand.

Farmer's weight hit her, pinning her to the ground, the shadows fleeing his features as he bared his teeth. She thrust an arm between them and smacked the heel of her hand into his nose. Blood flew, but he didn't seem to notice, just shifted slightly so he could tear into her arm. She hissed in pain, her stomach rebelling at the sound of his sucking.

She reached again for kinetic energy. The lances grew sharper, but she ignored them, lifting his body from hers enough to free her other hand. Flicking the second knife into her palm, she clenched it tight and with every ounce of strength she had left, thrust into Farmer's side.

He screamed. Silver flickered, running across his skin as the smell of burning flesh rent the night air. She hit him again with kinetic energy, thrusting him away. Another gunshot echoed, then came a heavy splat as Farmer hit the ground.

She didn't move. Couldn't move. Couldn't do anything more than suck in great gulps of air in an effort to ease the burning in her brain.

Jake kneeled beside her. "You okay?"

She nodded. He wasn't really looking at her, and he had the gun aimed to their left. "Farmer?"

"Being entertained by our ghosts." He shoved a hand under her back and helped her into a sitting position.

Farmer was lying at the base of a tree, his knee as bloody as his shoulder. Three ghosts ringed him. Mary kneeled beside him.

"Do you know," she whispered. "What it is like to wish for death?"

Farmer made a gargled sound in his throat. The shadows began to wrap around him, and Nikki hit him kinetically, holding him in place despite the fire in her brain.

"You said ghosts can't hurt you," Mary continued. "Perhaps we can't. Perhaps if I reached into your chest and wrapped my fingers around your heart, it is nothing more than fear that constricts the organ so tightly."

Ghostly fingers slipped into his shadowy chest. Farmer's eyes went wide, his face changing from angry red to pasty white. Sweat dotted his forehead and upper lip, and his expression had a touch of horror to it.

But nowhere near enough for anyone—not after what he'd done.

"This is not real. You're not real. None of you." He didn't seem to convince anyone he meant what he said, least of all himself.

"What if I squeeze your heart so tightly it bursts?" Though Mary's voice was conversational, there was nothing gentle in her expression. She'd been given the chance to avenge her death, and she was literally grabbing it with one hand. "What if I rip it from your chest and feed it to the first dog that passes by? You've never had use for it, so what would it matter?"

Ghostly tendons tightened. Farmer made a garbled sound, his lips turning bluish. Vampires couldn't die like this—but right now, he looked on the verge of a major heart attack.

Mary looked their way. Jake rose to his feet and walked over, the gun held by his side.

"Beg for mercy, Farmer," Mary continued. "Beg like you made us beg. Perhaps then I will let you live."

His gaze swept across the ghostly forms. "Please." His voice was hoarse, his breath rapid gasps of pain. "Please."

Mary snorted. "You always were a sniveling little coward, Billie. Guess you always will be, no matter what plumage you wear."

Her misty fingers slid from his chest, and Farmer's expression seemed to collapse with relief. But a flicker of cold amusement shone in his eyes. He thought he had them all fooled. Thought he could yet escape and gain the upper hand. The shadows half concealing his body grew sharper.

Sweat dripped down Nikki's chin and mingled with the blood running down her arm. She battled to keep her kinetic hold locked tight, knowing she had to keep him still until Jake got there. But her head felt like it was going to explode, and her whole body shook with effort. If she *was* siphoning Michael's energy, he was obviously in pretty bad shape, because she wasn't feeling any influx of strength.

The ghosts ringing the young vampire parted, allowing Jake through. He stopped beside Mary and raised the gun to Farmer's head. Ghostly fingers joined his on the trigger.

"She may let you go," he said flatly. "But I never will."

Together they fired the gun. The sharp retort echoed across the silence, and Farmer's body slumped. He was dead. It was over.

Jake lowered the weapon. For a moment, no one moved. In the distance, sirens wailed, drawing ever closer. The amphitheater looked suddenly brighter, as if a veil had been lifted. She hoped the dawn got here before the police. Hoped Farmer's body would burn where it lay, and his soul be consigned to an eternity of hell.

Mary's gaze met hers. Though she didn't say anything, Nikki understood the plea in her eyes. She took a deep breath, then reached for the last of her energy reserves and sent it Mary's way.

The older woman's form solidified. "There was so much left we had to do. So many things we left unfinished." She touched a hand to Jake's face, her smile sad, wistful. "So many angry words last spoken."

Jake made an incomprehensible noise in the back of his throat. He placed a hand over Mary's, his fingers shaking.

"I would never have really left you for long, you know," Mary continued. "No matter what I might have said."

"I wouldn't have let you go for long." He took a deep breath. "But there was no way in hell I was going to take the hotel job. I hate it."

"I know." She hesitated. "But would settling here have been so bad otherwise?"

He shook his head. "No. It was just the job that was too restricting."

"You would never have made a very good lawyer. You can't lie."

"No."

Mary smiled and leaned forward, brushing a kiss across Jake's lips. "Enjoy life while you still have it. Take care, my love."

Her body dissipated, became a shimmering mist that looked like a curtain of tears hanging in the rising light of dawn. But gradually that, too, faded until there was nothing left beyond memories.

Jake's anguished cry filled the silence. It was the last thing Nikki heard as the darkness crashed into her mind and swept her into unconsciousness.

Eighteen

Michael sat on the edge of the bed and brushed the hair from Nikki's forehead. She stirred but didn't open her eyes, though the awareness flowing through the link told him she was awake.

He skimmed a finger down her cheek to her lips. The alarming pallor of her skin had finally faded, but her cheeks still looked hollow. It was as if the ghosts had sucked every ounce of fat from her body—and she didn't have a lot to spare in the first place.

Three days had passed since she and Jake had battled Farmer and won. The police had arrived the same time as the sun, and by then the fog had burned off enough to destroy the young vampire's remains.

It had been easy enough to touch the minds of the two young officers and make them believe the reported gunshots had been nothing more than cars backfiring. And that Nikki's wound was nothing more than a scratch from a fall. With the gun safely hidden in Jake's jacket pocket, and Jake himself sitting on a park bench calmly smoking and sagely nodding in agreement with everything they said, the ruse looked more than believable, even without him enforcing it.

Farmer was dead. Jake and the ghosts had had their revenge. All that was left was the uncertainty that still stood between him and Nikki.

An uncertainty he had every intention of sorting out today. Now.

He leaned forward and gently kissed her. Her lips were soft, warm, and her response one that invited further exploration. But he resisted the temptation. She'd once accused him of using sex to avoid difficult conversations. He had a feeling she was attempting to do the same right now. Her tension surged through the link, even if she looked so very relaxed.

"Merry Christmas, sweetheart," he said softly.

A smile touched her mouth, and she opened her eyes. In the amber depths, pain and guilt still lingered. "Same to you. Though merry doesn't seem the right word to use right now."

"Perhaps. But I very much doubt if Mary would want this day wasted to sorrow."

"I guess not." She sighed and shifted, exposing one bare shoulder and the swell of a breast. "We don't even have a Christmas tree. And I left your present at home."

That she said home, rather than *his* home, had hope surging. Maybe the fight to keep her by his side was going to be easier than he'd first feared.

He raised an eyebrow. "Who said we don't have a Christmas tree?"

She stared at him, her smile growing. "We do?"

He nodded. "Went out early this morning and found one."

"Where? It's Christmas morning. Everyone would have sold out by now."

They were. But it was amazing what you could find when you had the money and the determination. "I couldn't let our first Christmas go by without a tree, could I?"

She touched a hand to his face, caressing his cheek with her thumb. "You really are an amazing man sometimes."

"And you, my love, are an amazing woman." He leaned forward and kissed her again, long and lingering.

She sighed when he pulled away. "You keep doing that—stopping, I mean. I guess it means we have some serious stuff to talk about before we get down to the fun stuff."

"That we do." He hesitated, not sure what to say first.

She solved the dilemma for him by placing a hand to his lips. "Let me." She ran her hand down his arm and wrapped her fingers around his. "I'm sorry for walking out on you the way I did. And I'm sorry for being so unreasonable with my demands. While I still truly believe we could work as a team on at least some of your missions, I can't expect these things to happen overnight. As you once reminded me, you've been on this Earth for over three centuries. Changing set ways takes time."

She was right. And yet it had taken so very little time to get used to having her in his life. He squeezed her fingers gently. "And I'm sorry for not taking your fears seriously. While I still believe much of my work is far too dangerous for you to be involved in, I agree with Jake in that there must be common ground between both our needs."

She raised an eyebrow. "Does that mean you *are* actually thinking about me helping you on some of your missions?"

He'd not only thought about it, but had spent hours discussing the pros and cons with an old witch. "You walking out on me gave me a glimpse of the future. I don't want that future, Nikki."

Emotion surged through the link—love and

regret intermingling—stirring his senses, warming his heart.

"My mom once told me only a fool runs from gold. She was right. What we have is too good to let go so easily." She hesitated, then added softly, "I guess I was just scared one day you'd walk out that door and never come home, and I'd be left to wonder for the rest of my life what happened. At least if I was with you, I'd know."

Then they shared the same sort of fear, though for different reasons. Still, the base was the same—love.

"I've been talking to Seline while you slept."

And she'd delighted in reminding him that she'd warned long ago this would all happen. That there could only be one end result if he really wanted happiness—and an end to the utter loneliness and despair that had begun to descend on him before Nikki came into his life. The old witch was right—as usual.

"So what did Seline say?"

Though her voice was carefully neutral, the tension running through the link increased. She still wasn't certain about his relationship with Seline, though it wasn't so much distrust as curiosity. He'd have to introduce them—if only because the old witch wouldn't stop harassing him until he did. He had a feeling the two of them would get on like a house afire, even if they were as different as night and day.

"First she chided me for being a stubborn fool. Then she agreed that there were some cases definitely too dangerous to risk taking you along."

"And?"

He had to restrain a smile at the edge in her voice. "And she said that you and Jake were one hell of a team, and I'd be a fool not to make use of you both on at least some of the cases."

She laughed, the sound warm and sexy. It touched her eyes with heat and sent a surge of desire through his body. "You really must introduce me to this Seline of yours. She's sounding more and more like my kind of woman."

"Yeah, and it's got me worried. I don't need two of you nagging me senseless."

"You deserve it sometimes."

"Maybe." He raised her hand and kissed her palm, then pressed her hand against his heart. "The way you and Jake dealt with Farmer proved you could take care of yourselves. But Farmer is far from the worst I deal with, and there will be times I cannot allow you to be with me. No matter what you threaten."

She nodded. "I know. I was just *so* angry that you wouldn't listen to me, wouldn't even consider ..." She shrugged. "I'm not a fool, despite the fact I may have been acting like one the last couple of days. And I have no doubt there are things I'm better off not knowing about."

That was a certainty. Some of the things *he* did she had no need to know. Sometimes the only way to catch a monster was to act like one.

"Seline wants you and Jake to become official Circle members. That'll mean undergoing some training, both in combat fighting and, for you at least, at a psychic level. And she'll probably want you to undergo some testing, so we have a better idea of where, exactly, these talents of yours might be leading."

She blinked. "Wow. When you agree to something, you go in full tilt."

"If you're going to join me on missions, I'm going to make damn sure you and Jake are primed to defend yourselves. I don't want to lose either of you."

"Have you talked to Jake about this?"

"Yesterday. He thought it was a damn good idea." He hesitated. "I don't think he wants to reopen the agency, anyway. Nor do I think he wants to return to Lyndhurst or his home there." Too many memories. And no ghosts.

She nodded. "Lyndhurst is pretty much a lost cause for us. After losing two clients in the manner we did, our name is basically mud." She paused. "But where is he going to live if not in Lyndhurst? Especially if he's going to become a member of the Circle?"

"Our headquarters is in Washington. We've apartments there he could use, or if he'd prefer to stay near you, I have a house in Cody in dire need of some attention. He could fix it up when we're not working." And Cody was little more than half an hour's drive from where they lived.

"Have you given him those options?"

"Not yet. He's not really ready to make such decisions yet, despite his determination to get on with life."

She nodded and raised her other hand, cupping his cheek. "Thank you."

"You may want to retract that thank you once you see what you've gotten yourself into."

"You're letting me in, Michael. Letting me see your whole world. That's what I'm thanking you for. I don't care about the danger."

She never did, and that was half the problem. But maybe Seline could drum some caution into her. He kissed her fingers. "We've only been living together for four months. At this rate, you'll have nothing left to discover about me two years down the road, let alone a century."

"I have a feeling there will *always* be something to discover about you." Amusement sparked in her eyes and flowed through the link, surrounding him in warmth. "You have three hundred years of living I know nothing about. At the rate I pull information out of you, it'll take me another three centuries to uncover it."

"Maybe." Probably. "In the meantime, why don't you drag your bones out of that bed and come see the Christmas tree?"

"Why don't you drag your bones *into* this bed and ravish me lustily?"

"Ravish you lustily? What on earth are you reading these days?"

Her grin sent his pulse rate sky high. "Something that's given me lots of ideas." She patted the sheets. "Hop in, and we'll try some out."

He was tempted. Very tempted. But there was still something left to do. He flipped the blankets away, exposing her to the cool morning air. Her yelp was full of amused indignation.

"Not before you see the tree and unwrap your present."

"There's a present? Why didn't you say so in the first place?"

She sat up, planted a fierce kiss on his mouth, then grabbed her robe and bounced out of bed. He followed her from the room, feeling a little like a scrap of paper drawn into the wake of a cyclone and loving every minute of it.

Her soft gasp made him smile. She'd stopped in the middle the room, her face tilted upwards as she viewed the massive and ornately decorated

Christmas tree. He stopped behind her and wrapped his arms around her waist, drawing her close.

"Merry Christmas." He kissed her ear, her neck, but resisted the temptation to do any more. Not yet. Not until she'd unwrapped her presents—the one under the tree, and the one in his pocket. The one he'd carried all the way home from Ireland.

"It looks like one of those department store trees."

"It is."

She tilted her head and met his gaze. "How on earth did you manage to get something like this on Christmas morning?"

He smiled. "I can be a very persuasive fellow when I want to be."

Her smile was saucy, stirring his already aching body.

"Yeah, I know. But that doesn't answer my question."

"No, but right now, it doesn't really matter." He dropped a kiss on her nose then moved around her and over to the tree. He picked up the long, brightly wrapped box and handed it to her. "Open your present."

Her expression was that of a kid in a candy store. She plopped cross-legged onto the floor and began unwrapping the gift. He sat down in front of her, amusement stirring as she tossed aside the paper and ribbons he'd spent so much time over and hurriedly opened the box.

Her gasp was soft. "It's beautiful." She lifted the delicate ivory silk nightgown from the box and held it up.

"Well, you were always complaining you didn't have any decent nightwear. I took it as a hint."

She grinned. "It was. Thank you." She leaned forward and kissed him briefly, then said against his lips, "How about I put it on and we see how long it takes you to get it off me again?"

He touched a hand to her face, caressing her cheek with his thumb. "I have something else to give you."

She raised an eyebrow and said archly, "Yeah, that's exactly what I was talking about."

Heat surged between them. He battled the urge to take her right there and then and said patiently, "I mean another present."

"Two presents? Why didn't you say so?" She sat back, amusement and love evident in her expression. "Well, come on, stop teasing and give."

He reached into his pocket and wrapped his fingers around the small velvet box. "It comes with a question you must answer."

She raised an eyebrow. "Christmas is a time of giving and receiving presents. I can't ever remember it being a time of twenty questions."

"Not twenty questions, just one." He withdrew the velvet box from his pocket and offered it to her.

She went still, her gaze darting from the box to his face and back again. She reached out, taking it from his palm then carefully opening it. The band inside was simple, plain. His family had been poor farmers, and had the simple tradition of taking the stone from their homeland to fashion it into rings for those that they loved. His grandfather had done it for his grandmother, his father for his mother. And he, who had outlived them all by many centuries, had finally fashioned a ring of his own for the woman he loved.

Disbelief, excitement and love surged through the link, burning his senses, encasing his heart. He didn't really need to ask the question, because he had it right there in that rush of emotion. In the tears and affirmation that glittered in her beautiful eyes when her gaze rose to his again.

But he asked it anyway.

"Nikki, will you marry me?"

DANCING WITH THE DEVIL

Having grown up on the tough streets of Lyndhurst, Private Investigator Nikki James believes there is nothing left to surprise her. That changes the night she follows teenager Monica Trevgard into the shadows and becomes a pawn caught in a war between two very different men. One fills her mind with his madness; the other pushes his way into her heart. Nikki knows how dangerous love can be but, if she wants to survive, she must place her trust in a man who might destroy her.

For three hundred years, Michael Kelly has existed in the shadows, learning to control his vampiric death cravings. Nikki not only breaches his formidable barriers with her psychic abilities, but makes Michael believe he may finally have found a woman strong enough to walk by his side. Will his love be enough to protect her from a madman hell-bent on revenge? Or will the secrets they keep from each other prove to be the greatest threat of all?

HEARTS IN DARKNESS

Life has never been so insane for Private Investigator Nikki James: a teenager is missing; a madman is kidnapping the wealthy; she's got a vampire to contend with; and her partner and best friend, Jake, is in the hospital dying. And just when it seems like nothing else could possibly go wrong for her, Michael Kelly returns.

The last thing Michael needs is a confrontation with Nikki – especially when his control over his bloodlust is still so tenuous. But when a kidnapper steps up his agenda to murder, they are suddenly forced into a partnership. Soon Michael discovers the biggest danger may not be from his need to 'taste' Nikki, but from his desire to make her a permanent part of his life – a life that is sure to get her killed. Nikki is determined to make Michael see that life apart is worse than death. But before she can make him see the light, a spectre from Michael's past rises that could destroy any hope she has of a future with him.

KISS THE NIGHT GOODBYE

Private Investigator Nikki James wants nothing more than to pass the Circle's strict entry exams so she can begin to plan her wedding to Michael Kelly. But when one of the testers attempts to kill her, she realises buying a wedding dress is the least of her worries. Especially when Michael is shot and kidnapped.

The trail leads her to the ghost town where Michael once killed a murderer. She's not surprised to discover that Weylin Dunleavy, the brother of that long-ago sorcerer, has set out to raise his brother's spirit from hell. Nor is she truly surprised to discover that a barrier of magic surrounds the old town, leaving her to battle Dunleavy with only her wits, strength and the one psychic gift she cannot fully control. The one thing that does surprise her, the one thing she cannot accept, is the fact that Michael no longer remembers who she is...